The Doctor's Estate

The Doctor's Estate

Heather Quinto

TruRealm Media
www.trurealmmedia.com

The Doctor's Estate

This book is a work of fiction. Any references to historical events, real people, or real places are used fictitiously. Any resemblance to actual events, places, or persons, living or dead, is entirely coincidental.
The text of this book is set in Saratoga Springs, NY in the year 2019.

Revised on March 12th of the year 2022.

Published by TruRealm Media

Clovis, CA

ISBN: 978-0-578-56799-0

Author's Note

Heather Quinto is a Yaqui Native American, and she resides in Fresno, California with her life partner and many cats. She has a BA in Creative Writing/English with a minor in Marketing from Southern New Hampshire University. She is the author of the paranormal/fantasy novel, *Inhuman,* and a spiritual/romance short story titled *In Love and Death.* She helped write *Doctor's Estate* with Jesus Martinez, who was the creator of the story.

Heather always had a strong urge to write and create imaginative stories ever since she could pick up a pencil. She started off by drawing picture books when she was four and began writing short stories when she was eight years old. Heather's main inspiration behind writing is to be able to leave the greatest impact on whoever picks up one of her books by challenging her readers to think differently. As a writer, Heather strives to add hidden themes within her books and layers of symbolism in the plot and characters to add more flavorful storytelling. You can read and reread one of her novels and find a whole new perspective of the story each time.

"Writing is a powerful tool. All I need is a pen and paper, and I can change the world." -Heather Quinto

Acknowledgments

The following people have contributed their time and knowledge to help make this book as best it can be. Special thanks to Joshua D'Andrea for his creative inspiration for the dark setting of this story. Thank you to Sam D'Andrea for his artistic talent in designing the story's ritual symbols. Thanks to Cheryl Lynn Carter, Karen Tomlinson, Shawna Rhoten, and Jackie Meador for your help with quality feedback.

Chapter One

Recurring Events

I saw the woman quickly speed down the steps while lifting up her dress. A loud deafening roar shook the home as a man I could not see set off yet another gunshot. She screamed as she pushed open the front door, and I followed closely behind her, unable to do anything other than watch as everything unfolded. The thin, screen door smacked against the paneled walling of the house. It was as if I, too, could feel the sharp pang radiating to her skull as the man grabbed a fistful of her hair and pulled her back.

Her back smacked onto the wet mud. Her now wet frizzy hair laid out in front of her face like string. She slipped on the ends of her dress as she desperately attempted to stand up. "Howard, *please*," I heard her beg. "What has happened to you? It's me. It's Lavinia!" Her boots slipped on the mud, and the thick and hardened sole from the man's shoe planted itself onto her back, causing her to crash onto the ground again. She flipped over onto her back, exhausted from her fight. "Howard, this isn't you!"

"Where's the journal?" he demanded. His once blue eyes had gone black. He pointed a 45-millimeter handgun at her and cocked back the safety. "Where. Is. The journal?"

Tears rained down her cheeks, staining her face with the color of her mascara. "Howard, I know you're in there. Please, you must fight this!" My heart ached for this woman I did not know.

A sharp clack echoed throughout the air.

Lavinia, with labored breaths, peered down at her core, which was now flowing with a thick red liquid. It soaked up her dress, discoloring the purple. She lay back and coughed. Blood bubbled out as my body, too, vibrated with pain. It was as if she and I were connected as one at this very moment. Howard, a face as cold as stone, stepped over Lavinia's body and pulled back the trigger one last time right into Lavinia's head.

"I'll just find the damn thing myself," he said. He spat on her motionless body.

I shot awake in bed as I gasped for breath. I gripped onto my soaked sheets and wiped the cold sweat from my eyes. It was the third time this week I had this dream, and I had no idea why.

I flipped the covers off me and walked towards my bathroom to get ready for work. Ever since I moved into this home, I've been haunted by the same nightmare almost every night. Each time I'd wake up in a cold sweat. I wrote down on my pad of paper, that I left on my nightstand, to buy a few pairs of sheets. It was annoying having to wash the same sheets every single morning from the clammy sweat.

Turning on the faucet, I splashed cold water onto my face. It was refreshing, and it opened my pores to wake me up. I got my comb wet before brushing back my smooth, brown hair. My hair was longer on top than it was on the sides, and I had the barber cut it this way, so I could flip back my hair, which was in style. I missed having my beard, but being where I worked, they required you to be clean-shaven.

I got dressed in my purple-colored scrubs. Most men wouldn't wear such feminine colors, but I enjoyed proving other men wrong. You can still wear pink and be manly. My muscles on my arms were proof enough.

As I went downstairs, the groaning of the worn-out wood floors further reminded me that the flooring needed replacing. This home was built in the early nineteen-hundreds, so it made sense that it was about due for improvements.

Once I got to the kitchen, I whipped up my typical protein shake with some spinach mixed in there. The protein helped with building up my muscles. I made a note on a different notepad that was placed on my refrigerator to set up my home gym. I chugged down my morning shake as I made my way to work. Today would be a good day. At least I told myself that every day. My mother always said to me that your day is what you made of it.

At work, I gripped tightly to the plastic handles of Mr. Walters' wheelchair as I steadily pushed him through the halls of the skilled nursing facility, or what we called SNF. One of its broken wheels squeaked as it glazed over the linoleum floors. I had to hunch over to reach the handles of the wheelchair, which left my shoulders curled at an awkward angle. I wanted to make conversation with my patients like I always did. I found it helped to lift their spirits. "Did you win at today's bingo?" I asked.

Mr. Walter's raspy voice always brought me comfort like a man whose words could give infiltering advice when you needed it most. "No, Ted. I didn't. That damn Rochelle got me again. I swear she's cheatin'."

I chuckled. He said that every day. It was always someone who was cheating. The fluorescent lighting that hit the newly mopped white-colored flooring made the facility seem well maintained. I am a clean freak myself, as well as a stickler for organization.

"Want me to report her?" I offered jokingly. "I can see if I can find you a winning card."

Mr. Walters wagged his finger. "Yes, yes. Do that." he began to whisper, which made me strain to hear him. "And sneak in another tapioca pudding while you're at it."

I let out another laugh as I pushed Mr. Walters to his room. "I'll make sure to do that, sir." I pressed down on the plastic stubs on the back wheels to keep the wheelchair in place. Turning to face the man, I said, "Ready to give it a go today on your own? Or would you like assistance?"

Mr. Walters smacked his wrinkled lips together. His pointed chin stuck out more after he had gotten his dentures. He waved his hand dismissively. "No, no. I got this." His hands shook as he moved them to the sides of the chair, and he slowly pushed himself up. I always made sure to stand by his side and took a stance ready to catch him at any moment.

The stubborn man shuffled his feet across the floor, and he gripped tightly to the bedding once he reached it. I pulled off the blankets for the man, and he crawled into the bed as I positioned the pillows just the way he always liked it.

"You're a good kid, son," he said. His shaky hand patted me on the arm. "They don't raise 'em like you anymore."

I grabbed the tray of food that patiently waited on the nightstand. The muscles in my cheeks tightened even more as my grin grew. "Thank you, sir. It was all my parents." I positioned the tray on Mr. Walter's lap.

"How is your Mom?"

I bit down hard and swallowed before forcing a smile. "As good as things can ever be."

Mr. Walters frowned. "It's a shame. To end up like that. Not remembering who your children are. I feel for you, my boy."

"Thank you, sir." I sighed and pointed at the two cups of tapioca pudding. "Got you an extra." I winked at him before leaving the room.

I checked the watch on my wrist. It was nearly five o'clock, which meant it'd be time to clock out soon. I headed towards the employee locker room, which was towards the front lobby down the hallway to the left. As I walked through the lobby, I saw the other nurses were preoccupied with the television. My curiosity was piqued, so I walked over to them, passing by the rows of chairs and couches and looked up at the screen, which hung in the corner of the room. "What's going on?" I asked.

My coworker, Ben, responded, "Another mentally ill homeless man went missing." He looked up at the television with his hand covering his mouth. "It's such a shame, you know. I wish we could take in all of them. It will continue to

5

happen. What did they think would happen after they passed that law a few years ago? It caused the release of a bunch of mentally impaired people that couldn't afford to be in homes."

"I know. It's been goin' on for the past eight years, but now it's gettin' steadily worse. It seems more people are bein' taken just this past year." Christina's southern drawl always made my cheeks warm up, and I tried my best to hide it by rubbing my face. "It's wrong that if ya' don't have insurance, ya' just left out in the streets like that. Some sicko must be pickin' these guys up and doin' God knows what to 'em. And they thought the first few kidnappins' eight years ago weren't connected to the ones today." Christina turned to me, and her face lit up with a smile. "Hey there, Teddy." She reached her arm out and playfully hit me on my arm. "Almost done with your shift there, 'hon?"

I swallowed, and my nerves fluttered in my stomach at the small contact. She always made me feel that way. I nodded while trying not to smile too eagerly. I didn't want to seem desperate to her. "Yeah. I'm just about to clock out and head home." *Now is the time to leave, Ted. Be casual.* I waved at everyone before turning around and heading towards the locker room area.

Right when I clocked out, my cellphone's jingle went off in my blue Jan Sport backpack. The caller ID said it was my Dad. I let out a sharp breath before answering, "What is it, Dad?"

The shaky tone of my father's voice caused me to straighten my posture in alarm. "It is your mother."

My chest constricted, and my feet became lead. "What happened to her? Where is she? Is she okay?" Each question blurted out quicker than the one before it.

"She's alright. She's… okay."

"Dammit, Dad! Where is she? You can't just start calls like this."

"I know. I'm sorry. I just…" He paused, and I was about ready to scream through the phone for an answer. "We're in the hospital."

I swung my backpack over my shoulder and charged towards the exit. "Which hospital?"

"The one in your town. She escaped again."

I unlocked my truck, and the rusted metal hinges ground together as it opened. The screeching of the engine made me realize I needed a new car. It wasn't that I couldn't afford one, but this was my first vehicle ever. I made sure to take good care of it like I did all things, and I couldn't get myself to part with it. I sighed as I buckled myself in. "Dad, you have to keep a better eye on her. Especially now that people like her are going missing. She could have gotten picked up by some stranger. I'm on my way." I slammed the door shut.

"I know. I'm sorry. I just—."

"I said I'm on my way." I hung up abruptly before taking off.

Once at the hospital, I raced to my mother's room and found her tucked under some sheets playing with the remote that controlled the bed. Despite the television being on, she was fully engrossed with the functions of the remote. She'd press up, and her lips curved with excitement. Then she'd press down and look over at her husband in awe. I

7

couldn't help but smile from both relief and at my mother's newfound innocence. Her long, graying hair sparkled where the bright silver strands hit the fluorescent lighting above her.

"Mom," I breathed as I made my way over to her. I dropped my backpack to the floor, knelt at her bedside, and took her hand. "How are you?"

"Oh, I'm fine," she said lightheartedly. The skin around her lips was heavily wrinkled, and there were creases around her eyes from all the years of happiness. "I wish they'd have better food. I want some pizza. I don't want…" She gestured towards her plate with a flick of her hand. "Whatever *that* is."

I grimaced. "I heard you went on an adventure today, Mom."

She continued to push the buttons on the remote. "Oh yeah. Parker needed to go to the store, so I offered to take him."

My brow furrowed, and I looked to my father who was behind me. All my father did was shrug. His glasses sunk a bit to the lower part of his nose, and he used his fingers to push them back up. I turned my attention back to my Mom. "Who is Parker, Mom?"

"The young boy who lives down the street from us. Don't you remember? You used to…" She trailed off and stared at the wall in front of her. "Used to…. Used to." She blinked, and it was as if she came back to reality. My breath caught in my throat. She looked over at me, and her old smile came back—The one that I grew up knowing. That smile could warm up any room it entered. "My boy," she said. "You came to see me."

I tightened my grip on her hand. "That I did, Mom. How are you?"

"Oh, I don't know," she placed the remote down at the side of the bed. "I was terribly dehydrated when they found me and quite fatigued, which is why they're keeping me here overnight. They want to make sure I don't get any worse. I just wish I knew why I was out there in those woods. I do, but..." She shook her head. "It seems so unimportant now and far away."

"Dad needs to keep a better eye on you."

My mother's hazel eyes shined brightly. "Oh, Ted. Be easier on him, will you? He's only trying his best." She placed a hand on my cheek, and that smallest touch, no matter how old I got, always brought a rush of comfort. "And it's good enough, okay? You worry about you and your life. Dad and I can handle ourselves."

I pressed my lips tightly together. "Okay, Mom." I knew better than to argue with her.

"Maybe we should move away from the mountains and closer to Saratoga Springs," she beamed. "I'd be closer to you."

I patted her hand before standing up and going over to my father. My father's half dome set of hair always made me apprehensive that I'd one day start losing my hair at forty years old like him. I was only ten years off from that fate. "Have you been giving her the medicine the doctor prescribed?" I whispered sternly.

My father stood there with his hands in the pockets of his windbreaker. "Yes, I have been giving Patricia her daily dosage three times a day, like instructed by the doctor."

I clicked my tongue against my teeth as I looked away from my father's eyes.

"They just don't work," he said.

My voice rose. "What do you mean they don't work?" We both peered over at my Mom. When she didn't turn her attention towards us and kept it on the television screen, I lowered my tone. Through greeted teeth, I said, "It's medicine. It is supposed to do what is prescribed." My father stuck his arms out in defense, but before he could speak, I said, "And if it's not, then you have to tell the doctor, so he can either up the dosage or change the prescription."

"Son, we are doing all we can."

I looked over at my mother. "Yeah, well, it doesn't seem like it's enough." I faced him again. "If you don't take better care of her, I will." I walked over to my mother to say goodbye by bending down to kiss her forehead. My tall stature made it so she could barely reach her arm up to pat my shoulder.

The following day at work, I found it hard to concentrate. I had first forgotten to clock in and lost some work time, and then I slipped up on a patient's medicine order. I was trudging down the hall when Ben's voice snapped me back to reality. "You forgot to change out Mrs. Sal's bedpan like you said you would," said Ben. "Are you okay?" His brow knit together in concern.

I blinked. "Yeah, of course." I shook my head to get my brain to function again like when someone hits the television to get a better connection. "I'll get to that." I picked up the pace as I made my way across the hallway to Mrs. Sal's room. I painted on a full smile when I entered to

10

hide my dazed look. "Hey there, miss. How are you doing today?"

Mrs. Sal cackled at me for calling her "miss." "You are something else, boy." Mrs. Sal was a heftier woman, and she was rich in spirit too. I always enjoyed seeing her every day. She finished sipping her orange juice. "Here, take this for me, will ya'?"

"Yes, ma'am," I said eagerly. I picked up Mrs. Sal's bedpan and carried it out of the room with me along with the empty cup. I made it a point to know all my patients' schedules like the back of my hand, so I knew Mrs. Sal would be coming out to get her medicine at any moment. She had to take it after every meal, and she was recently bedridden due to her bad hip. Despite having a walker, I could tell by her painful expression how hard it was for her to move. I took it upon myself to deliver her medicine for her.

When I entered her room, she was just about to get out of bed. She moaned in pain, and I raced to her aid. "Mrs. Sal, lay down."

She huffed as she reluctantly let me sit her back against the pillows. "I need my medicine."

"I know. I got it for you," I said as I handed it to her with a cup of water.

"Bless your heart, boy," she said. Her breath was still labored in pain.

"Want something extra?" I offered

She eyed me. "A handle of rum would be nice."

That made me laugh. "I was thinking more in the food department. I can swipe you one of your favorite dishes. I know you like the meatloaf."

"Mmm-hm! That I do." She took her medicine and handed me the empty plastic cup. "If and when you have the time, of course. Don't think I don't see you runnin' up and down these halls like a mad man." She pointed at me. "You workin' too hard. How much they payin' you, huh?"

I cracked a wide grin. "More than enough."

"Hm!" She rolled her eyes and turned her attention to the television screen.

Before I left, I asked, "Do you want me to adjust the AC in here, or are you comfortable?"

Mrs. Sal waved me off with her hand. "I'm good, boy. You keep workin'." Her cackle echoed throughout the halls as I left to go tend to another patient.

After a few minutes of checking on my assigned people and administering medicines, I got into the swing of things once more. However, the deteriorating health of my mother poked at the back of my skull like a never-ending pinprick.

It was this precise reason why I had bought that home in the first place. I had even used the computers at the SNF during my lunch break to find home listings in town. I didn't believe for one second that my father could take care of my mother. At least not to my standard of care. That wasn't the first time she was sent to the hospital for running off, and she seemed to be getting worse. A month ago, I took it upon myself to find a home where both my parents could live. This way, I could keep a better eye on her.

The homes in the area were expensive, but I had been saving up for years. I learned from my father's mistakes while growing up to always have a savings account for emergencies and extra expenditures. Despite having more than enough for a down payment on a decent home, every home in the area was so overpriced.

I began to think that I may have to move out of town as I scanned the listings. That was until I came across a property with a two-story home for only a little over two hundred thousand dollars. I had reread the price in disbelief. To me, there was no way a five-bedroom house with three bathrooms and a basement would cost so little. Especially not in a town so close to New York City.

There had to be something wrong with the property, but I decided to give the real estate agent a call anyway. If there were any problems, I'd find out soon enough.

Chapter Two
The Old Estate

O ne month ago, I pulled up in my old Toyota Tacoma to view what would soon be my home for the first time. It was an old mansion, but the land had since been sold off to build more homes in the neighborhood. The house now only sat on less than a half-acre luscious green plot, which made for a decent-sized backyard. Green Ash trees covered the side of the house. There was a large front patio with white rocking chairs, and large paned windows that allowed someone to see into the living room on one end and the dining room on the other. I marveled at the plain white paneling of the home. It was a solid color, which meant room for change if I wanted to add it.

A gray-colored roof covered over the patio to provide shade, and white painted wooden beams supported it. Four windows lined the second floor right above. A quaint cemented walkway curved up to the steps that were attached to the porch, and bushes lined the edge of the property.

I sat in my small truck, waiting for the real estate agent when my cell phone alerted me. It was my sister. "Hey Scarlett," I answered.

"Whatcha' up to right now?" I could hear her smacking on her gum.

I peered through my car window at the home. "About to look at a house. Why? What are you doing?"

"A house?" Her gum-smacking ceased. "Why? Are you finally ready to move out of that dank ass apartment you've been in since your mid-twenties? Big thirty-two got you finally thinking of getting your shit together and pretending to act like an adult?"

I laugh lightly. Scarlett was rough with her words, but she meant well. Growing up with just me as a brother made her that way, I guessed, but I enjoyed our playful banter. She was rough around the edges, but that's what made her perfect for New York City. "How's the city going, sis? Work going well?" I asked.

She smacked her gum some more. "Yeah. On my way right now." I heard honking over the phone, followed by a car honking from further away. "Yeah, you too bastard! Fuck off!" She laughed. "Sorry about that."

I smirked. "You have to be more careful, Scarlett."

"Yeah, yeah. So, this house thing. What made you finally want to purchase one? Got a girlfriend I don't know about?" I could hear the smile in her voice.

"No." I shrugged as I leaned back in the driver's seat. "I figured I'd get a house big enough for Mom and Dad to live in."

"Uh huh…"

"To help Dad take care of Mom," I added.

16

"Yeah, sure. To *help* Dad. I gotcha. You sure that's what this is about?"

A woman in a red Mercedes pulled up beside the house. "The real estate agent is here," I said.

"You have control issues, dude. You know that, right? You always had to be the one in charge. Dad is doing just fine. It's Mom that's not."

"Okay, okay. I gotta go," I said as I began to open the door of my truck.

"No! Let me finish dammit."

I let out a sigh as I sat back in my seat. I knew better than to hang up on her. She'd come barreling down the highway just to smack me for it.

"You should trust Dad more, dude. He is doing all he can."

I let out a snort. "Yeah."

"I'm serious, Ted. You need to hear this, and I'm only going to say this once. All this effort you're putting in is so you can take control over the situation and what's happening to Mom. You already put so much money towards sprucing up Mom and Dad's house to make it safer for her. You added in the walkway to the front door to replace the steps and shit like that. You are constantly riding Dad's ass on how he cares for her because all you see is her getting steadily worse, but it isn't Dad."

I was becoming increasingly more uncomfortable, and I breathed heavily into the phone as I fidgeted in my seat.

"You. Can't. Fix. Mom," she said.

Silence.

"She's going to die from this one day, and there is nothing you can do about it. So please try to accept it. I know it's hard to do, but there is no cure for what she has."

"Don't you think I know that!" I snapped. I cleared my throat and lowered my tone. "Uh…. Sorry about that."

"It's chill, dude. You're just pissed about the situation. I get it. Just don't lose a grip on yourself through all of this, okay? Do me a favor and ask yourself if you'd really want that house even if Mom weren't sick."

The real estate agent had gotten out of her car and was standing beside the porch with a clipboard in hand. "I have to go."

She smacked her gum once more. "Okay. See ya'."

I stepped out of the truck and slammed it a bit too hard. I took a deep breath before walking across the street to meet with the woman. She smelt heavily of hairspray, and her blonde hair seemed permanently stuck in its style. Not even the wind could move it. She smiled as she reached out her hand, "Hi. You must be Ted Rovers. I'm Cecile Linksy." After I shook her hand, she handed me her card.

She turned on her heel towards the home. "Well? What do you think?" Her red blazer and matching pencil skirt hugged her body well, but I focused on the house instead.

I didn't have much to say since I didn't know anything about the home. Did the electricity work or the plumbing? Did it have air conditioning? I grimaced. "Looks nice," I said without much emotion.

Cecile didn't seem to notice. "Wait until you see the inside," she squealed. She waved with her hand for me to follow her as she went up the porch steps. "The porch was newly renovated with all new wood flooring. I had a guy come in to fix that right up. The house was built back in the early nineteen-hundreds, and the last time the home was fully renovated was back in the seventies." She took the keys out of her pocket and unlocked the screen door and then the wooden one. The home smelled of old wood and dust. "It's been a while since anyone has been in here."

A flight of stairs greeted me upon entering. To the right was the living room and the dining room. To the left were the kitchen and small breakfast nook. I headed towards the kitchen first. The flooring was made up of orange and brown colored linoleum. The counters matched it along with its dark brown cabinets. The stove was only about five feet away from the sink, and there were only a few feet of counter space. "It's small," I noted.

Cecile smiled and let out a nervous laugh. "I know. It was refurbished in the seventies, so the coloring is a bit outdated as you can see. However, there is plenty of room to extend it. You can take out the breakfast nook to add more counter space to the kitchen or the parlor in the back."

I nodded as I tapped my finger on the counter. At the corner near the garage door was a small basket. Cecile pointed to it. "You can leave your keys there and phone," she said. "There were some things left behind by the previous owners. I thought the small basket was perfect there for people to put their keys after a long day."

I indulged Cecile and placed my keys inside the basket. I turned and smiled before walking past her towards the living room. The living room and dining room were combined into one with matching carpet. I figured I could make this into one big living room until my parents moved in.

There was a door connected to the bottom of the staircase, and inside was another set of stairs that led down to the basement. "Can I go down there? Is there proper lighting?" I asked.

"Oh yes," said Cecile. There was a light switch against the wall that lit up the way down to the basement.

I held on to the wooden rail, and with each step, the floor creaked with the slightest weight of my foot. Once I reached the bottom, the musky smell of wet cement hit my nostrils. Cecile walked past me to the middle of the basement and pulled on the metal string that was connected to the light bulb. The light wasn't nearly enough to cover the entirety of the room. Shadows still lurked in the corners, which made it hard to see. However, I could see a closet in the far back, and that piqued my interest. I walked over to open it, but it was locked.

Cecile gave a nervous smile, "I'll clear out what's in that room once the home is purchased. It's just paperwork and other old things from the previous owners."

"It doesn't come with the house? Usually, that does," I said. I wasn't too interested in old furniture and knick-knacks from previous owners, but I found it interesting that Cecile hadn't cleared it out sooner.

"If you wish to keep the items, I can leave them there." Cecile fumbled with her pen.

Her intake of nervousness made me curious. "Do not trouble yourself with the items. I'll keep them." Perhaps I could find something useful in there.

The basement was made entirely of cement, and I was wondering where its dampness originated. I thought of the things I could do with it. Perhaps I could live down there and my parents upstairs. Or maybe I could turn this into a home gym. First, I'd have to put in better lighting.

"There is also a washer and dryer hook up down here in that far-right corner," said Cecile pointing with her pen.

"Electric or gas?" I asked.

"I believe electric."

I nodded as I went up the steps. I didn't own a washer or dryer since my apartment complex had a laundry facility. When I got up to the ground floor, I immediately turned my attention towards the second floor.

The wood groaned with age with each step I took up the stairs. Upon reaching the top floor, the master bedroom was to my immediate left. Another bedroom was beside it. The hallway split in half at the stairs. There was a bathroom to the right along with the three other bedrooms and a bathroom across the hallway on the other side of the stairs.

"The bedrooms are newly carpeted," said Cecile. "I made sure to add that in because I felt it makes it homier."

I nodded my head and put my hands in my pockets. I stepped into the master bedroom and tapped my finger against my pocket jeans. It was smaller than I expected it to be, and there was a bathroom attached to the upper left side of the room. In the middle of the room hung a gold and brown colored ceiling fan, but no light bulb. I poked my head in each bedroom and made a mental note to buy bulbs.

"Any particular reason why you're interested in buying a home?" asked Cecile as we made our way downstairs.

I focused on heading to the backyard as I spoke. "I want to take better care of my Mom and help my Dad with it," I said with a sense of aloofness.

"Oh! That's wonderfully sweet," said Cecile.

I stepped outside, and the smell of fresh moss filled the air. The same trees from the front yard with the spider-like branches and dangling leaves covered the backyard. The sun was shining just right that the leaves left specks of shadow across the grass. "Plenty of shade," chirped Cecile. There was an awning made of wood that covered the small cemented area. I thought it would be a perfect place to put a picnic bench. I leaned against one of the wooden beams and noticed it wobbled a bit.

I immediately stepped back to inspect it further. I gently pushed the beam, and the awning quaked in its place. "I will want an inspector to come before I make any kind of offer," I said.

"Of course," said Cecile.

"There is something on my mind. Why is the home so cheap?"

Cecile's smile faltered.

"Homes in this area are never this cheap. At least not a five-bedroom home on such a nice property. Is there something wrong with the home? Mold? Rats?"

Cecile shook her head and fixed her grin. "Nothing like that. You have my word that nothing is damaging to the home. Trust me." Her lips fit into a tight line, and she stood with perfect posture.

I ignored her touch of apprehensiveness. "Alright. Let me get an inspector out here, and we'll see about an offer," I said. Even though I only saw one house, I felt this home would be good enough for my Mom, but my sister's words echoed in my head. I shook them away, and they scattered. I wanted this home for more than just my Mom. It was for me too. At least that's what I told myself. It was about time I left that small apartment. Plus, there might never be a chance to find such a cheap property in the future. If the home didn't have any serious damage lurking within the walls, I didn't care to find out further why it was so cheap.

"When will be a good time for an inspector to come?" I asked as I headed towards the small basket for my keys.

"This Saturday works," said Cecile.

My brow furrowed as I dug through the small basket looking for my keys. They weren't there. I patted my jean pockets and looked around on the floor.

"What is it?" asked Cecile.

"My keys," I mumbled. "They're missing."

Cecile inspected the basket and came to the same conclusion. I knew I had put them in there. I searched on the countertops and in the cabinets. I hurried up the stairs and checked every bedroom. It was unlike me to lose my things.

I went outside to the backyard and inspected the grass, but I couldn't help but shake the feeling that I left them in that basket. I knew I did. I came back into the kitchen and leaned against the counter with my hand. Tapping my finger tentatively, I thought about where I could have left them. I glanced over at the basket and lying neatly on top of Cecile's keys were mine.

I reached over to grab them. Assuming Cecile had found them and placed them there, I asked, "You found them?"

Cecile was busy in the other room. Her voice echoed against the empty walls. "What was that?"

I raised my voice a little. "My keys. How did you find them?"

"I didn't. I'm looking in this closet by the stairs."

I chewed on my bottom lip. "I, uh, found them."

"Oh, good!" I heard one of the aged doors rub against the old hinges as Cecile closed a door. Cecile walked into the kitchen, fixing her red skirt. "Before you hire an inspector, did you want to put a down payment on the home? It's fully refundable if you decide after the inspection that you no longer wish to purchase the home."

I juggled the keys in my hand and eyed the basket. "Yes, please."

As I signed the paperwork, I heard a creak upstairs. Cecile also paused and looked up towards the ceiling. I stopped midway through my signature and gazed upwards. "It's the old flooring," said Cecile with a flip of her hand. "Old homes sometimes creak for no reason."

I nodded hesitantly and signed the form.

The following Saturday, I went back over to the house to be there with the inspector. Cecile showed up as well. It was springtime, so it was a nice breezy day. However, the sun was clouded over from time to time. I zipped up my jacket as the inspector looked over the weak awning in the backyard.

"This is going to be a problem," said the inspector. "This will need to be fixed, but the good thing is that it

24

doesn't appear to be attached to the home." He pointed with his pen towards the end of the awning that was closest to the house. "It seems someone built this themselves, and they didn't do a good job at it." He made a note on his metal clipboard.

"Anything else?" I asked. I kept my hands in my pockets and held tightly to my keys that were inside.

The inspector read from his list. "The AC is strong, and the heater works well. The electrical wiring and plumbing all check out. Except in the basement, there seems to be a small leak, but it should be fixable. It appears to be just a loose bolt on one of the pipes, and the leakage is quite small. Come with me." We went into the kitchen, and the inspector flipped on each burner. "There is one burner that won't start. It's a gas stove, so the good news is that it is giving off gas. It's just not igniting. That's an easy fix. Just install a new lighter."

I nodded and noticed Cecile taking notes as well.

"Other than that, the house is in pretty good shape," said the inspector. "Some doors lack proper locks, but again, an easy fix."

After the inspector was paid for and left, Cecile asked a little too giddy, "What do you think? Want to buy? Or do you need a few more days to think it over?"

I couldn't help but be bothered about why the home was so cheap, but everything checked out. I shoved the heavy thought to the back of my head and reached my arm out to shake Cecile's hand. "I'll take it."

Chapter Three

The Haunting Dream

After I checked on Mrs. Sal one last time, I left work and came home to my empty home. I didn't own a whole lot since I lived in an apartment one month prior to this. The house remained bare once everything was put in its place. I had one small round table where I always ate. It was only me, so I didn't own a huge dining table. The couch was something I held ever since I first moved into my apartment, and it was still in decent shape sitting in the middle of the living room. I had the movers' help with positioning my flat screen against the wall. That was probably the only nice thing I owned.

Everything else was passed down to me from relatives: an antique bed frame, a large armoire, and my nightstand. With the home empty of people, I stood there in my bare kitchen feeling small. "It's just an excuse to buy more stuff," I said to myself. "That's a good thing."

I eyed the basket that sat at the corner. Cecile had left it there when I moved in saying it was a welcoming gift. Hesitantly, I took my keys out of my pocket and placed them there. That's when my phone rang. It was my father. "I heard you moved," he said immediately after I answered.

I kicked at the corner of one of the cabinets. I was hoping to keep this a secret until I was ready to have my parents move in because I knew my father would be upset when he found out. A guess four weeks was all my sister was willing to keep her mouth shut for. "Yeah, I decided it was time for a change."

"Scarlett tells me it's because you plan on having us move in with you."

Dammit, Scarlett. I cleared my throat and started to pace around the kitchen. "Yes, Dad. I was hoping to convince you to allow for my help."

"Son, we're doing fine."

"Not by my prognosis."

I heard my father sigh through the receiver. Right about now, he should be pinching the bridge of his nose, causing his glasses to lift. "Son, we don't need all this. Where did you even get the money to buy a house, huh?"

I stood in place as my muscles tensed. "I happen to be more responsible and have a couple of savings accounts, *father*. That's more than you can say."

Silence.

"I didn't have a problem with helping you fix up your house because you couldn't afford to," I said.

"Medical bills cost a lot nowadays, Ted." He sounded tired. There was no fight in his voice.

I ignored my father's comment. "And I won't have a problem with getting my house up to code for Mom's safety so you two can live here. This way, *you* won't have to worry so much about medical bills. That's all your money will be going to anyway. I can cover the rest."

My father let out another slow breath. "Son, is this really what you want? Use that house to build a family of your own."

I snapped back in anger. "Why don't you want my help, Dad?"

My father matched my tone. "Because it's not your job as our child to worry about things like that!" He calmed his voice. "If I were to be sick as well, that'd be a different story."

"It's your pride."

"And it isn't yours either? You are awfully prideful yourself, son."

I ground my foot into the linoleum and hung up the phone. I shoved it into the small basket with my keys. I trudged over to my couch and slumped into it, rubbing my forehead. Perhaps I was being unreasonable. Maybe I should be easier on my father. Maybe my Mom truly was untreatable. I shook my head as I leaned over and rested my elbows on my knees. Clasping my hands tightly together, I tapped my forefinger against my knuckle. There had to be hope somewhere. Anywhere. Maybe her living with me, and being around me more often, would keep her from forgetting me.

The night began to fall as I studied the empty living room around me. Other than the few boxes that were scattered around, the house was unpacked. I pressed the sides of my forehead with my thumbs. Maybe I was in over my head, but I had the house now. Either way, I needed to make it work.

A sudden rapping echoed from up the stairs. It sounded like wood scraping on the floor like a chair grinding on the ground.

Back and forth.

Back and forth.

I figured it was probably just the old pipes or the house settling.

Still, the sound never ceased. It got increasingly louder and faster. My body heated up as the adrenaline rushed through like a wave. I slowly sat up and perked my ears to listen in more closely. Should I go upstairs to inspect? "No, it's just the house settling," I told myself again. Still, though, my heart rate picked up.

Faster. Louder. More violent.

Bang!

The sudden clash vibrated throughout the house. I immediately jumped to my feet. There was no way I could ignore that. Gingerly, I made my way to the stairwell. I gripped onto the handrail while staring up at the second floor. Nothing was there, but I couldn't help but feel like something or some*one* was indeed standing there staring down at me. The hair at the back of my neck stood on end, and my jaw tightened as I swallowed.

I carefully took the first step, and I tried my best not to apply too much pressure so that no noise would be made from the creaky floorboards. As I made my way up the stairwell, my heartbeat was deafening in my ears. My breath had quickened with each step. Once I reached the top, I studied the area to find any abnormalities. It was probably just the wind. The only thing improper was the master bedroom door being closed, and I knew I had left it open.

Feeling braver, I made my way over to the door. A louder thump pounded the ground from inside the bedroom. I jumped back and let out a gasp. I took another gulp as I turned the doorknob. It screeched as aged metal on metal ground together. I pushed open the door and braced myself for whatever I may see.

Empty.

There was nothing in the bedroom except for my bed and a couple of boxes. I took a step into the room and scanned it quickly. I checked under the bed and in the bathroom, but there was nothing there. The window was closed, so it couldn't have been the wind. "Maybe there was an air draft of some kind," I said. "Or maybe the door isn't supported enough and closes on its own." I checked the hinges on the door, but they seemed secure.

"Air draft," I concluded. I left the bedroom door open on my way out. I made my way down the stairs shaking my head. Laughing at myself for being spooked by sounds from an old home, I decided to shove the experience to the back of my mind. Instead, I decided to make dinner. Keeping my hands busy was always a sure way of making me forget things.

I realized I wouldn't have enough cabinet space for my parents' things once they moved in because I knew they would need it for sure. I found my notepad on my refrigerator. Every room had a notepad in it just in case I needed to take note of something. I wrote down for myself to remember that I needed to install more cabinet space.

My stomach growled as I checked my fridge for anything. I found some eggs and bacon. I had rice and decided to make fried rice for dinner. As I cooked, I thought back to the time I spent time with my mother in the kitchen. She would show me how to stir the bowls full of cookie dough or salad properly.

"If there is ever too much of one flavor. Just add more ingredients to even it out," she'd say. Almost always, she'd add more bacon. "Bacon never hurt anyone," she'd say with a wink.

To level out the unhealthiness, she'd always put a side of spinach with almost every meal. She'd put bacon in everything because "bacon went with everything." I chuckled to myself as I chopped up more bacon to add to my rice. In my fridge sat a small bag of spinach, which I threw into the steaming pan.

I eyed my cellphone, which was still in the basket. I decided to pick it up and call my Mom. Leaving it on speaker, I waited as the dial rang off until I heard a click. "Hi, my sweet boy," said my mother. I breathed a sigh of relief. She was having one of her good days.

"I just called to see how you're doing. I'm cooking." I said.

"Ah, and are you maintaining the right bacon to spinach ratio?"

I peered down at my pan and added more spinach. "I am now."

My mother's laughter made my smile grow. "How are you? I heard you got a new home. Are you excited to be an official homeowner?"

"Yes, I am. It was high time I got my shit together, isn't it?"

"It'll be a good home to start a family in, won't it?"

I surveyed my nearly vacant home and shrugged. "I suppose so."

"How are things going with that one girl? What's her name again?" I could hear her snapping her fingers as she thought. "Chelsea was her name?"

"You mean Christina?"

"Yes! That one! Have you asked her on a date yet?"

I licked my lips and shook my head. My cheeks started to warm up at the thought. "No, not yet Mom."

"Oh, you need to ask her out on a date, and actually *ask* her. Don't do that thing nowadays that all the other boys do and ask to 'hang out.' Be a man! Say it's a date." Her voice was encouraging like that of a coach prepping up the team before the big game.

I couldn't help but laugh. "Yes, Mom. I will."

"Promise me?"

I turned the stove off once my rice was finished cooking. "Yes, I promise, Mom. I'll work up the nerve."

"Good because I won't be around forever, and your sister isn't having kids anytime soon. She's way too young. She's only twenty! She has her whole career ahead of her. You established your career already as a nurse. Now go get married." She giggled. "Don't feel pressured, though."

I leaned against the counter. "No. No pressure at all," I said jokingly. My mother fell silent suddenly, and my internal alarm went off. "Mom?"

No answer.

"Mom?"

Still silence.

I decided to be a little louder. "Mom!"

Finally, her voice broke through, but it didn't sound like her anymore. She sounded far away. "Oh… Hi there. Can I help you with something?"

"Mom, it's Ted. We are talking on the phone."

"Are we?" She fell silent again.

"Mom!" I began tapping my finger against the counter.

"You need me to help you find your mother, sweet boy?"

I tried my best to swallow the lump in my throat that began to swell up.

"I don't know what she looks like. Can you give me a description?" she continued.

My voice quivered. "Mom. Have you been taking your medicine?"

"What medicine?" she paused. "Who are you?"

I blinked the tears away before they could fall. I took a deep breath. "Give the phone to Dad, Mom."

"Who is that? Is that the Doctor? He gives me my medicine."

"Yes, I know, Mom. Give me to the Doctor, please."

"Oh okay," she said lightheartedly. I could hear her talking to my father. "It's a young boy looking for his mother."

"Hello?" I heard my father say.

"Dad," I snapped. "Has Mom been taking her medicine?"

My father sighed. "Yes, Ted. She has."

I ground my teeth together as I gripped on tighter to the counter. "She needs an update on her prescription. It obviously isn't working."

"Son, there's no cure for Alzheimer's. The medicine is to only help with some of the symptoms."

I squeezed a little too tight to the phone and said through clenched teeth, "I know."

"I don't think you do." His tone sounded grim with a touch of sympathy. I hated it.

"They're working on finding cures! They can find one for Mom!"

My father fell silent. After a minute, he let out another breath. "Ted, I know it's hard. It was hard for me to accept it too."

I heard a woman moaning in pain. "Is that Mom?"

"What? What do you mean?"

"I heard a woman cry in pain. Was that Mom?"

"No, son. She's right next to me watching the news."

I heard it again, and this time it was for sure coming from around the corner near the living room. My heart rate picked up. "I think it might be the neighbors," I said.

My father's tone had a touch of concern in it. "Does it sound like trouble? If so, call the cops. Don't go searching."

The same scraping as earlier filled the home. The rubbing of wood against the floorboards irritated my eardrum. "I have to go, Dad. I think the house may have mice or something," I said.

"Mice? I have some traps for that here. Swing by tomorrow," he said.

I was much too fixated on the strange noise to pay attention to what my father was saying. "Yeah, of course, Dad. Bye." I hung up and placed my phone into my back pocket.

I walked towards the closest wall. The scraping sounded as though it was coming from *inside* the walls. Thinking it may be rats, I placed my ear against it to listen for any scurrying. Again, the loud and deep raking noise returned, but I couldn't pinpoint where it was coming from. I decided to knock on the wall, thinking it'd scare whatever animal was inside and make the incessant noise stop.

Silence.

I stood there with my ear firmly pressed as I waited for any further sounds. A few seconds ticked by. All I could hear were the distant sirens from the town and my wristwatch ticking away. Suddenly, a large slam shook the house. I nearly jumped out of my skin.

It came from upstairs.

I slowly approached the staircase and looked up. This time, however, fear did not make me hesitate. Now I was irritated by the ruckus. I stomped up the steps until I reached the top and saw the master bedroom's door was closed again.

I took a deep breath to calm the racing thoughts in my head. Could this really be the wind? I took large strides over to the door and threw it open. It banged against the wall, and I scanned my empty bedroom. The window was closed, so I checked the air vent above the door. There was no airflow.

The scraping started up again, but it sounded as though it were right behind me. My pulse quickened as my instincts kicked in. I felt as though I were being watched, and someone was right behind me, ready to grab me at any second. The hairs on the back of my neck rose, and my palms sweated. Time froze in place as I slowly turned my head.

My peripheral vision must've been playing tricks on me because I could have sworn, I saw a shadow at the corner of my eye. My cellphone rang off from inside my pocket, and I invited the distraction. "Hello?" I answered.

"Ted! Come down to Parting Glass bar," said my coworker Ben. "I had a rough day at work, man. I need a night out. Frank and Carlos are here with me." Ben took on a teasing tone. "And Christina."

I smiled as I rolled my eyes. "Yeah, sure. I'll be right down." I hurried down the stairs and grabbed my keys out of the basket. I was more in a rush to get out of the home than I was to see my friends. The last thing I needed to be doing was chasing strange sounds and shadows. As I drove to the bar with my windows rolled down, I found the brisk night air calming as it cooled the adrenaline away. It cleared my mind, and I found myself laughing. "It's just all stress induced," I said to myself. "I need a night out it seems."

Once I arrived at the bar, I found my coworkers all huddled around one of the tall tables. The local Irish pub was always busy on nights like this with other locals who just got off work. The loud banter of the other patrons, live music, and laughter filled the room with a sense of comradery and leisure. One could easily take their shoes off in relax like they were in their own home. Most of the pub was made of wood like over the bar and the lower part of the walls, but everything else was painted dark green and tan. The flooring was colored the same dark green. Black strips ran across the floor leading up to where the dartboards were with lines to show where to stand at the appropriate distance for a proper throw. It was a decent sized place that we enjoyed because of the ambiance, but it was loud since it was such a popular place. I had a hard time hearing myself sometimes, so we all had to yell at one another.

I went up to the bar first. It was a squared shape bar, with a neatly kept wooden top, that wrapped around to the other wall. I squeezed in between the tall barstools. "A glass of your best IPA, please."

The bartender nodded his head as he filled my drink. "You got it, sir."

"Keep my tab open," I said as I handed the bartender a tip before turning my attention towards Ben and the others. They had taken a couple of the taller barstools to sit at the high-top tables. I took a sip of my beer and slid onto a barstool to join them.

"Ted, my man!" Exclaimed Ben. He hooked his arm around my shoulders and clasped down before letting go. He picked up his drink to clink it against my glass. "Thanks for coming. How is the new home coming along?"

I shrugged. "It's alright. I'm still slowly unpacking, which shouldn't take long since I don't own a lot of stuff. Although I think the house has rats or something in the walls."

"You should've gotten an inspector," said Carlos as he took a sip.

"I did, which is the strangest thing. Wouldn't an inspector check for that?"

"I heard it depends," added Frank. "When I bought my house, I had to hire two different types of inspectors. The real estate agents technically don't have to tell you shit."

Christina was the only girl there, and she smiled and winked at me. I swallowed hard before I took a sip of my drink and set it down on the green and white checkered tablecloth. I gave a shy smile in response.

"How are you enjoying being at the SNF, Frank?" I asked. "You started just last week, am I right?"

Frank placed down his glass. "Yeah, it's enjoyable. I do prefer the hours there and the benefits. Way better than the last place I was at."

"Weren't you at that one facility up the street from here?" asked Ben.

Frank nodded. "That place was a wreck. It was really the management. It was privately owned, so it was more business-like than actually caring for the patients." Frank curled his shoulders back. "I didn't like the ethics of the place, so I left. I wanted to work as a nurse because I care, not just because it's easy money. I do appreciate you all being so welcoming of me and inviting me out."

"It's no problem, man," said Ben. He gripped onto my shoulder again. "Me and Teddy Boy here started off together. Although they have me working weekends now, so I don't see him as often during the week, but when this boy first started, he was *so* shy. Hardly spoke to anyone. I had to practically drag him out of his home to come with me to the bar to hang."

Everyone laughed, and I grimaced as I stared down at my drink.

"I don't believe it for a second," said Carlos. He looked at Frank while pointing at me. "But you can learn a lot from him about caring for patients." He looked at me. "I don't know how you do it with all those extra patients. You volunteered to take on extras, didn't you? Shoot! I don't think I could handle that. I barely can keep up with the ones I have."

I shrugged. "It's really all in the timing. Once you get to know their schedules, it works easy. There's just no time for breaks."

"Yeah, Carlos," teased Ben. "You're constantly stopping by the break room."

Frank and Ben teased him by throwing a couple of peanuts at him.

Carlos laughed. "What? I need my snacks." He shook his head, still laughing. "But seriously, I can't work so much anymore now that my son was diagnosed with leukemia a few months ago. The wife is stressed too." He ran his fingers through his hair. "I've been working less nowadays. I need to be home, you know?"

Ben placed a hand on his shoulder and grimaced. "How is the little guy doing?"

Carlos shrugged. "He's responding to treatment, which is good, but it's still hard to see him go through it. He's only four."

My heart knotted up, and I thought of when I learned of my mother's diagnosis. They were all there for me, and we are doing the same for Carlos.

Carlos let out a light laugh. "He's still a kid and shows it. He doesn't let that disease get to him."

"How long have you and your wife been together?" asked Christina.

"A little over four years." he chuckled. "We were dating when she got pregnant, and it was only right I married her, you know?"

Christina nodded. "I understand."

40

"It's been tough on us, but it has really made us grow together rather than drifting us apart."

Christina got a huge grin on her face, and I couldn't help but smile in response. "That's good."

Wanting to change the subject because the look on Carlos's face told me he was finished expressing himself, I asked Frank, "What is your story? What got you into nursing? How's life?"

Frank laughed. "You guys don't mess around when it comes to conversation."

We all chuckled. That's what I liked about my group of friends. We hated small conversation and preferred to jump straight into the deep stuff.

Frank rubbed his hands on his knees. "Well, I started as an assistant nurse in Colorado. I helped take care of my grandmother, who lived with us while I was growing up. Over the years, I came to enjoy it and decided to do it as a living since I knew so much already. Years later, after getting my first job at a nursing home, I went to New York City for vacation and bumped into my future wife at a bar."

We all got smirks on our faces.

"She lived in New York, so I decided to move there. I was nursing there for a bit and attended nursing school, but then she got into real estate and wanted to move here chasing the money. I decided to work at the SNF."

"I recently bought a house. What is your wife's name?" I asked.

"Cecile. Why?"

I laughed. "She was my real estate agent when I bought my house."

Frank burst out into a boisterous laugh. "It is true when they say it's a small world."

"Damn right," I said. We clinked our beer bottles together.

"You bought a house? That is great to hear, Teddy," said Christina as she smiled at me. Her big smile was enough to make me forget about all the things I've been going through. This is what I really needed right now.

Ben turned his attention to her. "So, what got *you* into nursing, Christina? We've never asked."

"I know you haven't. So rude," she said with a thick tone of sarcasm. That made us all chuckle. She shrugged. "I don't know. It sort of happened." She paused as she picked at the label on her beer. "I've been caring for my younger siblings my whole life, and I wanted a job to get me out of the house."

"Makes sense, so you got into caring for old people now." Ben's cheeky grin gave away that he was teasing.

Christina's cheeks turned pink as she smiled. "Sure does. That about sums it up for Lil' ol' me. I wanted to get away, and I did for a little while. Nursing pays well enough."

"It does," I said.

"And it's a respectable career. I just never intended to be doin' this for as long as I have been."

I furrowed my brow. "What do you want to do?"

She shrugged. "I haven't quite figured that out. I don't know what I want to do when I grow up." She laughed. Her bubbly laughter was contagious and made us all join her.

Christina leaned over the table towards me as she played with her earlobe in between her two fingers. She always wore her hair in a bun at work, but since she was

42

clocked off, she let her naturally wavy blonde hair fall perfectly around her face. Her pink shade of lip gloss shined when the light hit it just right. Christina caught me staring at her, and I immediately looked back down at the table. My cheeks warmed, and her giggle made me chuckle in return.

"So, what happened at work, Ben?" I asked. I hoped the change in conversation would distract others from seeing me blush.

Ben sat back in his stool and sighed. His arms fell limp at his side. "Mr. Jacobson died today."

Everyone jumped at the chance to send their condolences to him. I knew this had to be particularly hard on him because he didn't deal with death well. When his adoptive father died, he refused to accept it. He didn't even attend the funeral, which ate at him later. I went with Ben to visit his grave some months later after the fact. Death had always been his boogeyman ever since his biological parents died in a car crash when he was a child. He was in the car too, so there was some survivor's remorse mixed up in there. He had no other family, so he was placed in an orphanage. This was the first time Ben has dealt with death since his adoptive father's passing.

I ordered him another drink as my way of sending condolences. He gave a tight-lipped smile when I handed it to him. His sorrow ate at me. I wished I could take it away and feel it instead of him.

Christina reached her arm out to squeeze Ben's upper arm. "I'm so sorry to hear that," she said with a visible frown.

Ben shook his head as he stared at his half empty cup. "It just happened in a snap. One minute I was seeing

43

him and picking up his food, and then the next he died. I had only left his room for maybe an hour." He paused. "It really makes you think, you know? About mortality and all that. One day that's going to be me." He leaned over the table and ran his fingers through his hair. "One day we'll all end up like that."

I thought of my mother, and my heart sank low to my stomach. I took a big swig of my beer.

"I mean what happens after that, you know? I know what procedure to do when a patient dies, but what about him?"

I furrowed my brow and looked at Ben. "What do you mean what about him? He's dead. Nothing happens to him." I knew that was insensitive, but I found that thinking of it logically made things easier. Perhaps he'd find the same comfort in it.

"Really? You honestly think you close your eyes that last time and then lights out. That's it?" Ben sat back in his chair again and crossed his arms, biting his lip.

"I think there's life after death, 'hon,'" piped in Christina.

Ben looked up at her. His eyes wide with hope.

"I watched this special on the Discovery Channel," she said. "And they talked about how energy works. It never dies even after death." She crossed her arms. "They even say after someone dies; they lose a small amount of weight. It's very minuscule, but it's significant enough to take notice. They don't know why. I believe that's the soul leavin' the body."

Everyone peered down at their glasses in contemplation, and Ben nodded his head slowly. "I believe that," said Ben. "I mean, I have to. I must think there's more to life than just dying. I have to believe there is more for Mr. Jacobson."

"There is more to life than death," I chimed in. I pushed my nearly empty glass of beer away. "Life is about experiences and the relationships you make." My eyes fell onto Christina for a split second. Her smile made my breath uneasy, and I snapped my eyes away quickly. "I believe that's all there is. I don't believe in an afterlife or a God who's going to come and punish you for not believing in him. It doesn't seem very healthy to me to worship something like that."

"So, you believe in nothing?" asked Carlos in disbelief.

I shrugged. "I guess so. There's no substantial evidence to prove it. It's just not practical. People are making things up to make themselves feel better because they're scared. I'm not saying for sure there is no afterlife. I'm just saying there isn't proof for either stance, so I have none."

"I find that bullshit," said Ben. "There's *gotta* be more. There has to." Ben was deep in thought, and it fell silent around the table.

"Let's go play some darts, huh?" Offered Frank. Everyone got up to proceed to the side of the bar. I ordered another drink at the bar, and Christina stood next to me as she ordered hers. I noticed how close she was standing. I could feel her body heat on me, and it made my palms sweat.

"For what it's worth. I think you're wrong, 'hon," she said. She had a playful smirk on her face.

I returned the smile. "Oh yeah? And why is that?"

When she got her beer, she took a sip. "I think you're just afraid to believe in somethin' greater than ya'self. You like to keep things where ya' can see them so you can keep ya' eye on it." Her grin reached her eyes, and I made the mistake of staring a little too long into them. Her cheeks turned pink, and she looked down for a brief second before playfully elbowing my side. "Come on, Teddy. Let's play us a game."

Ben went first. He had a total of four darts, and when he made a bullseye on his last throw, he bellowed out, "That's how you do it!" He took a swig of his beer. "The beer helps with your aim."

"In that case," I said as I took a big gulp. "Let me see how well I do." I missed the first throw and didn't even hit the dartboard. The boys around me chuckled. "Hold on," I said. "I was just warming up."

"Sure, sure," they teased.

The sound of metal sticking into wood made me raise my arms in victory. "See? I made it!"

"Yeah, but nowhere close to the bullseye," said Ben laughing as he pointed to the farthest red stripe near the twenty number.

I shot my finger in his direction. "But it's an improvement. It'll only get better from here." I heard Christina giggle, which made me lose my focus when I threw the dart. I missed the board again. My friends all clapped their hands slowly in congratulations. The beer was getting to my head and made my face flush. I found myself smiling without a care as I threw the next dart. This time it was mere inches from the bullseye. "Ah, see? Just warming up here."

"Yeah, yeah, but you're still further behind me," said Ben with a flip of his hand.

Christina stepped up to grab the darts from my hand. Her fingers slowly grazed over my palm purposefully as she eyed me. My buzzed smile got the best of me and made it obvious to Christina how much I enjoyed that small contact.

"Y'all mind if I step in?" she asked in her southern accent.

"Not at all," said the others. They all stepped away from the board.

She made her first throw and got a few inches away from the small red circle. The boys all cooed around her. "Beginner's luck," she said as she threw the other and completely missed the board.

Ben and the others looked to me, and Ben motioned with his eyes for me to go over to Christina. Frank and Carlos stood there grinning urging me to make a move. Christina wasn't paying attention as she went to the board to pull off the dart. Ben mouthed to me, "Go to her. Flirt. Help her."

I nodded my head before approaching her. "Mind if I show you?" I asked. "I have a few pointers."

Christina's cheeks turned bright pink, which made my chest flutter. "Okay." She placed the darts in my hand. "Show little ol' me."

I chewed on my bottom lip as I fought past my racing heart. I guided Christina away from the dartboard and helped her take a proper stance. "You should stand more at this angle, with your body to one side where you want to aim the dart at." I was unsure of my hands, and I thought better than to touch her without her permission.

47

Christina gave a wry smile and said, "Guide me with your hands."

I fought back my shakiness as I placed them on her hips. I moved them to one side and then ran my hand down her arm as I guided them to a throwing position. Ben and the others chuckled, and I glared in their direction. They all looked away with visible smirks on their faces as they drank their beer.

I held her hand in position as she gripped onto the dart. "You will throw it like this." I moved her arm for her slowly. "But do that faster." The backside of her body was pressed up against mine. I hoped she wouldn't be able to feel my heart beating rapidly against my chest. I reluctantly took a step back so she could throw.

She hit a bullseye, and the others cheered her on.

"See? You got yourself a good coach there," pointed out Ben. "You should come here more often to practice together."

I snapped a look at Ben, and he lifted his arms questioningly. "What?" Mouthed Ben.

I leaned over towards him and said in hushed tones, "You're trying too hard."

"And you're not trying hard enough," he whispered.

We finished off another round of beers as we played, and Christina blew us all away by her immaculate win. I was feeling a little buzzed by the end of my fourth beer and found it more difficult to aim correctly at the board.

"Let's call it a night," said Ben as he slammed his empty glass onto the table.

Ben, Frank, and Carlos grabbed their jackets before leaving out the door. I stood at the bar, closing my tab when

Christina walked up, holding her wallet. "I can pay for your drinks," I offered.

Christina's lips curved, and she said, "Thanks, but I've got it. Not that I don't appreciate you offerin', but I'm a proud girl." She held up her wallet and shook it. "I've got my own money."

"I respect that. Will you accept my offer to walk you to your car then?"

Christina's smile grew. "That I will accept."

After the tabs were paid, I held open the door for Christina as she walked out. I stood on her right side closest to the street as we walked around the back end of the building. I zipped up my windbreaker and placed my hands inside the front pockets. Warm air breathed out of me evaporating into the cold air as we continued down the wet sidewalk.

"How is your mother?" asked Christina.

I chewed on the inside of my cheek. "She's alright. She's as you'd expect her to be." I looked down at Christina whose nose was beginning to turn pink. I couldn't help but smile at that. Her soft blue eyes were so inviting and kind. I could easily open up to her. "I bought that house, so I could have her and my father move in." I paused. "I want to take better care of her." I felt a weight shift in my chest. It felt good to talk to someone about my problems other than my sister and father.

Christina reached her hand out and gently squeezed my arm. "You're a sweet man for wantin' to care of your mama like that. I just hope you don't take on too much."

"What do you mean?"

"You have to think about you, 'hon. You can't just think about others only. It's unhealthy."

I shrugged. "I don't only think about others. I bought that house for myself too."

Christina stared up at me with a knowing smile. "Okay, 'hon."

I felt defensive. "I also dedicate my life to my career."

"Yeah, but why did you decide to become a nurse? Because of your mama's diagnosis?"

I paused briefly. I became a nurse shortly after my mother began to show signs of her illness, but she didn't need to know that. "I always wanted to be a nurse," I said more to myself than to her.

Christina remained silent. All she did was nod her head, which only pierced at my anger more. When we got to Christina's car, she turned to face me. "Don't take on too much or you'll stress out," she said. She placed a hand on my cheek, and my annoyance immediately melted away. "Stress can lead to all sorts of things like loss of sleep, appetite, and even hallucinations." She gave a small grin. "I worry about you, not takin' care of ya' self. I hope I didn't overstep my boundaries."

I shook my head. The alcohol in my system splattered my emotions clearly across my face, which I knew I'd be embarrassed about tomorrow. "Thank you." My mother's words echoed in my head, and the alcohol made me feel brave enough to ask. "I was wondering if you would go on a date with me."

Her lips widened into a huge grin. "I'd love that. How does next Saturday sound?"

I took a breath of relief. "That's good."

Christina stepped up onto her tiptoes, and her soft lips gently grazed over my cheek. "Goodnight, darlin'." She unlocked her car door and got in.

As I watched her drive away, my first thought was to call my mother to tell her. However, I thought better of it considering the state she was in earlier this evening and how late it was.

I decided to use an Uber to get home rather than drive after I had been drinking. I waited a few minutes outside the bar for my ride. A young man pulled up and gave me a wave for me to step inside the vehicle.

"Fun night out?" asked the driver.

I peered out the window as I rubbed my hands on my knees to warm them up. My nerves were numbed a bit from the alcohol. "Yeah, it's been a tough few weeks." I furrowed my brow and shook my head. I was *never* this open with others. It must've been the alcohol.

The man looked straight ahead at the road. "I get you. Life can weigh you down." He looked over at his GPS and said, "You live off of Batson avenue?"

"Yeah."

"So, you live nearby that old mansion, right?"

"I live *in* the old mansion."

The driver widened his eyes in surprise. "I didn't think they'd ever sell that house to anyone after what happened."

I jerked my head towards the direction of the driver. "What happened?"

"The realtor didn't tell you?" he said dumbfounded. He whistled. "Pretty sure by law she has to, right? Anyway, the house was where a murder took place about eight years ago."

My heart sank low, and I blinked in disbelief. "A *murder?*"

"It was some girl who got murdered by her boyfriend there. He just went crazy one day, I guess, and started shooting at her."

I bit down and lowered my gaze to my knees.

"They never caught the guy."

I snapped my head back up. "They never caught him?" My voice cracked.

The driver shook his head. "The authorities went searching like crazy, but they never found him. He must've left the country or something. I also heard the house was once a mental hospital."

My heart lurched at what the driver said. A mental facility? I wanted to turn it into a makeshift one for my mother.

"Not sure about that fact, though," said the driver. "But teens always liked to break into it to find ghosts." The driver pulled up to my home, and I stared at it with reluctance. The beautiful paneling was now covered in menacing shadows that spread out like hungry arms out towards the street. The windows that were once welcoming took on a far darker and eerie energy.

"Well, have a good night," said the driver.

I swallowed. "Y-yeah… Thanks." I slowly stepped out of the car and retreated up the steps to my house. The sound of my front door closing echoed throughout the bare walls of my home. It was a stark reminder of how expansive and empty it was. I looked around at all the half empty boxes that still needed to be attended to.

I sighed as I ran my fingers through my hair. Placing my keys into the basket by the garage door, I went upstairs to my room. Despite the history of the house, I wouldn't and couldn't believe it was haunted. The home just had a bad history, and the dreams were just a coincidence. That was it.

Later, that night, I rolled over to my side, clenching tightly to the blankets. I tossed to the other side and pulled them up closer, but my teeth still chattered, and my body shook. I opened my eyes and sat up. The piercing feel of the cold air hitting my skin caused a shiver to roll down my spine. I threw off the blankets and walked out of my room to check the AC. I knew I didn't turn it on since it was the middle of spring, and it was still chilly in Saratoga Springs during that time. The snow had barely melted a few weeks ago.

I rubbed my arms as I walked out of my bedroom, but once I stepped out, I noticed a dramatic change in the temperature. The hallway was much warmer than my room. I stepped back into my room, and the chill hit my face like ice.

I checked every window and vent. I double-checked the thermostat, but it said my AC was turned off. I decided to turn on my heater to see if that'd help. Afterward, I walked over to one of my boxes to take out two extra blankets. I closed my bedroom door before I laid back down in bed and closed my eyes.

Right then, a raking sound like metal gliding against metal made me open my eyes in alert. The sound was small, but since my room was drenched in absolute silence, this made the squeaking all the louder.

I sat up in bed, and plain as day I saw my doorknob turning. The moonlight from my window hit the gold doorknob just right. I could see my reflection on the knob as it turned slowly to the right and then to the left. The aged metal screeched with every movement.

My heart stopped as I froze in place. I clenched tightly to my sheets before taking a deep breath. "This is ridiculous," I said to myself. I blinked wishing the hallucination away, but still, the knob turned. I refused to let fear overcome me, so I yanked off the blankets. I grabbed one of the lamps I hadn't plugged in yet to use as a weapon if needed. Then I charged towards the door, bracing myself for whatever I may see on the other side.

I threw open the door. I had my lamp held up ready to attack, but there was nothing there. While lowering my arm, my brow pinched together in confusion. I looked down the hallway, but there was nobody there. I placed down my lamp onto the floor and shook my head.

"It must be the alcohol," I said to myself. I went downstairs towards the kitchen to get some water. I gulped down one cup and then the second. "Perhaps the water will stop these drunken delusions," I thought. I splashed some water onto my face before heading back upstairs.

I decided that if there were any more noises during the night, I'd ignore them at all costs. I wasn't about to give in to fear and delusions. It was all due to stress, a mixture of alcohol, and that driver telling me about the history of my house. My mind was playing tricks on me. However, it wouldn't let up, not even as I dreamt.

As I slept, I had the same dream of watching that woman in a purple dress running down the stairs of my home in a panic. She screamed as she heard a gunshot set off. I wanted to face the attacker to try to help her this time, but I was forced to follow her. My adrenaline rushed throughout my body as I watched the woman struggle against a tall man with a buzzed haircut. He towered over her, and his muscles in his arms flexed as he pulled at her hair and knocked her down to the ground.

"Get up!" I yelled. "Run!" My hands shook with apprehension.

"Where's the journal?" The man demanded.

I tried to help the woman up, but nothing I did, worked. It was as if I had no strength. It was too late, and the woman got a shot right in the middle of her abdomen. I curled my hands into a fist, ready to fight the man, but as I swung, my arms went right through him.

"You bastard!" I yelled.

The man stepped over the woman's body and shot at her head, killing her. He said, "I'll just find the damn thing myself."

I snapped awake with a fury that pulsed through me, which made my sheets become soaked in my sweat. Despite the dream being over, I could still hear the gunshot ringing in my ears.

Chapter Four
Slipping Sanity

I threw off my blankets and looked out my bedroom window. It was morning already. There was nobody in my backyard or in the neighbors' yards from what I could see. Still, I couldn't get the sound of that gunshot out of my head. I checked all parts of my house, thinking maybe someone had broken in and let off a shot. Finally, I went outside, but there was no disturbance I could see. Everything appeared to be normal, but I couldn't help but think that the shot was real. I shook my head as I went up the steps. I had to get ready for work and stop chasing noises I heard from my dreams.

I called an Uber driver to take me to the bar before work so I could pick up my truck. Afterward, I headed straight to work.

During my shift, I couldn't shake the feeling of how real the sound of that shot was. I was covering for Christina at the front desk during the first part of my shift while she was on her break. I tapped my pencil on the counter as I mulled last night's and this morning's events. I decided to search online for probable causes for hearing a gunshot from my dream in real life. There *had* to be a logical reason.

I came across a site that spoke of dreams and their possible meanings. I exited out of it while rolling my eyes. Then I came across a website that discussed vivid and lucid dreams. I found that more appealing, especially since the article was about a study done on them rather than dream interpretations. "Sometimes our dreams can seep into our waking lives," it read. "Especially if a dream is vivid enough, it can take our brain time to readjust to the waking world."

The article said that when we are waking up from dreams, sometimes our brain is still giving off the Dimethyltryptamine molecule in our brain or DMT, which is the reasoning for why people may hallucinate or hear things that are not there, after just waking up. For me, this was enough to satisfy my uneasiness about the gunshot I heard. I was only in a deep sleep, and when I woke up, I was still half asleep, which caused for the overlapping of the gunshot from my dream state to my awake state.

Christina came back from her break, and I quickly exited out of my search before she could catch me. "Thank you for coverin' for me," she said. I stood up, and she took back her seat at the desk.

I put my hands in the pockets of my scrubs. "Anytime," I said with a shy smile. I opened my mouth to say more but thought better of it.

"Oh, Teddy. Will you give this chart to Monica for me?" asked Christina.

"Monica?" I asked questioningly.

"She's the new girl. Nurse Brooks gave me the updated chart for one of her patients. She has dark, black hair. You can't miss her. She works in the same area as you."

I took the chart and said, "Yeah, sure."

"Thanks, darlin'." I immediately left down the hall in search of this new girl. I glanced into every room I passed by, and Christina was right, I couldn't miss her. She was in the very last room in the hall, and her raven black hair against her alabaster skin was noticeable from even a mile away.

I knocked on the open door, and she turned to me while fluffing a pillow for one of her patients. "Monica?" I asked.

"Yes," she said. Her voice was meek and quiet, and I had to lean in a bit, so I could hear her better.

"This is for you," I said, handing her the chart. "It's from Christina. It's updated information on one of your patients."

"Oh, thank you," she said. "What's your name?"

"Ted Rovers... When did you start here?"

Monica turned to her patient, who was an eighty-year-old woman named Camille. She had been assigned to me when I first started, but when they changed my schedule, they also changed my patients. "Camille, is there anything else you need?"

The woman shook her head as she took a bite of her oatmeal.

"I'll be back to check on you later. Enjoy your breakfast." Monica walked out of the room, and I followed behind her. "It's nice to meet you, Ted. I started here last week."

I accompanied alongside her down the hall. I knew it was tough starting work at a new place, and she seemed shy like I was. I decided to engage in conversation with her. "What made you want to work here?"

"Um…" She was quiet as she thought. "I used to care for my parents. They're getting older so…"

I nodded my head in understanding.

"But being stuck in that house all day made me stir crazy."

I knew that feeling all too well since I was raised in the middle of nowhere up in the mountains in California.

"I was pretty good at taking care of them and enjoyed it, so I decided to become a certified nursing assistant," she said.

"I have a similar story," I said. "It was my mother's illness that influenced me to become a CNA. She has Alzheimer's."

Monica gave me a crooked smile to show her sympathy. "I'm sorry to hear that."

I shrugged. "It isn't easy, but I'm learning to deal with it. It was nice meeting you."

"Likewise. By the way, who is that?" Monica pointed down the hall to the recreational area where Ben was. He was watching us from behind one of the bookcases, and he quickly shoved a book back onto the shelf before scurrying off.

I chuckled. "That's Ben. He's another CNA here."

"He stares at me a lot but never says anything. I tried talking to him yesterday, and all he said was gibberish and wandered off. Is he okay?"

I couldn't help but laugh. *And Ben says* I *have no game.* "He is a bit socially awkward when it comes to women."

"Oh," said Monica. She let out a small laugh. "That's so funny, it's sad."

"It is, but he's harmless. If you were to approach him, he'd run away in the other direction. He has zero luck with the ladies."

Monica smirked. "I can see why. Well, I'll try not to scare him by being in the same room as him."

"Please do," I said. "And nice to meet you again."

My next patient was Hank. He was in the farthest room down the hall. The SNF was made up of the main lobby, which was the first room once someone stepped in to upon entering the facility. That was where Christina worked behind the desk. Next to her desk was a hallway for employees only—it was where the break room was. In the lobby, we had chairs, couches, and a television. Across the room was the main hallway that had a line of patients' rooms. The bulk of my patients were in that section near the lobby.

On the other side of that hallway was the recreational area. There were sliding glass doors in the recreational room that led to the outside fenced area. There was a hallway to the left and right of the recreational room. Both were lined with patient rooms. The medical counter and cafeteria were down one of these hallways.

Once I reached Hank's room, I knocked lightly on the door before entering. Hank was sitting there on his bed wearing his veteran's hat as always.

"Alright, Hank," I began. "It's that time of day."

Hank let out a huff before smiling. "We need to switch out my nurses. No offense to you, but I would much rather have a nice young lady for this job."

I let out a chuckle. "I don't blame you. I'd feel the same way."

Hank slowly got out of bed, but he needed my assistance with getting him to his wheelchair. I swept him up by the legs in one arm while using the other to hold up his back, and I carried him to his wheelchair. He was so light I could feel the fragility of his crippled body in my arms. I would carry him over to the tub, but Hank felt more dignified being taken in a wheelchair, which I respected.

I started up the bath and let Hank check the temperature of the water with his hand to judge if it was too warm or cold. Hank could get out of his shirt just fine, but he needed assistance with his pajama bottoms. "Remember I can wipe my own ass still," said Hank.

"I know, sir."

"You know the drill."

"Keep the briefs on. Got it. You do the rest."

Hank nodded. "Good man. I ain't no God damn baby. I saved lives Goddammit. I took them too. I don't need to be bathed by another man."

I asked, "Are you ready?" Hank let out a huff. I took that as a yes, and I picked him up to place him in the water. I had to stay nearby to make sure he didn't drown or that he didn't need any further assistance, but Hank didn't like me being in the same room. As a compromise, I took a seat outside the bathroom and would talk to him with my back turned.

"How is retired life treating you, Hank?"

"Bah!" Exclaimed Hank, which made me chuckle. "It's terrible. I want to die already. I've been waiting to die for the past twenty or so years. I never wanted to live to an age where I needed to be carried to the damn bathroom."

I nodded my head. "I completely understand, sir. I'd feel the same."

It was quiet. I could hear the water splashing as Hank washed himself. "But," began Hank. "I'm glad to have you as my assigned nurse. My last guy never understood that I was once a man and needed to be treated as such."

"You're still a man."

"That's real kind of you, but a man who needs help taking a shit ain't a man anymore. I'm the shriveled-up prune of what I once was, which is why I can't wait until my last dying breath to end this humiliation for me."

I truly sympathized with Hank. My heart twisted in pain, and a hollow feeling settled in my stomach. There was silence between us for a while. Suddenly, I heard a large splash, and I sat up in my seat. I called out, "Hank?"

No answer.

"Hank?" I asked again.

I heard him let out a small groan.

I immediately stood up in alert. "Alright. I'm turning around to check on you." I saw Hank hunched over with his arm dangling off the side of the tub. I raced over to help him up.

Hank shoved me off. "I'm fine, boy! Just got dizzy is all."

This did little to help ease my concern. My brow remained furrowed as I helped him sit up in the tub. "Why are you having dizzy spells?"

"It's that damn new medication they gave me. Look the other way!"

I immediately left back to my chair so Hank could finish bathing himself. "How long has this been going on?"

"About a week."

I raised my eyebrows and crossed my arms. "And you didn't think to tell me?"

"It was no big deal. Nothing I can't handle."

"What other symptoms do you have?"

"Nausea because of the dizzy spells. It makes my stomach hurt, which is shit because I enjoy those blueberry muffins they got. Last night, I threw it up." Hank grumbled to himself. "Damn old age."

I chewed on the inside of my cheek. I was silent for a few moments and then asked, "Are you finished bathing?"

"Yeah, yeah," said Hank. "Get me out of this damn thing."

I grabbed some newly washed clothes for him and made my way over to the tub. "Now, here comes the hard part," I said.

"Bah, get it over with," said Hank with a flip of his hand.

I looked away at the far wall as I took off Hank's soaked underwear and put on a fresh, dry pair. In my peripheral view, I could see Hank's distinct frown. I wasn't disgusted by changing him. I changed lots of patients, but I knew Hank hated it. Out of respect, I looked away.

After I was finished dressing him and placed him back into his bed, I went to the medicine counter where Frank was posted. "Hey, Frank," I said. "Can you bring me Mr. Charleston's chart?"

"Sure! What's going on?" Frank asked.

"I just want to check something." I looked over Hank's assigned medicine intake. "Is there any way we can switch out his meds? It's making him sick."

"I can ask, but it's not in our scope of practice. I can have one of the main nurses look over him."

Nurse Brooks was never around when I needed him, and even if he were, he'd yell at me for meddling too much in his patients' affairs. He was a stupid and prideful man, and the thought of Hank's suffering made me feel inept. I gave Frank my disappointed face.

Frank gave a sympathetic smile. "I get it, you're frustrated. But it's your job as a CNA to check on the patient and let the main doctor or registered nurse know what's going on."

I nodded my head. My inexperience showing, my frustration only got worse. I tried my best to contain it by clenching my teeth. "He should be off them *now*."

"As far as I know, they've tried nearly every medicine on the market, and it all makes Hank sick. This dosage has given him the least trouble."

I ran my fingers through my hair and said, "Fine. What should I do to make him feel better?"

Frank hands me a cool washcloth. "Use this to cool him down and give him a massage," Frank said. "I'll get him some peppermint tea for the nausea."

I returned to Hank's room. I needed to take my lunch break, but instead, I decided to comfort Hank with a massage and washcloth. This way, I could keep my eye on him. The peppermint tea did help, and I was more confident.

After my shift was over, I went straight home. I was far too exhausted to make myself something to eat, and I collapsed onto my couch the second I walked in through the front door.

An hour later, I woke up to my television being on, but I could have sworn I never touched the remote. However, my mind was far too fogged over to begin to question it. I sat up on my elbows as my eyes fluttered open. The news was on, and the anchorwoman was talking about another mentally ill man that went missing. I stood up from the couch and turned off the television.

Since it was Monday, I decided to plan out my week ahead on my planner, which I hung on the fridge. I took the magnet off the planner and sat at my kitchen table with a pen. I planned to finish the rest of my packing by the end of the week. I bit back a smile as I wrote down my date time with Christina on Saturday. Each day I put a small task for me to do: clean the backyard, transfer money into my savings account for home renovations, grocery shopping, call Mom, and clear out whatever was inside the basement.

After I was finished making my list, I decided to eat that fried rice I never got to last night with some fresh vegetables while I finished unpacking my living room.

As I cleared out one of the boxes, at the bottom of it, I stumbled across an old photo of me, my mother, my father, and Scarlett. I had to have been around twelve years old and Scarlett was nearly two. I had always begged for another brother or sister, and when I finally got one, I didn't like the result. Smirking, I stared at my twelve-year-old self-glaring over at my sister. She was playing with one of my old toys and smiling. At the time, I was going to throw out that toy because I was "too big" for kid stuff. It wasn't so much my idea as it was my father's. He decided I was too old for "dolls." He had gone through my bedroom and threw away all my stuffed animals, saying I had to start acting like a man. That was a hard day for me because my one security blanket, Effy the Elephant, was tossed into the dumpster. I couldn't sleep for that first week without it.

I thought back on that fight between my mother and father after he had gone through and chucked all my toys out. "He isn't ready yet! He's still a boy!" My mother exclaimed.

"Which is precisely why we needed to throw away his little girl toys. He needs to become a man." My father always had a way of sounding angry, even though he was having a normal conversation.

"He's only twelve!" My mother practically pleaded with him.

"And it's high time that he starts acting like it. My father threw away my toys when I was much younger."

"But he isn't you, and you are not your father." I still remember that deafening silence that fell between them after my mother said those words.

We never spoke of my grandfather, and I had no idea why. It wasn't until I was older that I learned my grandfather was an abusive man when he had too much to drink, which was all the time. My mother bringing him up was like a stake to the heart for my father.

"No more toys," was all he said.

My parents gave my G.I. Joe to my sister, which made me want it again.

My mind went back to that day in the park with Scarlett sitting on the blanket playing with my old G.I. Joe. "I want my toy back," I told Scarlett. She stuck her tongue out at me and then laughed.

I screamed before pushing her down. Instead of crying like I wanted her to, she stood up and hit me in the face with the toy. I held my right cheek in my hands. The stinging pain made my cheek throb. I cried out, "Mom! Scarlett hit me!"

"Maybe you shouldn't have pushed her," said my Mom as she fixed us sandwiches. "I saw the whole thing."

That was the last time I was ever violent towards my sister. She punched back.

Later, my mother went to the store to buy a whole new G.I. Joe. She had snuck into my room in the middle of the night, and I pretended to be asleep. She tucked it under my blanket and kissed my cheek before leaving. To this day, I still had that action figure. It was in a box down in the basement with my other memory trinkets.

I chuckled as the memory faded from my mind, and I dug through another box to find a picture frame to put the photo in. Seeing my family all together in one photo made me all too aware of how empty my home was now. The vastness of the house further pricked at the loneliness I felt in my heart. I hadn't realized it had gotten so dark. I flipped on the light in the living room, and then I gently placed the picture frame on my bookshelf beside the couch.

Drops of water kissed the windows as the rain poured. All I had were the sounds of the weather along with the occasional car that drove by causing water to swish in the distance to keep me company.

As I slowly unpacked my books to place on the shelf, a woman's scream filled the air, making me drop my book, and my heart stops beating. My body shook when a shot rang. I jumped to my feet and raced over to the basket where my cellphone was to call the police. There was no mistaking that sound. I wasn't asleep this time.

"911. What is your emergency?" asked the dispatcher.

I ran to the nearest window, but my view of the world outside was obscured from the rain on my window. My voice shook with each word. "I'd like to report the sounds of gunshots."

"Where are you located?"

"Twenty-one fifty-three Batson Avenue. I heard a woman scream before the shot went off."

"The police are on their way."

My hands shook as I gripped onto the window. "Please hurry. I think she may be hurt."

"Can you see her?"

I squinted my eyes as I looked out towards the total darkness. "No. I can't see anyone." I ran to the living room to look through the window. "I don't see anyone. I'm a nurse, so I'll go outside to see if she's okay."

"Please stay inside, sir."

I ignored her and ran out the door. The sound of the rain roared around me, making me deaf to anything else. I sped down the porch steps searching for the woman or perhaps someone with a gun. However, the more I walked up and down the street, the more I realized something: nobody was outside — not a single soul.

I was drenched by the time the police arrived. "Sir, are you the one that called?" one of them asked.

I nodded as my eyes still wandered around, looking for the woman. "Go inside. We have it from here," said the officer. A second officer approached me and helped guide me back to my home.

I sat on my front porch as the cops searched the area using flashlights. Several minutes ticked by. The police called for backup to search the nearby blocks, but still nothing. One of the officers walked up to the porch with his hands hooked to his belt. "We can't find a woman, sir," he said. "We even spoke to some of the neighbors, and they said they didn't hear anything. Are you sure you heard gunshots?"

I stared off towards the edge of my porch. "One. Just one gunshot and a woman screaming."

"Nothing like that happened here. Maybe your television was on, and you mixed it up."

I slowly shook my head. "No," I muttered.

"What was that?" The officer slowly leaned in to hear my voice over the rain.

I gulped. "Perhaps it was my television," I lied. The last thing I needed was being thought of as crazy, but then again, perhaps I was. The officers left, and I sat there hunched over, running my fingers through my hair. I heard it plain as day. I *heard* it. There was no denying it.

I walked back into the house and put my cellphone back in its place in the kitchen. I sat on the couch and thought about Christina's words. Perhaps I was overly stressed and was now hallucinating due to it. I didn't get the best sleep the night before, so that could explain it. That and it was raining. Perhaps it was lightning and the trick of the wind that made me mistake the sound as a gunshot. However, that didn't explain the woman, screaming.

I shook my head. "No, no, no," I said. "I am not about to give in to hallucinations. That's what this was, and I need to take better care of myself." Still, I found myself perking my ears at every little sound that croaked within the house.

I needed to distract myself, so I took my time as I got ready for bed. I even tidied up my bathroom before proceeding to floss every tooth twice. As I worked on the last tooth, I caught something purple at the corner of my eye. It fluttered like a wave down my hallway, and I could have sworn I saw the back of a feminine looking leg.

I ignored it as I swished my mouthwash. I spit into the sink, and when I lifted my head, what I saw made me take a step back in utter shock. I slammed my hand against my chest and gave out a loud yelp. It was unlike me to make such a noise, but the ghostly sight made my body freeze over like ice.

Right behind me in the mirror stood a woman who appeared to be in her early thirties. She was tall for a woman and nearly reached up to my height. She wore a purple dress with jagged edges at the end of the skirt like there were many uneven layers attached. Her hair was a rat's nest, but it complemented her face well. Still, the fading color of her nearly transparent skin along with the lifeless look in her eyes made me uneasy. Not only that, but there was a stranger in my home.

I caught my bearings after the first initial shock and yelled out, "What are you doing here?" I turned my head back to look directly at her, but she had vanished. I slammed my hands onto the counter and gripped tightly as I took a few deep breaths to calm myself. I searched for her in the bedroom by looking through the mirror. My body encased in ice; I couldn't move.

I didn't see anything through the mirror, which made me braver. After I calmed my rapid heartbeat, I searched throughout my bedroom but couldn't find anything. I looked down the hallway and in every other room too. If there was a woman in the home, then she couldn't have gotten far. I scanned every area downstairs, but still, no one could be found.

Before going up to my room, I made sure to lock every door and window. I wasn't about to accept that it may have been a hallucination or, heaven forbid, some kind of ghost. I did what any sane person would do, in my opinion, which was to double-check every possible entrance.

Before heading upstairs, I decided to grab my cell phone so that I could put on my alarm for the morning. However, when I looked in the basket, it wasn't there. My brow pinched together. "I must have left it upstairs," I thought to myself. I trudged up to the second floor fighting to keep my eyes open from my exhaustion as I searched my room for my cell phone. I couldn't find it anywhere. I clenched my teeth as I threw my blankets off from the bed and patted down the sheets. "I don't have time for this!" I exclaimed. I stomped down the stairs thinking I left it in the living room, but I always kept my things in their designated spots. It was rare for me not to. Then again, I had been having a couple of mental slip-ups. I could have easily left my phone somewhere else.

After searching the living room, I decided to retrace my steps of the entire night. Maybe I dropped it outside. If so, the rain would have rendered it useless by now. I went back to the kitchen to double-check if I overlooked something, and right there plain as day was my cell phone in the basket. I chewed on the inside of my cheek, and my hand visibly shook as I picked it up. Heat formed in my chest pressuring me, and I gripped so tightly to the phone that my knuckles turned white. I closed my eyes as I took a deep breath to cool down.

I stomped my way up to my room, crawled into bed, and set my alarm for the morning. I took a few more therapeutic breaths. "I need a night out or something," I said to myself before closing my eyes.

That night, I had the same nightmare that I always had of that woman in the purple dress being gunned down by the same man. Once again, I woke up in a cold sweat. *This has got to stop.*

As I made my breakfast in the morning, which was just a protein shake with a banana on the side, I laughed at myself over last night's events. I looked out the kitchen window, and the rising sun lit up the house with a soft orange color that kissed the old linoleum.

I shook the thought of last night from my mind as I blended my breakfast drink. "It was just stress," I told myself. I just moved into a new home, and I haven't been eating the best the past couple of days. I also got drunk only a few days ago. I need to take better care of myself. I convinced myself that everything I saw and did last night was due to stress and overwork. Perhaps a few days off would do me some good. I should revisit my mother. Maybe spend time in the city with my sister or go on a quiet vacation alone.

I went upstairs to my bathroom and looked through my medicine drawer, where I had a variety of vitamins. I took some B12, vitamin D, John's Wort, and Fish Oil with a giant swig of my shake. That should help jumpstart my system.

I remembered when I first got into the "fit" lifestyle as my mother put it. I did nearly every sport while in school, and my mother would tease me by saying, "Are you planning on competing in the Olympics?" All I wanted was a distraction and something to do, considering we lived up in the mountains. There wasn't much to keep us occupied other than work on the property by chopping wood, feeding the chickens, house repairs, and so on. I just wanted to be around people rather than in seclusion. An added bonus was being away from my father and being in sports was the only sure way of accomplishing that.

Plus, I wasn't all that good in the academic area, so I figured I could always fall back on being a PE coach or something one day even though that wasn't really what I wanted to do with my life. I was lost during my twenties, not knowing what to major in. That was until my mother got sick.

I was in a particularly peppy mood during my shift at work. I wanted to be more positive, and I hoped that'd spill out into my mental and emotional health as well. "It all starts with you," I said to myself, as I clocked in. It was something my mother always used to say. Happiness begins from within, not the outside world.

I checked on Hank by knocking at the door, and I waited to be allowed inside. "Come in," murmured Hank. When I entered, Hank grunted and said, "Now what are you so damn happy about? Wiping my ass fun to you?"

I chuckled. "No, sir. Just a good day is all."

"You got laid," Hank said it like it was a fact, and my cheeks burned. Hank nodded. "That's good for you. Lord knows I don't get any anymore."

I cleared my throat. "I came to check on how your meds have been doing for you. I made a note on your chart for your doctor."

Hank coughed. It sounded like something was trapped in his throat, desperately trying to escape with each breath he took. "Yeah, yeah. I decided to lower the dosage."

"And?"

"And we'll see. It's only been a day."

I breathed out and nodded. That was good enough for me. "You have a good day, sir."

"Bah!" Hank waved his hand dismissively.

On my way out, I bumped into Ben. "Oh, hey!" I said.

"Sorry, man," Ben said with a laugh. "I'm just late getting from my lunch break. I'm hoping to get back to my post before anyone notices."

"I was wondering if you and the guys wanted to go out for a drink," I said. I looked over Ben's shoulder at the new nurse Monica. "I can invite Monica and maybe a few other coworkers as well."

Ben rubbed the back of his head as he bit his lip. He failed at trying to hide his smile at the mention of Monica. "Yeah, alright man."

After work, I made myself a quick salad with chicken before heading out to our favorite pub. I was already feeling better, and my lips curved upward as I felt a newfound hope. While at the bar, I ordered a round of drinks for everyone. "Thanks, man," said Ben as he took a sip. Carlos, Frank, Christina, and Monica all raised their glasses in my direction as a form of thanks.

"You drinking?" asked Carlos.

I shook my head. "Not tonight. I can be the designated driver for anyone if they need it, but I'm trying to take better care of my health lately."

Ben nearly snorted. "How can you invite us all out for drinks and not drink yourself? That's madness!"

Christina was sitting next to me and rubbed my arm. "Everything alright?" she asked me in a low tone so others couldn't overhear.

I looked down at her with a grin. "Yeah, everything is fine." The way Christina's eyebrow curved upward told me I didn't convince her.

"And besides… Like *you* need to eat healthily," said Ben. "You're the buffest, guy, I know." Ben grabbed onto his stomach fat. "*I'm* the one that's unhealthy." He and the other boys laughed.

I chuckled nervously and shook my head. I hated being complimented. "Not so much anymore. Ever since I moved out of that apartment complex, I haven't been able to work out as much. They had a full gym, whereas my house doesn't."

Frank took a considerable glug of his beer. "We could all pitch in to build a gym at Ted's. It'd be nice because that way we don't have to go to a public one and pay all those damn extra fees, and we all live nearby one another. I know where Ted lives on Batson street, and I live a few blocks away."

"Plus, we can all go to the bar afterward. You know, to entice us to work out more," added Carlos.

"Or just go to the bar," said Ben. They all burst into laughter.

"I'm already renovating my house for my Mom," I said. "Adding a gym on top of it wouldn't be too far of a stretch. I was planning on putting one in the basement anyway," I said.

Ben slammed his hand on the table. "Perfect! Get my fat ass to Ted's Gym."

After the laughter died down, Monica spoke up. Her voice was small. I almost didn't hear her speak up, "Which house on Batson street?"

"The old mansion," I said.

Monica's face turned white, and her jaw muscles visibly tightened as she looked down at her drink.

"What's wrong?" I asked.

"My sister lived there," answered Monica.

"Holy shit? When?" asked Ben. His smile told me that he was unaware of Monica's grim expression.

Monica's jet-black hair fell in front of her face, and she tucked it behind her ears. "About eight years ago." She played with the condensation on her glass.

I drew in a sharp intake of breath. "Was she the one who…" I fell silent, unsure of how to finish that sentence.

Monica nodded. Her pink lips quivered a bit, and her already pale face became even more ashen.

"What happened to your sister?" asked Christina.

Monica stared up at everyone. "She was the one who was killed at the house by her boyfriend."

Everyone let out a gasp.

"Holy shit, man," said Ben. "Look, if you don't wanna talk about it..." Ben gestured to everyone around the table. "We'll respect that and drop it right now."

"No, it's fine," she said. "I just never thought anyone would be insane enough to live in that house since the incident." Monica looked to me, and the fear was apparent in her eyes. "Why are you living there?"

I was at a loss for words for a brief second. Maybe it was her question that caught me off guard, but I suddenly felt ashamed for living at that house. I stared at Monica for the longest time. "For my Mom. To help her. It's just a house," I finally said.

Monica chugged her beer and wiped her mouth. "She shouldn't move in there." Monica got up and swung her purse around her shoulder. "Sorry, guys. I must go. Thanks for the beer." She immediately left out the door.

"Way to go, Ted!" Said Ben. He sat back in his stool in defeat. "You chased away my date."

Everyone laughed except Christina and me. I couldn't shake the horrid feeling that knotted up in my chest. It twisted until it dropped down to my stomach. What Monica said sounded like a warning, but I couldn't figure out why she'd say that.

After everyone had enough to drink, I drove them home. Christina was the last to be dropped off. We sat in silence for a bit in my truck. I could see through my peripheral view that Christina was looking up at me and chewing on her lip as though she wanted to say something.

"What do you think Monica meant by what she said?" asked Christina.

I adjusted my posture. "I don't know. Maybe she feels the place is bad luck now or something."

"Probably," said Christina. She looked ahead. "How have you been feeling, Ted? I don't mean to pry, but you seem off today."

I eyed her questionably. "I'm not off. Today was a good day."

"If you say so," she said. "I'm still looking forward to our date."

That made me grin. "Me too. Do you have anything in mind you want to do, or do you want me to surprise you?"

Christina's lips curved. "Surprise me." She let out a light giggle, which made my heart flip. Once we pulled up to Christina's house, I turned to her, but I made sure to keep ample space in between us in case Christina felt uncomfortable being so close to me. Christina's hand hung on the car's door handle. "I will see you this weekend," she said with a wink. She jumped out of the car, and I waited until she was safely inside before I drove myself home.

That following Saturday, I woke up and felt lighter than I had all week. My positive thinking had done the trick. I stood a bit taller, and there was a skip in my walk. I decided to spend the day unpacking the rest of my home before heading out on my date with Christina. My knees weakened at the mere thought of a date with her. I planned to take her to a nice restaurant and end the night with a walk through the city's main park. Christmas lights still hung in the trees along the main walkway that ran through the middle of the park, and I thought it'd be perfect.

I played music on my phone and got to work unpacking the rest of my bedroom. It was mostly my clothes that needed to be hung up. I wasn't a man of excess, so there was very little to unpack. I crushed down the boxes and headed downstairs. The last thing for me to do would be to unpack the rest of the bathroom items and organize the basement.

I held all the smashed boxes in one arm as I made my way downstairs to the basement. I threw the boxes into a corner, and dust blew up into the air. I needed to clean this entire place.

Beside my miscellaneous box, which was filled with old memories, photos, high school yearbooks, and my sports trophies, I saw my old metal bat from my days on the high school baseball team. I held the bat in my hand, and the same white tape around the handle brought back a rush of memories.

As I swung the bat slowly, at the corner of my eye, I saw the door to the mysterious closet that was locked. I placed the bat back down against the wall and went upstairs to grab the keys the real estate agent gave to me. I had been so preoccupied with my mother and unpacking that I completely forgot about the mysterious room behind the door.

Then I had to, nearly, jam the small metal key into the misshapen doorknob. I grunted as I shoved the key further in and jiggled it to fix it in place. I turned the knob, and the aged hinges groaned as the door opened to reveal the room. I stood there with my mouth agape. It was a large storage room filled with abandoned hospital beds, blankets, metal handrails, and metal cabinets.

The room was unorganized, and there was a dusty, torn-up bed in the way that blocked me from the rest of the room. The wheels no longer worked on the bed, and it screeched against the cold, hard cemented floor as I shoved it away. I coughed as the dirt in the air filled my lungs. I searched for a window, so I could make the room less stuffy, but there was none. It was dark, and the only light that I was supplied with came from the small window in the other room at the other end of the basement.

I took out my phone to light my way through the cramped spaces. The room was rather large, and I found myself thinking of a home gym. I could clear it out and use this room as the workout area. I picked up a dusty metal pipe that laid at my feet. It curved at both ends, and I realized it was a handle to install in a bathtub. It was placed in every bathroom at the SNF. I could use it for my mother.

As I passed by the chairs that had leather straps attached and the box filled with the missing locks to the doors, I couldn't help but wonder why this was all kept here in this room. "Why not throw it out?" I thought to myself.

There were metal cabinets covered in cobwebs that I ignored. I wasn't interested in that, but what *did* interest me were the wooden boards on the floor. I lifted them, and a spider scurried out. I quickly dropped the board and stomped on the bug before it could get far. I lifted the large boards again and a huge grin formed across my face. "I can use these to build a ramp up the porch for my mother," I said aloud to myself. I looked around at the supplies in the room and thought of how I could make good use of them.

My excitement was quickly overshadowed by light whispers that made my stomach curdle. They floated in the surrounding air, and my ears perked as I tried to find the source for it. I assumed it was someone talking outside, but then I heard a woman's voice clear as day say, "Listen." I whipped my head around, but nobody was there. The whispers were incoherent, and they all jumbled into one another. I couldn't make out what any of them were saying, but the voices got louder and more persistent. A voice broke out amongst the masses and exclaimed, "Ted!"

My heart nearly lurched out of my chest, and I bolted towards the stairs without a second thought. I raced up to the ground floor, taking two steps at a time before barreling towards my keys in the kitchen. I sprinted down the porch steps towards my car. My hands shook as I struggled to put them in the ignition, and I dropped them before scurrying to pick them up. When I finally turned my engine, I sped off, causing my tires to squeal against the street.

I nearly lost control and barely got a handle on my wheel when I sped past a stop sign. A horn deafened my ears as I drove past a crossing car barely missing it by a few inches. This made me stop momentarily in the middle of the road. I let go of the wheel and closed my eyes. I needed to catch my bearings before I got into an accident. I took several deep breaths until my hands had calmed, and then I gently pushed on the gas pedal.

I didn't know where I was going, but I wanted to put as much distance between me and that house as possible. As I drove into the heart of Saratoga Springs, I saw numerous white tents over plastic tables. These tables had numerous baskets filled with produce on them. Each tent had different food on it, and dozens of people walked between each table buying items. I pulled over to the side of the street and got out. I had forgotten all about the town's weekly farmer's market. I took a deep breath of the brisk spring air. I zipped up my windbreaker and headed across the street.

Most of the Farmer's market was held indoors, but I enjoyed the sights of the newly harvested fruits that were displayed out front. Ahead of me was a giant public building that had ample space on the inside for a drove of people to come shopping for food. Most times, it rained, which is why they had held the market inside.

I bypassed every fruit and went inside. Amongst all the fresh vegetables, there was a butcher who was selling newly cut meat. I thought of the lack of food in my fridge at home and approached up to the table. "Are you interested in anything?" asked the man. "I am selling it by the pound."

I inspected every stack of meat displayed in the man's giant fridge. It had a glass top so you could easily see inside. The pack of bacon caught my eye, and I pointed at it. "Give me a pound of bacon, please."

"You got it," said the man. After the bacon was wrapped up in the white butcher paper and paid for, I couldn't help but smile thinking of my mother and her ridiculous cooking techniques. I didn't need a whole pound, but I thought I could go over to my parents' house a few nights out of the week to cook for my Mom.

I took my phone out of my back pocket and pressed the speed dial button to call my mother. It rang far too long for my liking because she usually picked up right away. When it clicked, and I heard my mother's voice, I breathed a sigh of relief. "Hi, Mom," I said. "I'm at the farmer's market, and I just thought about you when—"

"Who is this?" she asked

I began again. "This is your son, Ted. I'm at the farmer's market, and—"

"Can you pick me up some asparagus?"

I grew confused. "Asparagus?"

Her voice sounded far away like it did when she was having one of her bad days. "You're the delivery man, right? I need two pounds of asparagus. I have a party to go to tomorrow. Sarah is having another baby, and I said I'd make a dish for her shower."

I stopped in my tracks. I remembered our old neighbor Sarah, but that was nearly two decades ago. "Mom, Sarah's party already happened."

"What?" My mother gasped. "When? I missed it!"

"Mom, it happened twenty years ago."

"Oh…"

I sighed. "Hand the phone to Dad, please."

"Who is your Dad?"

I chewed on my bottom lip. "The man who lives with you."

"Oh! You mean the Doctor?"

I let out a slow breath and pinched the bridge of my nose. "Yes, the Doctor. Give me to the Doctor."

My mother was quiet, and I could hear fumbling over the phone — a few seconds ticked by before I could make out much of anything. Then I heard my mother humming. "Mom!" I yelled through the phone.

"Huh?" My mother's voice sounded as though the phone was placed down somewhere far away. I heard pots and pans clanging and water running.

"Mom!"

"Oh shoot," she said. I could hear the fumbling sounds, and then her voice came in louder. "Who is this?"

I was silent as I tried to calm my frustration. I gripped a little too hard on my phone.

The connection through the phone crackled, and my mother's voice became broken up in the loose connection. "Hel....lo?"

"Mom?"

"I... Can't help...."

"Mom?"

"Can't... Hear..." Then the line went dead.

A small crack could be heard as I strangled the phone in my hands. I took a deep breath as I found a seat on a nearby bench. I decided to call my father. When he picked up, I immediately said, "You need to get better cell service. The line just went dead between Mom and me."

My father's sheer lack of urgency only made my anger flare more. "Sorry, son. You know how... Up in these mountains. The reception gets... Sometimes."

"I'm coming to see Mom," I said, and then I hung up.

As I stood up from the bench, I saw that same translucent woman in the purple dress from my mirror. The hairs on the back of my neck stood on end, and I clutched tightly to the package of bacon. Her brown eyes bore into mine, and I felt as if she were silently communicating to me to follow her. She slowly turned and disappeared into the crowd. I walked towards her direction and caught a glimpse of her purple skirt behind a bunch of people. I shoved past the people in an attempt to follow the purple shimmer. Just when I thought I'd gotten close; I'd catch a peek of this mysterious woman in another large crowd and change directions.

I was so preoccupied with searching for a purple dress that I nearly crashed into a table. "Oh, I'm sorry," I said as I fixed the tablecloth.

"That's alright. Accidents happen," said the woman.

I recognized that voice. I looked up, and it was Monica. Her straight black hair was wrapped in braids, and she wore a red apron that said: "Holland Family Farm" with a sewn-on picture of a field and a sun on it.

"Hey, Monica," I said. "I had no idea you owned a farm."

She gave a crooked smile. "It's my parents'. I help with the farmer's market sometimes when they're too tired to come into town. My brothers help with the harvesting nowadays."

I nodded my head in understanding. "It's hard watching them get older, isn't it?"

She grimaced. "The child becomes the parent, and the cycle continues."

I eyed the table, and every basket was filled with different sizes of radishes. "So… a radish farm?"

She shrugged. "Sometimes. We also sell asparagus during the winter."

I snorted.

Monica smiled sheepishly and knitted her brow together. "What's so funny?"

"My Mom is need of some asparagus. She kept going on and on about it for some party that happened over a decade ago."

Monica joined me in laughing and then it died down. The laughter lifted an immense weight off my chest, and I felt so much lighter. It felt good to laugh it off.

"I'm sorry about your Mom," said Monica. "Ben told me about it. That must be hard."

I sighed before I plastered on a grin. "The child becomes the parent, right?"

Monica gave a grim smile. "Right."

I nervously played with the hem of the tablecloth as I contemplated asking the question that was on my mind. "Can I ask about your... sister?" I made sure to tread lightly.

Monica's posture straightened, and she nodded.

"I know this is going to sound weird, but what did she look like?"

Monica's strained face took on a happier expression when she smiled. Her eyes relaxed. "Her name was Lavinia. One thing I remember most about her was how tall she was. She was almost six feet. She had this..." Monica broke off and laughed as she rolled her eyes. "She had the messiest hair a person could have, but she'd brush it every day. No matter what hair products she used, her hair was always permanently curly and poofy. It reminded me of a rat's nest."

My heart stopped.

"She had dark brown eyes too like mine. We both got our eyes from our mother."

My world fell away, and everything became muffled. Without thinking, I asked, "Did she always wear this purple dress with uneven ends on the skirt?"

Monica turned visibly pale, and that moment of joy on her face immediately vanished. "How did you know that?"

I shut my mouth and swallowed. "I don't know."

It was silent between us. I could see the erratic rise and fall of Monica's chest.

"I'm sorry if I overstepped my boundaries," I said. I turned to go, but Monica reached her arm out to stop me.

"There's a reason you're seeing my sister." Monica let go of me. "Maybe... She needs your help."

Before I could come up with something to say, I heard Christina's voice. "Ted? Is that you?"

I quickly turned around, and my heart picked up its pace when my eyes laid on Christina. Right now, it was not a good time for me to be around her, and a bundle of nerves knotted in my stomach. What would she think about me and Monica's conversation?

"What are you doing here?" I asked, walking her further away from Monica's table.

She lifted her basket full of purchased vegetables. "I come here every weekend. I prefer to buy locally." I looked over Christina's shoulder towards Monica, who was still eyeing me warily. My phone burned in my pocket as I thought about my mother. "Are you okay, Ted?" Christina asked.

I blinked before turning my attention to her. "I'm sorry. I'm just distracted."

Christina took on a worried tone. "Is it your mother? Do you need to go be with her?"

"I think I do. They live far away, though." I kept shifting my body back and forth nervously. It made me uncomfortable that I was lying to Christina about why I was skipping out on my date with her tonight, but it wasn't a total lie. That conversation with my mother earlier had made me uneasy, but I didn't think it would be a good idea to go out on a date while I was hallucinating about a dead woman. I needed to get myself in order first and talking to Monica set me completely on edge.

"That's okay." Christina put her hand on my arm, and it immediately made my body relax. "Go be with your mother." She stood up on her tiptoes, and her lips gently touched my cheek. "I fully understand. We can reschedule." When she looked into my eyes, I could see her immense worry. I hated that, and I hated how I wasn't being honest with her. There was just too much on my mind to enjoy a simple date. "Do you want me to go with you?" Christina offered.

I shook my head. "Not this time. Maybe next time." I made sure to smile down at her to let her know that everything was okay. "But thank you for offering."

Christina smiled in return, and I caught relief in her eyes. "I'm glad to see you're still with me," she said. "You're finally making eye contact with me."

I grimaced.

"I'm worried about your well-being. You've been so spacey lately."

I rubbed the back of my head. "I know, and I'm sorry. I just…" I looked behind me towards the exit. "I just have to go."

Christina pursed her lips together. Her smile was gone. I didn't like the way she didn't say anything in response, but I didn't have time. I needed to see my mother first and then figure out why I was hallucinating about a woman I don't know. As I walked back to my truck, the thought of my slipping sanity made me grip tightly to my hair.

Chapter Five

Loss of Control

I raced up the mountain towards my parents' home in my truck. They had moved up there a few years back when my father retired. They always wanted a cabin of their own and lived only a few miles away from the lake. It was about an hour drive up the mountain, and I couldn't even enjoy the music on my radio as I shifted in my seat. I wasn't sure where to place my focus: on my insanity or my Mom.

Finally, I reached their home. The smell of the fresh air, pines, and wet moss hit me with a sense of nostalgia. The cool air blew through, causing my hair to shift in the breeze. As much as I enjoyed being in town with others, there was a part of me that still loved the woods. It was where I learned how to hunt, track, and take care of myself. It was where I became a man.

I let myself inside my parents' home. It was a decent sized place and much nicer than my childhood home in the California mountains, which was made completely out of cement. My father wasn't much of a carpenter, and he decided to make a cemented home with wooden floorboards.

It made everything cold and wet. The cabin my parents lived in now was already there when my parents purchased the property, and it was a nice two-bedroom home. My sister and I had already moved out by the time they moved up here after living in Saratoga Springs for a while. I liked that they lived here because if I ever needed to get away, I had a place to stay. My family wasn't the type where you had to call ahead of time before visiting. You could drop by any time unexpected. My sister and I even had our own set of keys to their house.

My father was in the kitchen when I entered the home, and the smell of oak hit my nostrils. The kitchen was to the left, and the living room was to the right. In the middle was the fireplace, which made the entire home smell like a campfire whenever in use. It was a smell I enjoyed. In the back of the house passed the kitchen was the small hallway that led to the two bedrooms.

"Hi there, Ted," said my father. "I wasn't expectin—"

I interrupt my father. "Where's Mom?"

He pointed with the wooden spoon he was cooking with. "In the living room."

I immediately made my way over to her. She sat there in front of the television with one of our family knitted blankets over her lap. The television was a small one from the early two-thousands. It wasn't even a flat screen. My parents weren't too much into technology. It sat on its own stand, off to the side near the fireplace. Everything in my parents' home was outdated. The bookcases were passed down from two generations ago. The kitchen table was stained with food and water rings from cups. I had carved my name underneath it when I was fourteen, which I got in trouble for, and it was still there. Even the couch was the same one they had for decades. I don't even want to know how old their mattress was. The one I had growing up was as stiff as a brick. It had belonged to my great grandparents, and when they died, my parents took it. Who takes an old mattress? One of these days, I was going to need to go shopping for them to get new furniture.

I knelt beside my mother and patted her arm. "Hey, Mom."

My mother was distracted by the television.

I glanced over at it, and it was the news. They were talking about another missing mentally ill patient who ran off. I tried getting her attention again, and she finally looked over at me and smiled. Her eyes were glazed over and had that far away gaze. "Hi, there. Are you here to deliver us our groceries?" she asked.

I pressed my lips tightly together and shook my head. "I'm your son Ted."

My mother's mouth fell open a bit, and her forehead creased together in confusion. She looked up at my father for help and then back down at me. "I am sorry, but I don't have a son. Not that I can remember."

It was as if someone slammed their fist to my gut, and my heart dropped. "I *am* your son, remember?"

"When?"

"Remember when your mother used to show us how to knit blankets?" I lifted her blanket, and she snatched it out of my hand with a frown.

"*Don't* touch my things. I don't know you," she said.

93

I swallowed the lump in my throat, which made it difficult to speak. "Remember when I would get hurt? You used to, always, sit me on the table and do the medicine dance before putting the ointment on my scratch?" I smiled, but the tears still broke through my eyes. "It was a magic dance, you said. It'd make it so the medicine wouldn't hurt my leg."

My mother's eyes scanned over me with unrecognition. Finally, her eyes lit up like a light bulb went off in her head. "Oh yes, I have a son. He was here a little bit ago." She looked around the room. "Not sure where he went."

"*Me. I'm* your son. I'm right here." I fought back the tears, but they just fell down my cheeks anyway.

My father came to my side with his arms reached out. "Son, this is how this illness works. I think it's best we—"

I clenched my teeth as my fists shook. I pushed past my father knocking back his arm. I marched into their bedroom and slammed open their closet door. I rummaged through it, throwing my mother's clothes onto the bed.

"What are you doing, Ted?" I could hear my father's stern voice behind me. It was clear by the tone that he lost all patience with me.

"Mom is coming home with me," I said.

"No, she's not." His voice was firm.

I turned to him. "It's obvious you can't take care of her! She's getting worse!"

"Of course, she is!" My father's voice matched mine. "There is no cure! We've been over this. You need to stop—"

I cut him off by shaking my head as I grabbed more of my mother's clothes from her dresser.

"You are in denial, Ted!" My father stepped into the room. "You and I both know Mom isn't going to get any better. You have to live with it."

I screamed at him. I yelled as though it would be enough to convince myself that my Dad's words were lies. Of course, I knew deep down that my mother wouldn't get better, but what if? What if she could somehow? What if there was some hope? There were advancements every day. Why not for Alzheimer's?

"Maybe you can, but I don't have to! I refuse to." I yelled. I grabbed a bundle of my mother's clothes as I made my way towards the door. My father blocked it by standing there with his arms spread out against the door doorway. "Move!" I demanded.

My father stood up taller. His chest puffed out. "Not until you calm down and put your mother's clothes back. You are acting on impulse. This is unlike you."

"Move now! Or I'll make you move!"

My father took a readied stance. "How are you going to make me move, huh?"

The ground my teeth together and my rage blinded my every rational thought. All I could think about was getting him out of the way, so I could finish what I needed. I threw down the clothes. The hangers landed haphazardly on the ground below us. The edge of one stabbed into my flesh, as I swung my fist, and made contact with the cartilage in my father's nose. I felt his nose give way to the pressure of my knuckles, and he stumbled back with his head cocked back. He grabbed ahold of his nose, and blood seeped out through his fingers. His eyes were wide in shock, and I instantly dropped my fist and froze.

For a minute, we just stared at one another. Both unsure of what to do next—Both surprised by the turn of events. I stared down at my fist as though it were a stranger to me—A separate entity that acted on its own accord. I opened my mouth to say something, but no words would come out. My father had already made his resolve. He pointed towards the front door. "Get out," he said with a steady voice.

I swallowed hard. I held my head down, hoping my father wouldn't see the clear pain in my eyes. Rushing towards the door, I yanked it open and stomped out of the house. The tires on my truck spun out as I sped off the property. My body jerked and swayed as I drove down the steep, dirt road.

My knuckles turned white, and my fingers were red as I gripped onto the wheel. Once I arrived home, I slammed open my front door causing the windows to rattle. I paced back and forth in my living room, and my chest rose and fell erratically with each thought.

This is how this illness works.

You can't fix Mom.

The medicine is to only help with the symptoms.

I gripped onto my hair and pulled until a searing pain gripped my scalp. I let go and shook my arms jumping a few times, hoping to rid myself of the sour heat that formed in the pit of my stomach.

I needed to do something—Anything. Perhaps pacing some more would make my anger and panic better, but my ears only grew hotter, and my breath shortened. The emotional build up was too much, and I found myself blacking out again from both rage and now utter panic. I stomped over to the bookshelf and threw it over. I chucked my side table next. I heard a crinkling at the bottom of my shoe and looked down to find that I was stepping on the glass of a picture frame.

I bent down to pick it up. My mother's face was now shattered right through the middle, and a clear cut ran through my face. I smoothed my fingers over the shattered glass. I plopped down onto the arm of the couch and hunched over, staring down at the photo. A drop of water plunked onto the glass, and I wiped the next tear from my eye. To my astonishment, I was crying. I couldn't fight it back anymore.

I was alone. Nobody would see or hear me, so I let them fall. One by one, the tears rained down over my broken frame and the mess of my life. I dropped my arms at my sides and let out a low howl. The thought of my Mom's deteriorating health punched me in the gut once more.

A few minutes passed, and the hum of the refrigerator was what filled the silence. I sat there, numb. All feeling had been vanquished slowly through every teardrop. Suddenly, my ears perked as I heard slow thumping upstairs. I sat up and looked towards the ceiling.

Thump. Thump. Thump.

I slowly stood up so as not to make the floorboards creak from underneath me.

Thump. Thump.

The sound of shuffling led me to believe someone was upstairs. "Hello?" I called out. The footsteps sped up at the sound of my voice. My heart froze, and my stomach churned. I could hear it run straight across the hallway towards the master bedroom where the bash of the door slamming shut made me jump.

Instead of cowering in fear, I ran to the kitchen to grab my knife. A hot pool of rage settled in my core. "Leave now!" I yelled. I stomped my way up the steps. "Leave! Go away!" I thought of what Monica said. Images of my mother's face from when she was younger flashed before my eyes followed by the slow regression of her happiness as she became sicker. "I can't do anything for you!" I yelled at this invisible trespasser as I advanced towards the master bedroom. "I can't do anything to help you!"

I broke through the bedroom door to find nobody in there. I lowered the knife and rubbed the back of my head. The cesspool of fury immediately left me, and instead, it was replaced with embarrassment. I heard the door creaking, and I turned my head slightly to see the door moving on its own.

At the corner of my eye, I could see an all-encompassing black abyss in the form of a silhouette. Frozen stiff from the shock of it, I had no time to react before it darted towards me. Its arms swung side to side, and its legs picked themselves up higher like a rabid animal. I heard the pounding of its feet hitting the ground with each step. I couldn't make out if it were an animal or a person, but whatever it was, it pounced on top of me. Ice coursed through my body leaving me in a motionless state.

A flash of light covered my eyes transporting me. I was in the same house, but the lighting was brighter. Everything was different. The sun poked through pink curtains, and a queen-sized bed sat on the opposite side of the room from where I had placed mine. There was a desk beside the window and standing in front of it was a curly haired woman scrambling through papers and throwing things off the desk searching for something. She picked up a black leather-bound journal and hid it in her gray colored sweater. She wore a familiar-looking purple dress, and my breath caught in my throat when the woman turned around, and I saw it was Lavinia. My eyes widened, and I froze in place waiting for her to scream at me for intruding in her home, but she didn't seem to notice me. Massive bags hung underneath her eyes, her collar bone stuck out more than what I deemed to be normal, and her arms were like twigs.

She scurried past me without a glance in my direction and tiptoed downstairs. She was hunched over concealing the journal in her sweater, and she looked both ways before continuing down the steps. I followed her as she ran on to the basement door. Her dress danced in the air as she raced down the steps towards the basement storage closet. She took out a bundle of keys on a round, silver ring.

On the door were five different types of locks that bolted it shut. Lavinia's ravaged eyes peered behind her as she hurried to unlock everything. She pushed open the door, and the storage room was filled with so many more items than mine was now. An entire box was dedicated to thin metal hammers, orbitoclasts, antique syringes, metal hand drills, and sharp pins. Another box had hospital trays and gowns. I noticed something new in Lavinia's basement that I did not have, and that was a metal table that appeared to strap in a person like an animal. It separated each leg and seemed to have straps to pin down the wrists along with a metal bar with screws to keep the head in one place.

99

I shuddered at the thought of what took place on that table. I focused on Lavinia instead, and she was far off in the corner of the room near the metal cabinets. She had taken off her sweater, which still had the journal inside of it, and stuffed it inside one of the drawers. She locked up the cabinet with another key. She heard a male's voice call out in a sing-song voice. "Lavinia. Where are you?" The sound of the voice made a cold, menacing shiver run down my spine. Lavinia froze for a split second before racing out of the room and locking every bolt again. She then slipped the keys into the top portion of her dress before running up the steps.

An invisible force pushed me, and the image of Lavinia faded away. I snapped back to reality, falling to my knees in the middle of my bedroom. I couldn't help but cough and heave at the utter shock of what I just experienced. My whole body shook uncontrollably as I crawled over towards my bed. I clung to the bedpost as if it were my life raft back to sanity. I darted my eyes around the room searching for that shadowy silhouette, and I silently begged for it not to return.

After what felt like hours, I eventually got a grip on myself well enough to head downstairs. I patted the walls and the handrail as I descended to make sure everything was still solid and real. When I reached the kitchen, I opened the top cabinet to grab a glass of water. I fumbled it in my shaking hands and nearly dropped it before placing it under the faucet. I chugged down two full cups of water and splashed more on my face.

I eventually crawled into bed, but all through the night, my eyes would snap open at the tiniest sounds. Never had I gotten such vivid hallucinations. That's what that was, right? It had to be because there was no way any of that was real. What would you call seeing visions while awake like that? Waking dreams? I wasn't sure which was more frightening: the shadowy silhouette or me losing my mind.

In the morning, I swung my feet over the bed and sat there hunched over. I blinked several times and stared at the dust that floated in the air. The late afternoon sunlight covered my feet. I had slept nearly all day but was still exhausted. I picked up my cell phone that sat on my nightstand to call work.

"Saratoga Springs Skilled Nursing Facility. How can I direct your call?" It was Christina.

"H-hi…" I cleared my throat. "It's Ted."

"Oh!" Christina's voice perked up. "How are you feeling today?"

"I believe I'm coming down with something," I lied. My coarse and exhausted voice made it believable.

"Oh my. Do you want me to stop by after work to give you some soup or something?"

I faked a cough in order to sell it more. "No. I don't want to give you what I have." *Total insanity—It can spread like wildfire.* "I just need to call to schedule today off from work. I don't think I can manage it."

"Of course. I'll let them know." Christina took on a soft tone. "Feel better, Teddy."

"Thanks." I hung up and tossed my phone onto the bed beside me. The day off would help me get a better mental grip on myself. Time outside would do me some good.

101

I got up and went down to the basement to grab my old metal bat. I dug through my old box of memories and found my batting helmet. The blue paint on it was slowly chipping away, but it still fit me. I threw the bat and helmet into the back of my truck, and I drove to the local batting cages.

The cool breeze hit my face as I made my way towards the cashier to pay for a couple of rounds. The wet air hit my nostrils and soothed me with the smells of fresh spring. The sun provided ample warmth as it sat uncovered in the sky.

"Two rounds, please," I said.

"It's automated, so you pay as you use it," said the cashier.

I grimaced. "Sorry, it's been a while."

The man forced the typical polite smile that was expected of a customer service worker. "It's alright. You just need a few rolls of quarters. It's a dollar for every ten balls."

"Sounds good. Can you convert this five-dollar bill to quarters for me?" I handed him the bill.

"You got it," said the man.

I stretched my arms out and did a few lunges once inside the batting cage. I placed one-dollar worth of quarters into the automated cashier inside my batting cage. The hum of the machine turning on made me take my usual stance. I hit the first few, but then missed the last of them. With batting cages, if the person couldn't keep with the rhythm of the machine, it messed up with the whole groove.

I placed in another dollar, and this time, I only missed a couple. As I practiced, I got better, and my hits got stronger. The ball would fly farther and higher with each swing. Sweat beat down my face, and I quickly wiped it away with my sleeve before the last round of balls could start.

I found the exercise to be uplifting. It served me well to spend time outdoors grounding myself to the Earth—To reality. Afterward, I went across the street to a local bar for a drink and some lunch. I sat down at one of the high tables and waited for a waitress. I'd been to this bar before, so I knew their menu already. A petite young woman approached me. "How can I help you?"

"I'll take one of your best IPAs and your double guacamole burger."

She gave me a big grin and with a flip of her ponytail said, "Right on it!"

I made myself relax by watching the baseball game that played on one of the televisions. The waitress came back with my beer, and I took a swig of it as I continued to watch the game. A news channel that played on another television caught my eye. I read the captions as a man stood outside a home holding a microphone and speaking towards the camera. "I'm outside the Shire's home where an older woman has gone missing. She lives in this home, and her daughter has been taking care of her since her mother was diagnosed with dementia just a few years ago."

My heart deflated at the news. The fact that the older woman had an illness like that of my mother was all the more heart-wrenching.

"I'm here with the daughter, Sara. Sara, walk us through the night she went missing."

Sara had her arms crossed, and she had to speak up over the wind that was picking up. "She always tended to

103

walk off. I always had to keep my eye on her. I had put her to bed for the night, and usually, once she's asleep, I clean the house and get ready for the next day. While I was showering, she must've woken up and snuck out the back door. It was wide open, and I looked everywhere, but…" Sara sniffed. "She was nowhere to be found."

The man reached his arm out towards her. "Thank you for telling your story, and I hope your mother is found safe soon."

Sara nodded her head, and the camera focused itself on the reporter only. "This is just one of the many people that have gone missing recently. All of them have one contributing factor, and that is mental illness. The police are hard at work searching the woods and homes, hoping that anyone can point them towards a clue. Anyone who has any information, please call the number that is displayed below."

I thought of my mother, and I decided to give her a call. "Hey, Mom," I said once she picked up.

My mother's voice sounded light-hearted. "Hi, sweetie. How are you?"

"I'm fine." I leaned back as the waitress placed my burger on the table. "I'm about to eat, but I just wanted to know how you were doing today."

"I'm fine. Are you sure *you're* okay? Dad told me what happened." Her tone was short, with no hint of joy in it. I was in trouble.

I let out a deep sigh. "Look, I know I was over the line—"

"You're damn right."

Well, at least she's having one of her good days. "I'm just…" I trailed off as I searched for an excuse, but I didn't have any. I knew I was in the wrong. "I'll apologize to him soon. I just need time. He's probably still pissed."

"Oh yeah, and rightfully so. You better apologize soon, or I'm gonna drive all the way to your house to beat you senseless." Despite the clear anger in her tone, I could also hear the humor behind her remark, and it made me smirk.

"I will. I promise."

Her tone became solemn. "What's going on with you, Teddy? It's not like you to be violent."

I didn't know if I wanted to tell her about the visions I'd been having, so I settled on, "I'm just under a lot of stress, and I worry about you."

"Me being sick isn't an excuse to hit your father. You have control issues; you know that? I love you, but someone needs to tell you."

I rolled my eyes. "Scarlett does plenty."

"I'm sure she does, and it seems you need to hear it more often. I'm *fine*. Your father takes good care of me, and you need to stop barging in and making a mess of my clothes."

Again, that frustrated tone with a touch of humor made me smile. "Okay, Mom. I'm sorry."

"I forgive you, but if you do it again, I'm kicking your ass." She laughed lightly. "You can't see it, but I winked."

I chuckled. "I love you, Mom."

"I love you too. Take care of yourself."

"I will. I must go. My food is here."

I hung up and quickly dug into my burger. I tried my best to focus on the game, but my mind kept wandering back to the missing people. I drank a glass of water and waited an hour after my meal before driving my truck home.

Once I got to my house, the sun was beginning to set, which made me feel apprehensive. My palms began to sweat, and I took a deep breath to calm my beating heart. I turned on every light in my house and kept the television on. I was far too distracted by the strange vision I saw the night before to even pay attention to what was on the TV. I thought that it had to have been a dream, but it was far too real. And I was clearly awake. My hands shook, and I held them tightly together to stop it. It wasn't the visions that scared me but my loose grip on reality.

I looked up at the ceiling as I sat back on the couch. The thought of Lavinia flashed across my mind. I wondered how true my visions were. What if it was just a coincidence that Lavinia fit Monica's description? I didn't want to believe ghosts were real because that scared me far more. I decided to take out my cell phone to search for any information about Lavinia. Perhaps I could debunk what I have been experiencing to give me some peace of mind.

I typed in her name along with "murder" and "Saratoga Springs." An article from eight years ago popped up, and it featured a photo of Lavinia. It was the same woman I had been hallucinating about. My heart stopped. I ground my teeth together as I debated whether to read on. The article was titled: Local Woman Killed by Boyfriend Outside Home.

There was a photo of Lavinia's body lying on the muddied grass. I recognized it as the front yard. Her upper body was blocked from sight by a couple of officers standing beside it in the photo, so all I could see were her legs.

However, I saw the same jagged edges of her purple dress, which made my muscles tense.

The article detailed how many times Lavinia had been shot: twice. One shot in her mid-abdomen and one in the head. The same as in my dreams. I developed a cold sweat. At the end of the article, it said that the boyfriend was still at large. I scrolled down and saw the photo of the killer. I dropped the phone out of my now shaking hands. My breathing quickened, and I closed my eyes as I tried to calm myself.

The boyfriend was the same man I had seen in my dreams. I'd recognize those piercing blue eyes anywhere. I slid off the couch to grab my phone, but my hands were shaking too much to get a good grip. How could I dream about someone I'd never seen?

I shook my head as I tried to make sense of everything. This was ridiculous. I must've heard about it before on the news years ago, and it must've stowed away in my subconscious. That was all. I finally got ahold of my phone and read the name of the boyfriend: Howard Jefferson.

A feminine voice hissed in the air. "Ted," it said.

I shot up and looked around the living room.

"Ted."

I turned the television off. Silence enveloped the room, and all I could hear was my heart beating against my chest.

Again. "Ted."

It was coming from the basement.

I crouched as I slowly approached the basement door. I debated whether to go down there, but I told myself I had to in order to make sure it wasn't a burglar. My muscles tightened as I inched myself down each step. My mind fought against the idea of some unknown person saying my name, but I clearly heard it.

Once I reached the bottom floor, I froze in place at the sight before me. The sight of Lavinia's ghostly figure in the middle of the basement made me nearly gasp. It was dark in the basement, but somehow, Lavinia's body glowed.

There was no expression on her face. Her head snaked towards the direction of the storage room door before vanishing. I stood completely still as my eyes darted around the room searching for her. I had an inkling that there was something about that closet she wanted me to see. Maybe she'd leave me alone if I gave in.

I steadily headed towards the basement storage door. I gripped onto the doorknob, and a wave of visions rushed through my mind. Voices soon followed, and they came at me in droves like a giant wave crashing into me one after the other. They swarmed my mind. I closed my eyes and clenched my teeth as I tried to get a grip on myself. They wouldn't go away, and I fell to my knees and shook my head, as my last-ditch effort to force the voices out of my mind.

That was when the vision started. I saw women and men in hospital gowns being injected with some unknown liquid by a doctor. The doctor looked to be in his mid-forties, and the way he was dressed along with the gowns of his patients told me that this was a hospital in the early 1900s.

A second vision came flooding in. This time, the same patients laid pinned to a metal bed while the doctor strapped their heads firmly to the bed. The sight made me squirm. The patients struggled to get out while others were so heavily drugged that they drooled. The doctor began grinding into their skulls, and they all laid their limp.

One after the other, the images came crashing and taking over my sight — images of bodies being cut up and buried. Then visions of charred corpses filled my mind. I planted my hands onto the ground and began to heave.

A feminine woman's voice broke through among the chaos. It was raspy, and it sounded familiar to the one that called out my name. "I need your help."

I gingerly crawled towards the stair steps. "The people missing…." Said the voice. Again, I was slammed with more images, but this time it was of the reported missing people wandering towards the woods. "He's back," said the voice.

I vomited violently on the floor, and I looked up to see Lavinia's face. I felt a pressure in my head as I stared at her. A muffled knock caught my attention, but I still couldn't look away from the apparition in front of me. Lavinia's mouth moved to speak, but her voice was muffled too. All I could see were her lips moving. I squinted as I stared at her. The smothered banging came again followed by rapid, high-pitched rings. I blinked, and suddenly, Lavinia was gone. The pressure ceased, and I could hear someone knocking on the door, followed by numerous doorbell rings.

I quickly stood up and wiped my hands on my jeans. I shook my head, hoping to rid myself of the memory of what happened as I made my way upstairs. Before opening the door, I wiped the last of the vomit from around my mouth.

"Hey, dude!" Scarlett said. "Mind if I come in?" She didn't wait for me to respond and walked right past me. Without missing a beat, Scarlett threw her jacket and purse onto my couch and turned to me with her arms out. "So, what the fuck, dude? You punched Dad in the face?" She dropped her arms to her side. "Why is Dad calling me freaking out saying like…" She deepened her voice to imitate our father. "You need to check on Ted. He's been acting strange, and he is in over his head, and blah, blah, blah." She widened her eyes at me. Her voice turned back to normal. "So, what's going on there, huh? The fuck?"

I rubbed my forehead. "I'm not in the mood right now."

She rolled her eyes. "Okay, whatever. Well, I'm here to check on you because Dad said so."

My head fuzzed over, and I gripped onto the wall to stabilize myself. Scarlett's brow furrowed in concern, and she reached her arms out towards me.

"Woah, dude. You okay?" she asked.

"How did you get here so fast?" I asked. "I went over to Mom and Dad's not too long ago."

"Dude, it's Sunday. You went over to Mom and Dad's on Saturday, remember?"

I pinched my brow together. "Really?" I nearly tumbled over.

"Dude, go to the couch. I can't lift your big ass over there." Scarlett had her arms around me as she guided me. Once my body nestled into the cushions, I peered at my wristwatch. Scarlett was right. It was Sunday evening. I had a giant lapse in time that I couldn't account for. I remember coming home from my parents. I remember the batting

110

range, but they all felt like dreams. They were far away events that felt like they happened ages ago, but I knew they were recent. My stomach churned, and I winced at the queasiness.

"Are you hungry?" Scarlett asked. "I'll make us something." She headed towards the kitchen and called out. "What do ya' got in your fridge?"

My mouth twisted as I stared at my watch. There was no way a whole day passed. The sun was still up when I got home, wasn't it? How is it so dark already? It was past ten o'clock at night. The thought of losing my grip on time left me in a panic. I heard sounds of Scarlett slamming the refrigerator and then pots clanging. "Dad is overreacting," I said, needing to change the subject.

"Huh?" Called out Scarlett.

I raised my voice. "Dad is overreacting. I'm fine."

She poked her head out of the kitchen. "Is he, though?" She lifted her eyebrow, and I glared at her before rolling my eyes. Scarlett turned her attention back to making dinner. "I say…" I heard a loud crash of a pot hitting the stove top. "We put Mom in a home," she said. I heard sizzling followed by the aroma of melted butter with garlic. It made my mouth water. "She almost wandered off again."

I ground my teeth together and balled my hands into fists. "If Mom is going to be put into *any* home, it'll be mine."

Scarlett was silent. Her doubt was palpable even from the other side of the house. After a moment, she snorted and said, "You can't even handle yourself. Look at you, dude; you're losing your shit and punching Dad. How are you gonna take care of Mom like that?"

She was right. I couldn't take care of things. I was losing my mind over this. The dreams. Lavinia. The murder. The visions. I was in my own hell.

"What's really going on with you dude?" she asked. "You were never the violent one. You always had things under control. I hated you for being so perfect."

"I can't talk about it," I said. "A lot of things are going on in my life. I'm trying to understand it myself."

"How are you not doing well? Are you sick?" She took a pause. "Or are you in love?" she asked teasingly. "Who is it?"

I wasn't going to get into my feelings for Christina at this moment. I wanted to tell her about the house and Lavinia, but I knew she would say it was all in my head. I wish it were the case. "I'm under a lot of stress. It's work-related." I lied. Hopefully, she bought it.

"Well, worrying about Mom is only gonna make it worse," she said.

A bottomless pit formed within me, and my shoulders curved inward as I hunched over. "I know she won't get better," I said.

We shared a silence filled with pain.

"I'm sorry," she said after a while.

A knot formed in my throat, and I swallowed to force it down. "Me too."

Scarlett and I sat across one another at my small, round kitchen table. My arms were limp at my sides as I stared at my plate. The cooked chicken with collard greens made my mouth water, but the dark, twisted pit in my stomach made it difficult for me to muster the strength to eat.

I could hear the clinking of Scarlett's fork hitting against the glass plate as she ate. She didn't say a word, and I was thankful for that. Scarlett was good about not asking too many questions about our emotions, and I liked that about her the most. She dabbed her fork at her cut up chicken before taking a bite.

I eventually lifted my heavy arm to pick up the fork. It felt dense in my grip as I took a bite of the greens. Scarlett had turned on the television to listen to the news, and they were talking about the missing mental patients. It made my stomach curl inward, and I thought of what Lavinia had said to me in the basement.

"It's madness," Scarlett said. "Someone must be doing something to those poor people."

My cheeks began to ache as the vomit rose up my throat. I placed down the fork and wiped my mouth with a napkin. "I'm not very hungry," I said. I excused myself up to my room.

My empty bed looked inviting, and I crawled under the covers without bothering to dress into my pajamas. At some point, I woke up to a light knock. "Hey, Ted. Dude," said a soft voice.

I stirred and looked up to see my sister. "I cleaned your kitchen and shit. I gotta go because I got called into work in the morning. You gonna be okay here?"

I groaned as I nodded.

"Call me if you need me, yeah?"

I let out another groan before my head fell back onto my pillow.

"Feel better, dude," Scarlett said, and she quietly closed my bedroom door.

Hours later, the sound of whispers woke me. I flipped onto my back and stared up at the ceiling as I listened some more. The whispers got louder. It sounded like several voices speaking all at once in a rush. My eyes flew open, and when I sat up, across my bedroom, I saw dark shadows. At first, I thought it was the moonlight casting shadows of my furniture, but as I stared further, my blood quickly ran cold. Clear, distinctive masses of blackness took their stances throughout my room.

"W-who's there? Who are you?" I called out. My voice faltered, and I tried my best to control my shaking body.

There was no answer. I thought it could be Lavinia, so I called out her name. The whispers started up again, and they got louder and filled the entire room. I could only catch glimpses of what was said.

Experiments.

He's still here.

Ashes hidden in the walls.

"Go away!" I yelled. I squeezed my eyes shut. When I opened them, the shadows had vanished. I took a sigh of relief, but then a dark mass began to form low to the ground by the bedroom door. My breath caught in my throat, and I clenched my bedsheets in my fists. The dark silhouette steadily got larger as it inched its way closer to the foot of the bed. It was dead silent in the room, but my heartbeat deafened my ears.

My shivered as the room's temperature suddenly dropped. The shadow's hand pressed itself onto the sheets, and its fingers stretched over my body like spider webs. The force of it was strong, and I was knocked onto on my back. I felt a heavy weight on my chest, and to my immense horror, I realized my body was paralyzed. I couldn't blink. I could barely breathe.

The shadow only grew more and more until it encompassed the entire room. It was pitch black and so dead quiet that there was ringing in my ears. It was as if the world stood still at that moment. My heartbeat was erratic, and my head felt a sudden pressure. The sides of my temples pulsed violently, and my mind fuzzed over. The black abyss was quickly replaced with an image of that same doctor from my previous vision.

He was reading a black book with silver writing etched on the cover in the basement. In the book were strange symbols that I couldn't recognize, but one of them I knew was a pentagram. The book was filled with these symbols and a language I couldn't recognize. However, the images in the book gave away the truth of what was written: pictures of half-human and half-beast creatures torturing naked people surrounded by flames.

I saw this doctor flip through the pages erratically as he chewed on his fingernails. He stopped when he reached the final page. On it was a photo of a snake-like demon with its serpent tongue sticking out. The snake had protruded out scales that formed into wings, and large nostrils that fire came out of. Its face was contorted into a menacing grin. The doctor placed the book onto the floor of the basement and began muttering incoherently. It sounded as though he was chanting. He grabbed an old dagger. It was glowing red as he placed on what looked like a ritual altar. The dagger seemed medieval or maybe older.

All I could do was watch as the man drew a giant circle all around the room along with the cultish type symbols from the book. To me, what he was writing was gibberish, and I thought this man was insane for participating in such ridiculous practices. He stood in the middle of the circle and said, "I call on the Beast of Eternal Life to come forth and give me the power of life to continue my work. In return, I will deliver him, souls, for him to feed on." He grabbed the dagger and pierced the skin on his palm. He winced as he trickled the blood in the middle of the circle. "If I fail to complete my end of the deal, he may possess my soul." He shook his hand a final time as a few drops of blood dripped onto the floor. "As is the price that needs to be paid."

I felt an invisible force pull me back away from the vision. It got smaller and smaller until I eventually gasped and was back in my bedroom. The sun shined across the room, and I immediately sat up. Had it been all a dream? I got out of bed and stretched. It had to have been a dream. A wave of relief rushed over me, but concurrently, a muffled panic settled in because I couldn't recall ever going to sleep.

Chapter Six
Searching for the Truth

I looked over at my clock, and I had an hour before work started. I took a shower first, and the heat from the water encompassed the room. I took in a deep breath as I leaned against the wall of the shower. I thought about the images of last night. I had never experienced such vivid dreams before, and who was that man? What did this man believe this beast would do for him and why?

I rubbed the back of my neck as I stretched my muscles. After some time, the water hitting my back had made my skin go numb. I turned off the water and stepped out. Using a towel, I wiped the fog from the mirror and saw my reflection staring back at me. I hardly recognized myself. My eyes were bloodshot and there were purplish-red colored bags underneath them. To me, I looked like I aged a decade. I sighed, then started brushing my teeth.

I eyed my phone that sat on the counter and threw my toothbrush down. An hour had passed, and I was running late for work. I rushed to my room to throw on some scrubs and put on my shoes without bothering to tie them. I raced outside the front door and took off in my truck to work.

I pounded my fist against the steering wheel. How could an hour have passed in the shower? I was only in there for five minutes. I took a deep breath as I ran my fingers through my hair. "It'll be okay," I said. "Lapses in time are normal when you're stressed. It'll be okay." However, my own words did little to comfort me.

When I arrived at the SNF, a security officer stopped me at the door. "You work here?" the tall man asked. He was dressed in an all-black uniform with a handgun in a holster on his right hip.

"Y-yeah," I said as I pointed to the front doors. "I work here. I'm running late."

"Can I see your badge?"

I furrowed my brow. "My... My badge...? Oh, yes!" I patted my pockets, but nothing was there. I usually brought my backpack to work, which I kept my badge in. I held up a hand. "Hold on," I said. I ran back to my truck and dug in the front seat. My backpack wasn't there, so I pulled the passenger seat forward and looked in the back. However, my backpack wasn't there either. I must've left it at home. I banged my fist against the back of the seat.

A thought occurred to me: I never needed a badge to enter the building before, so I trudged towards the officer and said, "I work here. I left my badge at home. I need to go inside."

The security officer stopped me by stepping in my way of the front doors. "I'm afraid I can't let you in there."

I had lost all my patience. Usually, I was much calmer than this, but with everything that had been going on in my life lately, I lost my nerve much more easily. Panic rose to my chest. "And why not!"

The officer took a step back and placed a hand on the gun. "I'm going to have to ask you to go back to your car."

I raked my hands through my hair. "Why? I work here! I'm late! I need to go inside!"

I noticed other security officers approaching slowly. "I'm going to give you one last warning," said the man.

Right then, Christina ran out through the front doors. "Ted's with me," she exclaimed. She stepped beside me. "He does work here. He left his badge inside. I vouch for him."

The security officer looked at Christina and then eyed me warily. He lifted his hand off the gun. "Okay, miss." He turned to me. "But you need your badge the next time you want in."

I nodded my head, and Christina took me by the arm to lead me inside. Once we were past the front doors, I asked, "Why are there so many security officers?"

"Because of all them missin' patients lately. The owner of the SNF decided to take extra precautions." Christina looked out the glass doors. "It's annoying, really. Are you doin' alright?"

"Yeah, I'm fine," I said, feigning a casual tone. "Why?"

"Because you're..." She eyed me up and down.

I looked down at my scrubs and realized I was wearing a different colored top than my bottoms, and I had mix-matching shoes. I bent down to finally tie my shoelaces together. "Sorry about that," I said.

"No need to apologize," said Christina. "Are you sure you're doin' alright?"

I shrugged. "I guess… I'm late. I must go. Thanks for your help." I glided past her and towards the break room to clock in.

As I checked on my patients, I came across Monica. All life drained from her face as she made eye contact with me. She put her head down as he picked up her pace to get away from me. That was odd. Maybe it was because of what I said about seeing her sister. I didn't entirely blame her because I would've done the same thing.

That day I did the bare minimum of my job. I gave my patients their prescribed medicine and their food. I made sure to help them to their scheduled appointments and then back to their rooms. My last patient was Hank, and when I walked in, Hank blurted out, "You look like shit, boy. Where have you been?"

"I needed some time off," I said. My voice dragged low. I walked over to Hank to lift him up into his wheelchair.

"Girl trouble?"

"I wish." I plopped Hank into the wheelchair and pushed him towards the bath. I turned the faucet on and waited for the water to fill up, not bothering to let him test the water temperature as usual.

"Boy, I need help with the shirt, remember?"

I snapped back to reality and mumbled an apology as I helped Hank lift his shirt and finally his pants. I carried him into the water and sat outside the bathroom like always.

"You know, when I was your age, I had a lot of trouble with my PTSD after the wars. I found myself being spacey, and I couldn't do much of anything," said Hank. I could hear the gentle sloshing of the water as he cleaned himself. "I fought hard against it, but eventually it won. I had to be checked into a mental facility for a bit, and it did me a lot of good. I only wish someone would've told me it was okay to check myself in."

I sat with my elbow resting on my knee and my head in my hand.

"What I'm trying to say is, you've been looking like shit lately, and it's getting worse. I don't know if it's grief because of 'yer Mom or what, but you need to take care of yourself. You can't go dying on me before I do." he chuckled. That made me finally smile for the first time in days. It felt nice.

On my way home, I thought of what Hank said. Maybe I needed a mental health check. As much as I didn't want to admit it, I had been hallucinating. I was a man of practicality. I made lists, I had a planner I followed, and the last thing I could handle was disorganization of any kind. My thoughts and my mental health were simply that: disorganized. I tapped my finger against the steering wheel, and I thought about my mother. Maybe my mother felt the same way about her losing her grip on reality. How did she deal with it? Was she even coherent of it?

I parked outside my house and trudged up the porch steps. The last thing I wanted was to be in my home. I sighed heavily as I pushed my keys into the lock. I turned it but realized I had left the door unlocked all day. I lightly knocked my forehead against the screen door, silently chastising myself for being so forgetful. I pushed open the door and made sure to check every room for signs of entry or someone in the home.

After checking upstairs, I stood at the top of the steps that led down to the basement. I stared down the dark descent into the cool room below. My hesitance was there, and I gripped tightly to the wooden handrail, unsure if I truly needed to check down there or not.

"This is ridiculous," I said out loud, and I stomped down the steps. The overly loud footsteps I made eased my fears somehow, and I hurried to pull on the metal wire that turned on the lone light bulb.

Nothing.

I closed my eyes, and my muscles relaxed. I eyed the storage room door before running up the stairs.

I threw some leftover rice into a pan to warm up for dinner. I preferred to cook it that way because it made the rice less dry than when using a microwave. As I cooked, I thought back to what Hank said. I decided that if things got worse, I'd see a doctor. There was no way any of this with Lavinia was real. There *had* to be an explanation, and the best one I could come up with was that I was crazy.

The odor of charred oil filled my nostrils. The fire alarm went off behind me, which sprung me into action. My rice had turned a dark brown color, and smoke rose from it suffocating the air around me. I turned off the stove and picked up the pan with my bare hand. I yelled out in pain and dropped the pan back down onto the stove. I waved my hand in the air before running over to the sink to cool it under the water. The cool touch of the water splashing over my injured hand relieved me. I picked up an oven mitt and placed the pan under the water. It seared angrily as it made contact with the pan. I opened the windows and used my oven mitt to wave away the smoke from the alarm.

After the alarm was off, I decided to order delivery. I kicked myself for being so spacey that I wasn't paying attention to the food I was cooking. How much time had passed since I started cooking? I had never done that before, and it frightened me that it could happen again.

I filled my evening with late-night television and Chinese food. Once finished, I continued to stay up binge-watching shows until my eyelids grew so heavy that I couldn't keep them open. The last thing I wanted was to be alone with my thoughts, and TV was the perfect thing to keep my mind distracted. I eventually passed out in the living room with the television still on.

I tossed on the couch as another unsettling dream blanketed over me. It was the same dream as before. The same doctor as before was now sawing apart the bodies of his patients in a massive bathtub. He was drenched in blood as he incinerated the chopped-up bodies in a giant pit outside, burning only a few limbs at a time. The doctor then took the ashes of the dead and sprinkled it across the circle and did more incoherent chatting.

Afterward, he ground away the filling in the brick wall of the basement—*My* basement—to hide the ashes behind it, and then buried the charred bones around the land that surrounded the home. I recognized some of the trees from my own backyard.

The sight of this left me feeling sick to my stomach, but I couldn't make them stop. "Wake up!" I yelled at myself. "Wake up!" I lunged forward off the couch with my eyes wide open, but I was immediately pushed back onto the couch by an invisible force. A pressure pressed into my chest. I gaped my mouth open to breathe, but some unforeseen force squeezed my lungs.

My eyes bulged out as a dark shadow loomed over me. There was no face and no distinct features. It was just a silhouette of something pure evil. My adrenaline rushed through my body, but I couldn't move a single inch. Whatever this was, it was powerful, and it frightened the shit out of me.

The shadow dissipated, and I could finally gasp for breath. I flipped off the couch and heaved on my hands and knees. I coughed and clung to my throat, checking to see if it felt sore. I ran to the nearest bathroom, and there was no bruising on my neck. I checked my chest, and there wasn't so much as red markings from the pressure or any sign of trauma.

I continued to take in deep and slow breaths. I needed to get out of this house, but where would I go? It was the middle of the night. I ran out to my truck still unsure of where I was going. Rain pounded down from the sky, and I was nearly soaked by the time I got to my vehicle.

I didn't have a destination in mind, so I just drove. I drove around the town going up and down the same streets. Most of them were empty except for the occasional car. It was somewhat hypnotic to me—Driving at night with no end in sight. Almost an hour passed before I realized I was still driving. I had been stuck in a trance the entire time, and I was surprised I hadn't hit anything.

I looked down at the gas meter, and my truck was nearly empty. I found the nearest gas station and pulled into it. It was eerie out there in the dark with no one else around. I couldn't see beyond the lighted gas pumps. All that kept me company were the patters of the raindrops.

I got back inside my vehicle and sat there deep in thought. Maybe I should check myself into a mental hospital, but I wasn't feeling suicidal. I wasn't that far gone yet, but I needed a break before I did go over the edge.

I put my truck in drive and decided to head up the mountain to my parents' home. I had a key to their home, so I didn't need to knock and wake them up. It was well past one in the morning when I pulled up to their dirt road. I turned off the ignition and headed towards the cabin. My boots sunk deep into the mud as I made my way towards the front door. I fumbled with my key ring searching for the correct one.

Once inside, I collapsed onto their couch and quickly fell asleep.

In the morning, the sound of sizzling and the aroma of bacon greeted me. I sat up on the couch and peered over into the kitchen to find my father preparing breakfast.

My father's back was turned towards me as he cooked. I sat up on the couch, and he turned his head slightly. "Come to kidnap your Mom again?" he asked with a bitter yet somewhat playful tone.

I groaned as I sunk my body into the cushions. "Yeah, about that…" I sighed. "I'm sorry for what I did." My father had fully turned himself to face me. It was hard to be serious when my Dad wore his white apron that said, "Good cookin' by Mr. Good Lookin'." I bit back my smile as I shook my head.

My father peered down at his apron and grinned. "Oh, yeah this. Your mother got it for me a few years ago before…" He fell silent. I met his eyes, and he grimaced. He meant before she was diagnosed. Before she started to show symptoms and her memory began to fade away. He pressed his lips together and sighed. "Son…" He trailed off and then poured a cup of coffee. "Coffee?"

I nodded.

He came towards me as he handed me the mug. He took a seat beside me. "I'm not mad. I get it. I was the same way when your Mom was first diagnosed, and I took it out on her doctor assuming there was more that could be done. To make a long story short, we had to switch doctors when I punched him in the face after he said there was no cure." We shared a laugh. He faced me with a morose smile. "The apple doesn't fall far from the tree."

"There has to be something," I said. "There has to."

My father clasped his hand onto my shoulder. "I know, son." Silence filled the room. "Eventually, your mother and I will need to move. I'm finding it difficult to transport her from up here down towards town for her appointments. It seems she has more and more appointments every week. And soon I won't be able to upkeep this property. Eventually, we will need to move into town, and maybe then we will make use of your home you got for us." I looked up at him with hopeful eyes. "Most people's sons wouldn't go through so much trouble for their parents. Most parents get shoved into retirement homes."

I frowned as I looked at the bruising around my father's nose. "Yeah, but most people's sons don't punch their fathers in the face either."

My Dad let out a chuckle as he gingerly touched his nose. He cocked his head to one side. "That's true." My relationship with my father was always like this. We'd fight and then find something to laugh about and make up. My father changed his tone to a more lighthearted one. "Did you want some breakfast?"

I ran my fingers through my hair and blew out a sharp breath. "Yes, please."

"Rough night?" my father asked.

"You have no idea."

"Want to talk about it?"

I shook my head. "No, I don't. I need a break is all. That house…" I trailed off and looked out the small window that was beside the front door. The sun was high in the sky, and its rays beamed brightly across the living room.

"What about the house? Repairs? You need help with it?"

I spaced out as I stared at the blank television screen in front of me.

"Ted?"

I blinked. "Sorry. I'm just tired is all."

My father eyed me, warily. "You sure it's just exhaustion? Is there anything else going on? Scarlett told me she came over after I told her about, you know… I just wanted her to check up on you because I knew that wasn't you back there." My father pointed back to the bedroom where I had attacked him. "She said you were sick while she was there. You hardly ate, she said."

I rolled my eyes. Of course, Scarlett would rat me out. "I need a break is all. Mind if I stay here for a day or two? The clean air may help."

My father grinned and patted my shoulder. "No problem, son. You can help me chop some wood and do the house chores." He left back towards the kitchen.

My mother came shuffling into the room wearing her robe and house slippers. Her hair was in disarray with half of it sticking up and the other side much tamer. It made me smile. Her eyes squinted at the sunlight. I became apprehensive at who would be greeting me that morning: my mother or someone who thought of me as a stranger. She smiled and said, "My Teddy."

I exhaled and returned the smile. "Mom." I got up and hugged her. My bulky body consumed her thin frame in my embrace. "How are you feeling?"

She swayed her head side to side as she thought about it. "Better after I have some coffee." She turned around and saw the freshly cooked bacon. "Oh! And breakfast." She snagged herself a piece of meat. "What are you doing here? Not that I don't love you being here."

I shrugged and shoved my hands into my pocket jeans. "I needed to get away for a bit. I've been stressed lately."

My mother slowly shuffled over to me and reached her arm up to place her hand on my cheek. Concern washed over her face. "I'm glad you're here then. I can bake you some cookies later."

My grin grew. "I'd like that."

After breakfast, I called into work again while faking the flu. I figured that'd get me at least a week off. I wasn't one to take days off, but the main nurse still yelled at me over my lack of presence at the SNF. "I'm putting a write-up in your file," said Nurse Brooks.

"Why? I still have paid sick days."

"Who is going to take care of your patients, huh? We can't keep covering for your hangovers."

Hangovers? What kind of person did he think I was? "It isn't a hangover. I'm not well. Do you want me spreading the flu to our elderly patients?"

He was silent on the other end, which meant I was right, and he was finding something else to yell at me about. "Well when you finally decide to come to work, make sure you're not doing the bare minimum. My patients deserve the best." With that, he hung up. I squeezed my phone in my hand, and the muscles in my jaw tightened.

I shut off my phone after that and threw it into my car. I didn't want anyone to disrupt my mini vacation.

After breakfast, my father led me outside to the back of the cabin. "Alright, son, this is the wood I'd be chopping for tonight's fire. I'll have you give it a go instead, so I can focus on cleaning out the shed." My father handed me an ax. I had chopped wood many times before when my family and I used to live in California up in the Sierra Mountains. We had moved to Saratoga Springs when my father got transferred for his job when I was thirteen, and we'd been there ever since. My parents preferred the forest to city living, and in a way, I did too.

I placed the log upright on the stump. I gauged where I'd hit it before lifting my ax all the way up and slicing it hard into the log. It didn't go all the way through, but it did so enough for me to rip the giant splinter apart. I knew to make a few thin slices of wood along with some thicker pieces for the fire.

A good half hour went by before my arms became too exhausted to continue. I cradled a bundle of wood in my arms and carried it inside to put by the fireplace. Inside, my mother was knitting on the couch.

129

"What are you making there, Mom?"

She flipped over the thin rectangular cloth. "I have no clue."

I chuckled as I neatly stacked the wood together.

"It started out as a blanket... Well, that was my intention, of course, but it's not looking like it's going to be that."

I eyed over the missing and distorted knots. "Is this your first time knitting?"

My mother laughed. "You'd think so, huh? This is, actually, my fifth attempt, and..." She lifted the crooked disaster. "You'd think I'd get it by now."

I laughed.

"I guess I'm not the knitting type."

"No, you're not, Mom. You're more of the chopping down trees and fighting forest fires type."

My mother gave me a small smile. "That was a long time ago."

"You're still that woman, though."

"Thank you, Teddy." She looked out the window. "Sometimes I wish I could do all that again. I miss it."

Seeing the longing in my mother's eyes gave me a sorrowful feeling in my gut. "I can take you on a walk, so we can collect some more twigs for the fire."

My mother threw off the blanket that was over her lap. "Let's get to it, then."

I took my mother's arm as I helped her out of the house. As we walked by the shed that was at the edge of the property, I yelled through the door. "I'm taking Mom on a walk. We'll be back in a few."

"Alright!" My Dad hollered.

We made our way to the road, and my Mom took a left.

"You sure you want to go that way? It's uphill," I said.

"I can handle a small incline," my mother said with finality.

We walked for a while up the hill, and I had to stop a few times to wait for my mother to catch up. I made sure to listen in to hear if my mother's breathing ever became labored, but she didn't seem to grow tired at all.

"I've meant to ask you why you're really here," my mother said. She took on her no-nonsense tone, which I knew all too well. That meant I had to answer quickly and honestly.

"It's hard to talk about."

"I'm sure I can manage."

I gazed up at the tree line. Looking away made it easier to respond. "It's the house. I've…" I trailed off, unsure of how to continue.

My mother gestured with her hand for me to proceed. "Yes? You've?"

I smirked. Now I knew where Scarlett got her sass from. "I've been having dreams. Really strange dreams about a woman being murdered and seeing her in the house."

"Was she killed in that house or something?"

"Apparently so."

"I've been watching Ghost Hunters lately. I believe it's all real."

I couldn't help but laugh, and I eyed my mother questioningly. "You're kidding, right?"

"No, no. I've had those experiences before. When I was younger, and this was way before you were born, your father and I lived in a small dingy-ass apartment in Los Angeles. It was an old building that had been built in the early nineteen-hundreds. At night, lights would turn off and on in the hallways."

"Faulty wiring in an old building. That makes sense."

My mother shook her head. "No. The repairmen constantly checked the wiring and always did routine checkups, but everything always checked out. I used to think it was faulty wiring too. I never in my life would have believed it was paranormal until I saw a ghost." My mother pointed to a trail that was off the road, and we headed down it. The light instantly vanished among the tall oak trees. "I was heading out to work one day, and there was an elevator that I always took down to the ground floor. I live on the top floor, and when I got inside it, there was already a man standing inside. I didn't think much of it. I assumed he was going to work too. He wore a black, pin-stripe suit with a fedora hat. He also had one of those old leather-bound suitcases. He didn't speak to me, and I noticed he hadn't pushed any buttons to which floor he'd want to go to. Then I realized he had been in the elevator when it arrived at the top floor, which didn't make sense unless he was planning to get out on the top floor. Still, I ignored that and pushed the button myself. I asked what floor he was going to, but he didn't say anything. I figured he was just an ass. There are lots of those in LA."

I chuckled.

"Once we reached the bottom floor, he stepped out and started walking and then vanished." My mother snapped her fingers. "Into thin air. I was in so much shock I couldn't move. There was no mistaking what I saw. He was walking in the lobby one minute and then the next minute he vanished. Mid-step too."

I started laughing more.

"You believe me, right?"

"I believe that you believe you saw something."

"Oh, please." My mother smacked my arm. "Don't give me that crap. That's the same thing your father said." We stopped walking once we reached an area with a dense number of twigs and dried up pine needles. She pointed at me. "You're seeing things too, and you're here because you think you're going crazy. You're not, and I would know because I'm the one over here, losing my memory." That comment took a jab at my heart. My mother started to pick up handfuls of twigs while wearing her thick gloves for protection. She looked over at me and said, "Make sure you pick up longer twigs than that. We don't want small baby ones. We can break them ourselves. It makes it easier to carry them back when they're longer."

"Okay, Mom," I said. Suddenly, I smelt charcoal mixed with a horrid Sulfur smell in the air. I covered my nose. "What is that?"

My mother sniffed the air. "Oh, that must be the neighbor again. He lives several miles up the mountain, but you can always smell whatever it is he's burning. My guess is he does control burns every week on his property."

"Control burns of what?"

My mother situated the bundle of twigs in her arms. "He may have crops up there, and when they die, you burn them."

"He must suck at farming then if it's every week."

My mother tilted her head back in laughter. "Alright, Teddy. Let's head on back."

Once on the road with a clear sight of the sky again, I looked behind me saw the smoke rising from further up the mountain.

Later that day, I helped my father with making dinner by cutting the extra fat off the pork shoulder. My mother was in the living room watching television as she attempted to knit again.

"How long are you planning on staying with us?" my father asked.

"Just a few days. If I feel better by tomorrow, I'll probably leave the following morning."

My father nodded as he poured the chopped vegetables into the steaming pot. "Sounds good… Ready to talk about it yet?"

I shook my head. "Nope."

The fire that burned in the fireplace reflected off my mother's face causing her skin to take on an orange glow, and I noticed her eyes were glazed over in that way it gets when she was no longer present with us.

"She had a good day today," my father said. "She was here more than not."

I stood up and wiped my hand on the towel that was on the back of the kitchen chair. "Yep. She spoke to me about seeing ghosts back when you two first got married." I grabbed the marinade for the meat.

My father chuckled. "Not that story again. She's convinced she saw a ghost. I say she was just tired if anything."

I shrugged. "She saw what she saw, whether real or not. It was real enough for her."

"If that is the case, then Bigfoot and the Loch Ness Monster would be deemed as real."

I rubbed the marinade over the pork. "It's impractical to say something is either real or not real without facts to support either side."

"So, it's both real and not real until then?" My father questioned.

I flipped the shoulder over to get the other side. "It's illogical to say something is not real when you have no proof to back it up just like it's illogical to say something *is* real with no evidence."

"The lack of evidence is proof enough," he said.

"I disagree because there are enough eyewitnesses to prove something did happen. Take Mom's situation, for example. She did see something. Now whether that was an actual ghost or something else entirely is up to debate, but something did happen to provoke an emotional response from her. That part was real." I began to chop up the pork into smaller pieces to be cooked in the soup.

"I see where you're going with it. It may not be a ghost just like it may not have been Bigfoot or Nessie, but it's a fact that people experienced something. Whether or not it's what they claim it is, is not based on fact."

I nodded. "Exactly. The experience was real, but what it could have been is an open-ended question that can't be proved either way. No one can say for sure."

It was silent. "Is that why you're here? Because you saw something?" I could tell my father chose his words carefully, and I wasn't sure if that irritated me or not.

"I don't know." I gave the bare pork bone to my father. "It's just stress, so I decided I needed a vacation."

My father nodded. "Fair enough. Glad to know you can separate reality from delusions, son." He looked over his shoulder at his wife. "I can't say the same for your Mom."

The following morning, I went to the front of the property where the dumpster was holding two full gallon trash bags. The smell of the fresh morning dew helped to clear my head. The sky was overcast, and I figured I'd stay another day and leave in the morning to go home. My boots sunk into the mud as I made my way towards the dumpsters. Already, I felt lighter in my chest, and a weight had been lifted off my shoulders.

As I threw the garbage bags into the dumpster, I saw a beat-up truck drive by. Its engine whirred loudly down the mountain. Its blue coloring was faded as red rust took over in its place. I saw a glimpse of a long-bearded man in his late thirties behind the wheel. His face was concealed behind long, scraggly hair that he kept somewhat tamed in a beanie.

The man caught me staring at him and snapped his head in my direction. Those piercing blue eyes looked vaguely familiar to me, but I couldn't put my finger on it. I felt a sense of uneasiness as the man continued to eye me as he drove by. I found it odd that there was what appeared to be a cage divider in the truck that separated the front seat from the back. I only ever saw that in police cars. I shrugged the encounter off and figured he was a hunter of some type.

On my way back into the house, my father was putting on his trucker's hat. It was the one he used to always wear whenever on the road for his job. "I'm heading into town to buy some groceries," said my father. "Keep an eye on Mom, will you?"

I waved my father off and went to the back of the house to chop some more firewood for the night. After a half-hour, I headed inside with a fresh bundle. "Mom?" I called out. She didn't answer. I set down the wood and went down the hallway towards my parents' bedroom. The bed was empty. I knocked on the bathroom door. "Mom?"

Silence.

I knocked again and waited a few more seconds before opening the door. There was no one inside. I checked the second bathroom out in the hallway, but that too was empty. I went into every room, and my panic quickly set in when I realized she was nowhere in the house. I ran out the front door and called out for my mother.

I rushed over to the shed and threw it open, but my mother wasn't inside. I went to the back of the house where I had been chopping wood and found fresh prints in the mud. My father had taught me how to track during our hunting trips. The smallest rustle of the leaves could tell me who was there and what had transpired. I was a bit rusty, but the clear bare footprints in the mud made it easier. Nobody else on the property had my Mom's small feet. I followed them a few feet into the woods. It didn't take long for me to find my mother standing there looking up at a tree. I let out a breath of relief, and I jogged over to her. "Mom, you scared me. Don't go running off."

She had that same glazed-over look, and she inched herself away from me. "Who are you?"

"I'm your son," I said.

She shook her head. "I don't have a son." She looked around. "Where am I?'

I sighed. "Come inside."

She shook her head, profusely. "No, I don't want to. I want my husband."

"He's shopping. He'll be back with food. I'm watching you in the meantime."

This seemed to calm her. "Oh, okay," she mumbled, and I followed her back to the house all while keeping a close eye on her.

I sat her down on the couch and put a blanket over her lap. "Can I have my pudding?" she asked.

"Of course," I said. I went to the kitchen and came back with a spoon and her opened pudding cup. I fluffed her pillow and placed it behind her for support. "Is there anything else I can get for you?" I took time off work only to be doing my job as a nurse for my mother.

"The remote, please?" She reached her arm out towards its direction, and I handed it to her. A strong gust of wind blew through, causing the windows to rattle.

"I'll get a fire going," I said. "Before it gets too cold."

"I used to chop down trees to do control burns during the off season. I used to be a forestry worker and fought the forest fires," my mother said.

I pushed a bundle of dried twigs together with some dried pine needles. "I know. You told me."

"Oh…"

I used a lighter to ignite the fire and blew on it. The flames grew, and I threw in some more twigs. Once the fire was steady, I put in a log.

Since it started to rain, I spent the rest of the day in the house in silence. There wasn't much to be done outside. I felt like I was back in my childhood days with only a television to keep me occupied, but I wasn't even allowed to watch a show I enjoyed. I sat on the couch beside my mother as she continued to attempt knitting a blanket. "I have a son that looks just like you," said my mother.

"I am your son, Mom," I said.

"Oh…" She smiled and patted me on the arm. By the end of the day, I was used to my mother, not recognizing me. I never thought I'd become desensitized to it, but there I was sitting on the couch casually correcting her memory as though I were talking to her about the weather.

I looked up at the wall above the fireplace, and there hung the deer antlers from the full-grown buck that my father and I shot over fifteen years ago. The antlers were the biggest I had ever seen, and it had been one of the longest hunting trips we ever took together.

I was around seventeen years old, and my father took me out on another one of our hunting trips. Hunters were needed to keep the deer population down in the area because it was getting out of control and affecting the ecosystem, so every year we would go out. We'd keep some meat for the family, but the rest we gave away to neighbors. That year was my first shot ever. Before, it was my father who would always make the final kill. We had tracked that deer down for days. Hunting wasn't easy, and most times we'd come home with nothing. That was why the meat we hunted for was so much sweeter than the prepackaged stuff at the supermarket. The act of having to physically go out to find, hunt, and work for your food made the meat taste that much better.

During those times when my father and I would go hunting, he and I would actually get along. Whereas at home, he was constantly on my ass about something whether that'd be school, chores, etc. It wasn't like he was abusive or anything towards me. He was just much harder on me than he was on Scarlett. I guess he expected more of me. He didn't care what I decided to do with my life if I lived up to his standards of what a man was.

In my adult years, he softened up on me. Maybe it was due to his old age, or maybe he felt he finally achieved what he needed to do as my father.

I smirked as I looked at the antlers. That was a good hunting season. I looked over towards my mother, and she gave me a subtle smile. It was the ones she gave to strangers at the grocery store. That distant gesture punched me in the gut, but I didn't let it show on my face.

The following morning, I decided to head back home. I needed to get back to reality at some point, and I also needed to put on a fresh pair of clothes. Wearing my father's old jeans and T-shirts didn't fit quite well.

"You take care of yourself, son," said my father. "You're welcome home any time." I hugged my father, and it was the first time in ages that we embraced one another. We both paused somewhat baffled by the contact. I wasn't sure what caused us to hug. We both did it without thinking.

As I got into my truck, my mother raced out the front door holding something in her hands. "Teddy!"

I rolled down my window. "Yes, Mom?"

She handed me a silver crucifix. It was on a leather string, but I found it a little too big to be a necklace. "Stay safe. I remembered our conversation." She winked at me.

I studied the crucifix before I carefully placed it on the passenger seat. "Thanks, Mom." I didn't plan on using it, but I knew it'd comfort her.

She kissed my forehead. "And use it when you need to. We're not Christians or anything, but I find that it can help ease any fears."

"Okay." I nodded my head at my parents before backing out of the driveway and onto the dirt road that led to the paved one.

When I pulled up to my house, I sat in my truck, tapping my finger on the steering wheel. Now even during the day, the home took on a looming parasitic vibe that overshadowed the once welcoming house. It made my stomach churn. I looked over at the crucifix, and I rolled my eyes at myself as I picked it up. Was I humoring the idea of using such things to give me a false sense of safety? I figured I was already nuts for thinking that my house was haunted, so I might as well start using crucifixes. I clutched it in my hand as I got out.

I made my way up the front porch and took a deep breath before entering. The morning light shined a whitish-yellow across the old oak floors. I could see the dust in the air, and there was silence. Nothing creaked or groaned. There weren't any unpleasant feelings of someone watching me. I walked over into the living room and put the crucifix on the table by the couch.

The rest of my day at home was quiet, and I welcomed it. For the first time since I moved in, there weren't any sounds nor any uninvited visions. I had made myself dinner, which was my usual rice with mixed vegetables, and sat down on my couch to watch television. As I fell back into the cushion, a small smile crept across my face. Maybe a simple break was all I needed.

The following day, I went back to work. I tended to my patients who were all too glad to see me. Hank, as usual, was his bitter self. "Where have you been? I had to get bathed by Ben, and you know how much I hate that man. He doesn't seem to understand that I'm still a man and deserve some dignity."

I gave him a sympathetic smile. "I'm sorry. I was taking care of myself as you said."

"You done being crazy?"

I sighed as I gave him his medicine. "I hope so."

"Good because he didn't even let me test the bathwater and threw me into some cold ass water."

"Well he and the other nurses were covering for my other patients, so he probably was just busy and forgot."

He huffed, then took his medicine.

As I walked out of his room, I saw Monica again. She was headed in my direction, but when she saw me, she quickly turned and headed the opposite way. I decided right then that I *had* to talk to her. I didn't want her to feel uncomfortable around me.

I was so focused on Monica that I didn't see Christina in the hallway. As I turned around to head to another one of my patients, I ran right into her. She almost dropped the file in her hands. "Oh, I'm sorry," she laughed. I noted how her light purple scrubs complimented her eyes, and her blonde hair was down today, which cascaded beautifully around her face. "How are you feelin'?" she asked.

"I'm good. Much better. I'm sorry about canceling our date and not getting back to you."

She forced a pleasant smile, but it just came out as a tight line. "It's fine."

It sure didn't sound fine.

"I figured you're just not interested," she said.

"No, I'm *very* interested." A coworker walked by, and I lowered my tone. "I've just been having a rough go at it lately. It's a bad time."

She smiled passively, which meant what I said insulted her. "Take all the time you need." She walked past me down the hall.

I closed my eyes and quickly turned around to stop her. "I want to make it up to you."

She looked me up and down.

"Please," I implored. "Allow me to take you out and show you that I have a genuine interest in you because I do. I'm just… I'm not good at this."

"No, you're not." She continued to walk past me, and I decided not to stop her again. It was over, so there was no point. That's when she halted and turned to me. "Tomorrow night. No excuses. Meet me at that Italian restaurant on fifth street at eight. If you're not there, consider my interest in you gone."

I took a breath of relief. I still had a chance. I heard Hank whistle, and I turned my head towards him. His door was open the entire time, and he gave me a playful grin, thoroughly pleased with himself that he caught that conversation.

143

I decided not to allow Monica to dodge me anymore. I needed to tell her about the visions because maybe she'd be able to help. I wasn't sure how, but I was desperate to make them stop. I didn't have any visions when I came back from my parents, but I wasn't sure how long this peaceful period would last. And I didn't want to start losing my sleep again because of it.

During our lunch break, I found her outside sitting at one of the picnic tables eating a salad. "Mind if I have a seat?" I asked. She looked up at me, and there was a look of clear apprehension on her face. I sighed as I sat down. "Look, I'm sorry for whatever I said to you that made you feel uncomfortable. I just..." I trailed off as I thought of what to say. "I was just desperate for answers, and I still am."

She swallowed. Her forehead creased with concern. "I'm sorry for how I've been avoiding you. It isn't fair to you, and in all honesty, I believe you. I just wasn't ready to hear about my sister again."

I could understand that. If my mother were to pass suddenly, I don't think I could handle even thinking about her let alone talking about her. "I'm sorry for bringing up old wounds," I said.

She gave me a small smile. "It's alright. It was needed because I am not over what happened. I needed that push to remind me to work through my feelings, so thank you."

I nodded. "You're welcome."

"And if there is anything I can do about you seeing my sister, I will let you know. Maybe she wants your help with something." Monica paused as she fumbled nervously with her fingers in her lap. "I want to tell you what she was working on before she died." She shrugged. "I feel like I should tell you. My sister was a reporter and journalist. She liked to pick up strange stories and solve mysteries, and then write about it. She was good at it. Some stories were more serious than others like working with investigators on cold cases. She always loved a good mystery." This made Monica smirk. "I believe the last story she worked on was what got her killed."

I frowned as I furrowed my brow. "Why?"

Monica shook her head. "I have no idea what the story was exactly because she wouldn't tell me, but it has something to do with the house you live in. She was very apprehensive before she died and constantly looked over her shoulder. I think someone was after her for what she knew."

My interest was piqued at this point. "Did she move into the house before or after she started researching the story?"

"After. She had moved in with her boyfriend, which my parents were *not* happy about. We're travelers. Some call us Gypsies." She rolled her eyes. "We're of the Catholic faith in my household, and my parents were *not* happy about her cohabiting with him. They're old-fashioned folks. She wasn't even married yet when she moved in with him, and she was in her thirties. We get married at a very young age. At least in my family we still do. Lavinia was never one to follow customs, so she was a bit of a black sheep."

I wanted to get Monica back on topic about the murder. "What I'm not understanding is, why her boyfriend would kill her for what she knew? Unless he had a connection to the story."

145

Monica leaned over the table and whispered, "I believe there were dark forces at work."

I leaned back. I didn't know how to respond to that. I couldn't help but think Monica was a little ridiculous for hinting at that because it seemed so absurd to me. However, I didn't have time to discuss it with her further since our lunch break was over.

"We'll talk about it later," she said. "Perhaps I could come over to your place, or we could meet up somewhere?"

"I'd like that," I said. I wrote down my address and phone number for her and left back to continue my shift. It was a great relief to me that she was willing to discuss this more. I began to think that maybe spirits *did* exist. Perhaps Lavinia's soul wanted me to contact Monica to help her heal from her grief. It was a stretch, but I was willing to believe anything other than dark forces at play.

That night, I made myself a spinach and kale salad with some chicken. It didn't fill me up much, so I decided to order a pizza on top of that. I figured that I ate something healthy, so a pizza wouldn't hurt. As I finished up my last piece, a knock came at my door. I wasn't expecting anyone, but then I figured it was Scarlett coming to spy on me again.

When I opened the door, I raised my eyebrows when I saw Monica standing there with her hands in her pockets. She was still wearing her scrubs from work, and her black hair was pulled back into a tight ponytail. "Hey," she mumbled. She sniffed as she peered down at her sneakers. I noticed how awfully pale Monica was as she stood on my dark porch. I wondered if she ever went outside. She had the same narrow face as Lavinia's with the same plump cheeks and round nose

"Hi," I returned. "What are you doing here?"

She looked off to her right before finally looking up at me. "I came to have that chat with you about Lavinia." She looked past me to the inside of my house.

It was a little late for guests. When I gave her my number and address, I thought she'd call ahead before dropping by, but there she was standing at my doorstep. She shuffled back and forth on each foot. There had to be another reason why she was here, and it would've been rude of me to just shut the door on her, so I invited her inside. Monica scanned my living room and peered into the kitchen as she chewed on her bottom lip.

Once I closed the door, I asked her, "Did you want something to drink? You can tell me how the rest of your shift went, and if Ben finally got the guts to ask you out or run away." That was my play at humor, but it didn't go over well since Monica didn't so much as smile.

"No, I'm fine," She answered. "I'm just here to talk about Lavinia." She peered at the basement door, and I noticed how her shoulders curled back as her eyes widened. She blinked and forced herself to face me.

"What about Lavinia?" I asked.

"You've been seeing her," she said.

I chewed on the inside of my cheek. "Yes," I said slowly. *We have discussed this already*.

She took a step towards me. "I just want to help with that, and I haven't been able to think about anything else since we spoke. How often have you been seeing her? What is it like? What's the context of it?"

I looked away from her, unsure of whether to tell her the truth. My mouth opened to speak, but no words came

147

out. How does someone tell another that they are seeing their sister's ghost and dreams of her death?

However, I didn't need to say anything. It was as if she already knew what I was thinking. "That's what I thought," she said.

I grew confused. "What do you mean?"

She ignored my question. "I dove, recently, into my sister's murder again, and there was something seriously wrong with the whole thing."

You mean other than being killed by her own boyfriend?

She stepped away from the basement door and took her hand out of her pocket sweater to point towards my small kitchen table. "Mind if I sit down?"

I pulled out a chair for her and sat across from her.

"Before, I relied on the police for answers when she first passed away. I was younger then and didn't think much about it until recently. Meeting you and finding out you live here made me want to dive into her story again because I remember Howard. He was such a kind man. He was strong and a real manly man, but he was gentle. He would never hurt Lavinia."

"Oftentimes the people we least expect can commit the most atrocious acts."

She shook her head. "No, there was something she was working on. Maybe Howard was framed for it or something, and whoever was involved killed him and hid the body to make sure he wouldn't talk. There were no signs of any problems between them. I've spoken with her friends and colleagues, and there was no indication of any issues in their relationship leading up to the murder. It was when she started working on that story that she started to feel paranoid a lot. I think it's related to that."

"What was she working on exactly? You seem to know more than what we previously discussed earlier."

"She was researching this house, as I said. She didn't tell me much because she didn't want me to get caught up in the story and know something that could get me in trouble. It has something to do with Dr. Ransteen, who once owned this house and held his practice here in the early 1900s. I've been looking at her notes, and there are some disturbing facts I found, which has led me to this conclusion: I think Dr. Ransteen is still alive somewhere and orchestrating all of this."

I let out a long breath as I leaned back in my seat, wide-eyed. "There's no way he would be behind this if he had his practice in the early 1900s. That means he has to be well over a hundred years old."

"Maybe he has a grandson or someone he passed the practice down to, and this person wants to keep these secrets hidden."

My curiosity was piqued. "What secrets?"

"I'll show you. I can bring by the box filled with all her notes tomorrow after work."

I wasn't sure why I was so interested in this, but maybe figuring out this secret would get rid of the nightmares before they came back. I was willing to try anything.

The following day at work, instead of avoiding me like she usually did, Monica gave me one of her small smiles. She had this way of tilting her head down whenever she'd look at you as though she were afraid to make direct eye contact. It made her come off as modest, reserved, and shy.

Since Christina, Carlos, Frank, Ben, and I shared the same lunch break as Monica; I decided to have us all eat together in the employee lounge. It had to be tough being new at work with no friends, and Monica seemed a bit cut off socially from everyone else. It could be because she was shy, and I was rather quiet myself. People like us need someone to push us into social gatherings, and I thought sharing lunch would be a perfect way of doing that without overwhelming her.

Christina came waltzing in with her lunch bag. Her lips parted as she smiled at me. She took her seat beside me and said, "You haven't forgotten about our date tonight, have you?"

I smirked. "How could I?"

She giggled. "I'm looking forward to it."

Ben and Carlos came in with fast food bags. Ben was winded as he took his seat across the table. "We ran across the street to Five Guys really quick. I made sure to call ahead of time." He tapped the side of his head. "See? Smart."

I leaned over the table and lowered my voice. "Monica is joining us. This is your second chance with her. Maybe ask her out on a date."

"Yeah, and not run away," added Carlos.

Carlos and I chuckled, and Ben rolled his eyes. "Yeah, whatever man," said Ben. "As long as you don't go chasing her away with talk about your house." My smile instantly vanished. Any mention of my home only reminded me that I was totally fucked and that the nightmares were waiting for me. Right then, Monica and Frank entered. Ben lowered his voice to barely above a whisper. "House talk is off limits," he said. He turned his attention to Monica and pulled out a chair beside him for her to sit.

She gave her usual quiet smile and took her seat. "Thanks."

"No problem," said Ben. "We wanted to make you feel welcomed, so we decided to put together this lunch for you." Even though Ben made it sound like it was his idea, I let him have it since he seemed to like Monica a lot.

"Thank you," she said towards Ben. He beamed, and she turned her attention to everyone. "Thank you. It really is hard to make friends as an adult."

"And keep them," added Christina.

We all got a good laugh out of it. Monica took off her gray sweater, and I noticed for the first time a scar that ran up her lower arm to her elbow. I pointed at it and asked, "What's that?"

She peered down at her arm and shrugged. "Oh, this?" She tried to conceal parts of the scar with her hand. "This was from a horse-riding accident years ago. I was in college still." The scar was whiter than her already pale skin, and the skin rose where the jagged lines crawled itself up her arm.

"What happened?" I asked.

"I fell off while the horse was leaping a hurdle. My sister and I…" Her voice got quiet, and she put her arm down. "We used to breed and train horses together." That took me by surprise because Monica didn't seem like the type that did a lot outdoors. She didn't look like she went outside at all.

"That's impressive," said Ben. "How many horses do you own now?"

Monica put her head down as she shook it. "I don't have them anymore." She began to fumble with her fingers. "After my sister passed, I sold all of them."

Christina reached her arm out. Concern mixed with sympathy seeped into her voice. "Why, hon'?"

Monica grimaced. "It just wasn't the same without her. She helped a lot with caring for them, and it just…" She went quiet. "It was hard to continue because her memory was all over that barn. I just couldn't." She shook her head as she wiped a tear. "I'm really sorry. This is embarrassing."

Everyone jumped to console her and say it was fine.

"I have to use the restroom," she said as she got up and scurried out of the room.

"Great. Now we can't talk about horses. Thanks a lot, Ted," said Ben. "You always make her cry." The playful smirk on his face told me he wasn't distraught, but he was right. This was the second time I made her upset like this. It was becoming a bad habit of mine.

When she came back, there was the faintest color of pink on her cheeks. "I'm sorry about that. I just never talk about my sister. I've been avoiding it for a long time. I barely know you guys, so this is *very* embarrassing."

Everyone jumped at the chance to give her reassurance.

"Hon', nowadays there isn't anyone our age without some skeletons in their closet," said Christina. "We talk about our issues. You should too because that's what friends do."

"It's true," added Carlos. "We don't do small talk here. We get it. It's hard when a family member dies. These guys were there for me when my father passed."

"And they were here for me about Mr. Jacobson," chimed in Ben.

"And so, we'll be here for you, sweetheart," said Christina. "It'll make the friendship that much easier." She reached her hand out to Monica's and squeezed it with a smile.

"Thanks," said Monica. "What do you guys do other than eat lunch together every once in a while?"

"We mostly go to the bar," I said.

"Sometimes dates," added Christina. She swayed her hip my way to nudge me playfully.

The boys cooed, and I rolled my eyes at them. "Yeah, yeah."

Ben slammed his hand on the table. "Finally! It took like what? Two years?"

"Okay Mr. Run Away from Monica," I teased.

Ben's face burned bright red, and even Monica burst out laughing. Her ashen face eventually matched Ben's crimson color, which made her laugh even harder. It was the first time hearing her laugh like that, and it took me by surprise.

Monica bit back a small smile. "Ben, you don't need to be so scared of me. I'll go out on a date with you," she said. "If it's true that you are interested in me."

Carlos and Frank raised their eyebrows at one another and leaned over the table to catch what Ben would say.

"Oh. O-okay," said Ben. "I'll give you my digits then."

"But don't stand me up by running away once I get there," said Monica.

We all teased Ben by laughing at him, and he proceeded to throw a French fry at each of us jokingly.

The lunch was a good idea. We got to know Monica in a whole new way. We had no clue she used to be a horseback rider, or that she competed in shows. My circle of friends was small, so I was elated to have expanded it a bit.

"Out of all the horses you trained, did you have a favorite?" asked Ben.

Monica took a bite of her salad and neatly placed down her fork. She rubbed her hands together, but not in a nervous way like usual. It was from excitement, and that made me grin. "Oh, yes!" she said. "Her name was Penny. She passed a year after my sister, which was when I decided to sell the rest of the horses. Before I was on the fence about quitting, but it was an easy decision after Penny left."

"What happened with Penny?" asked Ben.

Monica covered her mouth using her hand as she chewed. "Just old age is all. Nowadays, I take care of my parents and their farm with my brothers. I live here in town, but on the weekends, I go to help them. I wasn't in college or doing much of anything for years after Lavinia passed." Monica shrugged as she picked at her nail. "My life was put on hold for a bit there. This is my first job since the... You know."

"The murder," finished Carlos.

Ben smacked Carlos in the stomach.

Monica nodded her head. "Yeah, *that*. It's still hard to talk about it because I shut down. I hadn't been off my parents' property until I started this job."

Everyone widened their eyes in surprise.

"So, you just been on their farm this entire time?" asked Christina in dismay.

"As I said, it was a hard time for all of us," said Monica. "I was afraid to be on my own. I used the excuse of taking care of my parents as the reason for staying sheltered for so long, but honestly, it was me that was afraid of leaving and never coming back like my sister."

I understood that more than anything. "We all grieve differently. You shouldn't be ashamed of that," I said. "It was a rough time."

"And it still is, but it's getting easier." She gave me a meek smile. "I can finally talk about her."

"That's good," said Christina.

"And if you ever want to talk about her more, we're here," added Ben. Monica seemed genuinely touched by that, and for the first time, I saw her give a bigger grin than that small curve of a smile.

"Changing the subject: you take care of your parents too, right Ted? How are they doing?" asked Carlos.

"My Mom," I corrected. "Well I'm trying to at least, but my Dad wants to stay up in the mountains. Eventually, he'll come around."

Christina rubbed my back and smiled at me in comfort. I hadn't realized how hard I clenched my fork in my hand at the mention of my mother until Christina had put her hand on top of mine.

After lunch, we all went our separate ways. "We should definitely do this again," said Ben as he threw out his empty fast food bag. "Maybe later this week we could all hit the bar." For once, since I moved into that house, I finally felt normal. I was going to go on a date, I made a new friend, and I had plans to meet with perfectly sane people doing a normal thing like going to a bar. Maybe things would start to get better for me.

That night when I got home, I took a shower right away. I only had a few hours before the date, and I did not want to chance missing it. The scent of lavender mixed with spice-filled the bathroom as the steam rose from the shower. Once I got out, I wiped the mirror, so I could see my reflection. I gently placed shaving cream onto my face and took hold of my razor. The last thing I wanted was a cut from my razor during my date, so I made sure to go slow and steady.

The soft stinging of the aftershave seeped into my pores as I patted it on my skin, and then I combed back my hair. As I walked into my bedroom, I found one of my many notepads and wrote on it to schedule a haircut. I never liked my hair going past my ears because I didn't care for the way my hair looked long. It got too curly and unmanageable. If it went straight down rather than furl up into a 'fro, then perhaps I would rethink my short hairstyle.

As I got dressed into some khakis and a nice buttoned-up shirt, a rapid tapping came at my door followed by ringing. I wasn't expecting any visitors, so I was perplexed as I made my way downstairs towards the door. I saw the silhouette of a long haired person beyond the fogged glass. I unlocked and opened the door to find Monica standing there with a cardboard box.

I held the door partly open. "What's going on?" I asked.

She lifted the box a bit. "I came here to show you the information I have."

"Can this wait? I have a date in…" I peered down at my wristwatch. "In less than two hours."

"This will only take a second. I want to leave it with you." Using the box, she shoved past me. *Of course, just walk on in.* She plopped the box down onto the kitchen table. She patted it and said, "This is what Lavinia was working on before she died. This is all her paperwork. Some of it is missing I think, but for the most part, this is it."

I came over to the table and opened the lid. Inside were papers and sticky notes haphazardly stacked on top of one another. There was no form of organization with any of it, and I found my chest constricting a bit at the sight of its disarray. Disorganization always made me a bit apprehensive. Monica stared at me expectantly, and I took that as she wanted me to dig through the box. I lifted out a big stack of papers, and a couple of them fell to the ground. I went to pick them up, and one of them caught my eye.

It was a black and white photo of a man with a long pointed beard and a thick mustache. His hair was slicked back, and he wore a black suit and tie. The photo was only of his face and part of his shoulders. He had a very solemn look in his eyes as though one could sympathize with him; however, there was also something sinister about them. What was more disturbing was that this man looked familiar to me.

He was oddly similar to the man I saw in my visions, cutting his hand while performing some ritual.

"That's Dr. Edgar Ransteen," said Monica. "The man in question."

I studied the photo a bit more before putting it back down on the table. "What did he do?" *Other than be into weird occult stuff.*

"As I said before, he owned this house and converted it into a mental institution for his Mom." I lurched painfully in my chest. The similarities were starting to become uncanny. Monica scattered the papers across the kitchen table searching for something. "Here it is," she muttered. She picked up a photo and handed it to me. "That's his mother." She pointed at a frail woman standing beside Dr. Ransteen. It was a group photo of what appeared to be his family. He was the tallest out of all of them, and he stood there with his white jacket that I had seen him in during my vision. His mother wrinkled with age, and she hunched as she stood there. Her eyes were glassy, and her one hand rested on a cane. Beside Dr. Ransteen was a young man who appeared to be in his teens. He dressed like a true gentleman with his suit. There was a young girl that stood beside the Mom who couldn't be older than twelve.

"These are his siblings," said Monica. "I think the brother…" She pointed at the young man in the suit. "Owned the house after Dr. Ransteen passed. He could still be alive somewhere. I can't seem to find his information, though. It seems my sister only focused on him." She placed her finger on the doctor.

I placed down the photo and picked up what appeared to be Dr. Ransteen's death certificate. He died in the late

1940s in his eighties. All the certificate said was "natural causes."

"His mother had Schizophrenia, and Dr. Ransteen spent his whole life growing up with her. His father would get abusive with her whenever she had her psychotic episodes, and according to my sister, the doctor would always step in between them and suffer the blows instead to protect her. He wanted to find a cure for his Mom, so he studied medicine and psychology. He bought land out here and decided to have a house built. He designed the home himself and moved his mother in."

"He doesn't sound so bad. What's the big secret?" I thought about how similar his goals were to mine. In fact, I felt a sense of pride at having bought this house with the same intention that he had.

"His mother died is what happened, and he spiraled," she said as she handed me a copy of a newspaper article. The yellow-colored news clipping with its faded ink was photocopied onto a sheet of paper. At the bottom was a stamp from the public library. The article told about a woman who jumped from a two-story building at the Ransteen Institute. The woman was hospitalized, but she died from her injuries.

"She jumped off from the roof of this house late one night," said Monica. "She would often chase and talk to invisible birds, according to Dr. Ransteen. Here are his notes from his practice. It appears some of them are missing, though." She handed me photocopies of the aged notes. The edges around the notes themselves were frayed, and neat cursive was displayed perfectly across the small pieces of paper.

I frowned. I began to sympathize with this man. I, too, would spiral if anything happened to my mother. However, as I read his notes, an internal alarm went off. With each passing day, it seemed his writing got more scrambled to the point that it became chicken scratch. Before, he wrote well-thought-out prescriptions for the patients, but it was later replaced with "give them three pills" and then eventually "a shot of morphine." Soon every patient was given shots of morphine instead of actual medication for their ailments.

"What the hell happened?" I asked. "These were unethical practices."

"What the hell indeed," said Monica. "At the time, society was beginning to develop a better moral understanding of asylums and mental illnesses. However, they were very poorly monitored, and many institutions got away with abuse towards the patients. This was around the time when they started doing lobotomies and electroshock therapy. And most mental patients were dumped in institutions by families that didn't want to deal with them anymore — leaving these patients without any families to check on them. I think Dr. Ransteen did something to his patients because they are all on morphine twenty-four-seven, which meant that they were not lucid at all. He had them on high dosages."

"I think I know what he did," I said. My stomach churned as I thought back to the dreams I had. "I've been getting visions ever since I moved in here and started dreaming about your sister. I've seen her death so many times." I swallowed hard, and my voice shook. Monica reached her hand out to me in comfort. "He killed his patients somehow. I'm not sure why, but I think he did things to them that caused them to die. I think your sister wanted to figure it out, so maybe that's why I'm being haunted by all this." I dropped the notes down onto the table and ran my fingers through my hair laughing nervously. "This sounds insane."

"No, it doesn't," said Monica with all sincerity.

"Before I wouldn't have believed in any of this, but now…" I looked up around the house. "I don't know anymore, and I just want them to stop so that I can go on living. I'll try anything at this point."

"Then maybe we can help one another. I've been wanting to research and find out what exactly happened to my sister. I've gone as far as tapping into the paranormal and trying to speak with my sister's spirit, but I can't hear anything. Nothing I do gets picked up." I looked down at her ankle and noticed Lavinia's name tattooed in cursive followed by a rose at the end. Below that in small print were the years Lavinia had lived: 1979-2011.

If I were that desperate to figure out what led to my own sister's murder, perhaps I would have resorted to such outlandish practices like ghost hunting as well. I had no right to judge her because she obviously was still grieving, and we all grieved differently, but I couldn't help but find it a bit silly that she thought talking to dead people—if that were at all possible—was the answer.

I looked down at my watch. I had to leave now if I was going to make it in time for my date. I was always very punctual, and tonight I needed to be even more so. I couldn't chance being even a minute late, and I wanted to leave a half-hour early just in case. "I have to get going," I said. "I have somewhere I need to be."

Monica looked down a bit disappointed. "Oh, okay," she said. "Sorry for bothering you."

I rubbed the back of my head. "It's no problem, I guess."

She gave me a small and somewhat embarrassed smile as she bundled up the papers. "I bothered you, I know it, but thank you for hearing me out anyway. I appreciate it. I had no one to talk to about this, and I figured out of all the people I could talk to, it was you. I guess it's because you seem approachable. Plus, you were already seeing my sister, so I figured why not come over here to try to figure this out." She plopped the papers into the box. "I'll leave these here for you to look over. If you find something I overlooked, give me a call. Do you have a pen and paper?"

I pointed towards the refrigerator behind her. She walked over to it to write down her number before leaving. At that moment, it felt like I was juggling two worlds: one where ghosts possibly existed and haunted me, and another where I focused on real-life matters like a date. After Monica left, I put on my shoes and walked out the door.

I was a bundle of nerves as I drove up to the restaurant. I stayed in my truck for a few moments longer as I took deep breaths. My palms were clammy, and I breathed into my hand to check if my breath was still fresh. I was about ten minutes early, which was what I wanted. I wanted to show Christina I could commit to her. I wanted to grab us a table and not allow her to wait for me for even a minute.

When I went inside, I scanned the restaurant from where I stood at the entryway to see if Christina had a table yet. When I didn't see her, I took a breath of relief. My plan was working so far. I told the host I was expecting someone, and he wrote down Christina's name before taking me to a table in the middle of the restaurant.

It was a beautiful place. It was one of the fanciest food establishments in our small town. The bright red carpet reminded me of the color of their famous pasta sauce, which matched the curtains. Some vines painted the cream-colored walls and painted fake windows that looked out to nowhere. They painted faraway hills and a bright shiny sky behind the fake glass.

Christina came walking in moments later, and she had a black lace shawl around her red dress. Her hair was over one shoulder and curled beautifully down her chest. She looked over at me, and my breath caught in my throat. It was my first time seeing her in makeup or anything else other than scrubs or her jeans. She was absolutely stunning.

I waved her over when she looked in my direction, and she gave me a small smile. I took that smile as, "I'm glad you're here, but you're still on thin ice." The host walked her over to our table, and I stood up to pull out her chair. Her lips curved a little more as I gently pushed her in towards the table. "Thank you," she said.

Our waiter came just in time, asked us for our drinks, and handed us a basket of complimentary bread. "I love this bread," said Christina as she immediately reached for it. She ripped it open, and steam rose out of it. Sniffing it, she made a satisfied smile. "I just love the smell." I beamed at how much she enjoyed that simple pleasure. She and I both ordered red wine, and we clinked our glasses together after it was poured.

"How was work for ya'?" she asked as she took a sip.

"It was rough getting into the swing of things again, but I got there."

"Are you going to tell me what happened or are we stickin' with you were sick?" Even though she was still upset and being sassy towards me, her southern drawl made me forget how angry she was. I just thoroughly enjoyed hearing her speak and being around her. Nothing else mattered. I ignored the slight annoyance in her tone.

"I wasn't sick," I confessed.

She raised her eyebrows. I could tell she was more surprised that I was telling the truth. "Do you want to tell me what happened?"

"Sure." I drummed my fingers on the table. "This is not, really, a first date conversation, but to hell with it. I've been having a lot of…" I thought of the right words to say. "Nightmares since I moved into that house, and they've been keeping me up. I had a horrible one and left to go to my parents' house to get away because I needed a mental break."

She furrowed her brow as she glared. "I still don't understand. So, nightmares have been bothering you? Are they more like night terrors? Because my little brother has those, and they wake up the whole house."

I shook my head. "It's hard for me to talk about, but I think it's the house causing it, or my stress…" I trailed off.

"Or your stress *about* the house," she said.

I decided to go with that. It was much better than telling her the actual truth, and I didn't want to mess up my chance with her. "Along with my stress about my mother. I had a bit of a breakdown, so I needed some rest."

She nodded her head, and I could see that her compassion came back. She no longer held her tight-lipped line. Instead, she leaned back in her chair and gave me a morose smile. "I can understand that. How was it spending time with your folks?"

"It was good. My Mom had her good and bad days." I shrugged. "I got used to her not remembering me, which I never thought I would."

Christina reached her hand out to me and grabbed my arm. "I'm sorry, hon'."

"It's alright, but enough about me. I know what you do for a living…" She and I both laughed. "So, tell me something I wouldn't know. Something that I would never have guessed about you."

She sat up with a wide grin across her face. I admired the way her lips puckered out a bit. She noticed my gaze, and her cheeks became flushed, which made my heart flutter. "I collect seashells, and I bedazzle them up to sell them online."

I got a huge smile. "No way! I want to see them."

She bit her lip as her cheeks became red. "Okay, okay, but try not to laugh." She took out her phone and scrolled through a few pictures until she found one to show me. It was of a perfectly round seashell that she glued jewels onto. In the middle was an amethyst with an array of different silver-colored jewels that flowed out onto the rest of the shell.

"It's beautiful," I said.

"You think?" Her voice was small, and I saw her shoulders were bunched up near her ears as she aggressively chewed on her bottom lip.

"Show me more," I said in a soft tone.

Her eyes met mine, and they were bright with hesitant excitement. She scrolled through and showed me a couple of more that were all decked out in bright crystals. "This one is my favorite. I made it as a joke." She laughed before she even turned her screen towards me. Her giggle made me smile even more. When she finally showed me, I started to laugh too. It was a seashell with googly eyes glued on and a few yellow strings as hair. "Her name is Danielle. I made her when I was in high school."

"So, this is something you've been doing for a long time?" I was pleasantly surprised to learn this small secret about her. I don't think anyone at work even knows.

She nodded as she put her phone away. "Yep. It sure is. The first time I went to the beach was when I was fourteen, and my family could afford to go all the way from Alabama. I collected as many as I could, and I wanted to do something with them. I had a bunch of left-over beads and fake diamonds I got from toy stores during my childhood, so I used those." She giggled. "It's something that has stayed with me. Although, I try to be more professional about it and not make anymore Danielles."

I smirked. "What made you move to Saratoga Springs from Alabama?"

She shrugged. "I originally wanted to move to New York City."

I nodded with a knowing smile. "Of course."

She giggled. "Don't laugh! I ain't no typical country lovin' girl that wanted to try her hand at the big city."

"Looks a lot like it," I teased.

Her face turned crimson as she laughed, and I was thoroughly pleased that I could get her to do that. "Well, I spent a week there looking for schools and said, 'nope! The big city isn't for me.' I decided on something near the beach, and I got into the university at Bridgeport. That's where my little hobby really kicked in. Whenever I was stressed about finals, I'd go out onto the beach and scavenge early in the morning for seashells after the tide went down."

"How did you make it here to Saratoga Springs?"

"I was looking for work, but Bridgeport was expensive to live in. After I graduated, I needed to find a job and a cheaper place to live. I was looking around local cities and ended up in a small town outside of Bridgeport for a couple of years. Then I heard my little brother was moving to Saratoga Springs for college, and my parents wanted me to move in with him since it was his first time away from home." She shrugged. "He's the precious baby, so of course he got coddled. And of course, I had to be the one to help take care of him like my parents wanted me to."

I nodded in understanding. I related all too much with that. "It can be rough being the eldest. How many siblings do you have again?"

Christina took another sip of her drink. "Three. Two brothers and a sister. My sister is still in high school, and the youngest brother is even younger in elementary school."

"You still live with your brother?"

She shook her head. "He moved out once he got a girlfriend. He's still living with her."

I raised my glass a bit. "Well good for him then, and for you, on getting your own place again."

"What about you?" she asked. "Has your family lived here forever?"

"No, I'm California born."

She got a big smile and tilted her head back. "Oh, now it all makes sense."

I got a playful smirk. "And what does that mean?"

She put her hands up in defense. "It just means you're a typical Cali boy with your muscular arms, protein shakes, and whatnot."

I laughed. "Is that a Cali boy to you?"

She giggled, and her hand rested on top of mine, which made me take a sharp intake of breath. I didn't want to blow this moment, so I turned my palm over and held her delicate fingers in my hands. She visibly blushed and looked down at the table. Right then, the waiter came to take our order. I got the usual spaghetti and meatballs. I had been on lots of dates before, and usually, the women would get a salad to keep it light. Christina decided on the chicken Marsala with fettuccine. I was a bit surprised.

"I love any kind of chicken dish. Especially if rosemary is involved," she said. She turned to the waiter and said, "And a tiramisu to go, please."

I raised an eyebrow at her.

She took on a defensive look. "What? A girl's gotta eat, and I ain't sharing my dessert with you. We can order one for both of us, but that tiramisu is coming home with me."

I let out a chuckle. "Alright, alright. I respect that. I don't mind paying for your dessert."

"I wanted to go Dutch," she said.

168

I paused momentarily. I had no idea how to respond to that. Was this not a date? Usually, the men paid for the dates, but I also didn't want her to feel disrespected by my insistence. "I hope this doesn't come off as rude, but why do you want to go Dutch?"

She shrugged. "Because I am the keeper of my own money, and I feel we're past the time when men pay for everything. I have a job, and you have one too, so why can't I help pay? Besides, I'll feel less guilty about adding a dessert to go."

It was a hard pill to swallow, and I wasn't sure if this was a test or not. My mother always raised me to believe a woman knew what she wanted because *she* always did. My Mom never played those mind games. However, maybe Christina did. Maybe she wanted me to fight to pay for the check. I wasn't sure how to go about this. She noticed the contorted look on my face as I struggled with this modern-aged dilemma, and she bit back a laugh. "Hon' I ain't playin' with you or nothin'. I'm being perfectly honest about everythin'. I know what I want, and that's why I don't play games."

I took a sigh of relief.

She played with her earlobe as she spoke. "Datin' always tired me out. I never understood the games people would play like not calling back until after two days, and I also got tired of the slowness of it. I mean who dates without meanin' to marry? That only ever ends in heartbreak. If ya'll ain't in it to win it, then don't go into the ring."

"So, you want to marry?" I knew this topic would come up eventually, but I wasn't expecting it so soon.

She lifted her eyebrows as if to say "yes, obviously."
"Oh, yes. I plan to get married and have children. If you
don't, then let's continue to have a nice dinner to ourselves
as friends and then go our separate ways." She let out a deep
sigh. "I hate how long it takes for people on dates to figure
each other out. Put all your cards on the table, Teddy." She
smacked her hand next to her plate. "Tell me what you want
out of life and tell me good because I don't mess around. I
don't have time on my hands here." She winked. "No
pressure or nothin'."

That's what attracted me to her in the first place.
When we first met on my first shift at work, she told me
what she wanted me to do and how to do it. She was always
brutally honest about herself, and that's what I liked in
women. "I want children, for sure. Marriage is a bit scary
still."

"We're in our thirties, Ted. Best get over that fear
there."

I laughed lightly. "That's true. I just never found the
right woman, but I have family on my mind. I definitely
want some kids one day."

She sat back in her seat. "Sounds like you haven't
figured yourself out yet."

I took on a defensive tone. "I have."

She raised an eyebrow. "Have you? You either want
to get married or not. You either want a family or not. Do
you see yourself doing something else with your life
someday?"

I thought long and hard about it. I became a nurse
because it was a passion of mine to help others. It all started
when my mother became ill. Before that, I had no clue what

to do with my life in terms of career. I knew being a nurse in a home wasn't the highest career point to some, but I never thought further than that. I never actually *planned* my future, and that made my stomach unsettled because that was what Christina wanted: a future. She wanted someone who knew what they wanted.

I let out a sharp breath. "I guess you're right. I always went day-to-day and never actually took life into my own hands. I just went with whatever was happening *to* me and not making things happen *for* me. Does that make sense?"

She nodded. "Oh yeah, it does. I was the same way, and that was why I went to help my baby brother instead of going my own route. I let my family tell me where to go. I didn't have my own compass. I needed someone else to guide me. There comes the point in your life where you want to make your own decisions for *you* and not anyone else. Let me know when you get there." She smiled.

My stomach dropped, and it pulled my heart down with it. "Is that your way of saying no second date until I get myself together?"

"It means we have an expiration date if you don't, and a pretty short one."

I nodded. I looked down at my lap as I nervously chewed on the inside of my cheek.

Christina's tone softened. "I'm sorry I'm so harsh. I'm in my thirties, and women who are still single in their thirties are a bit impatient." She smirked. "I don't get past many first dates. I come off as too strong."

I laughed, which felt good to do. "I wonder why."

She laughed at herself. "There are tons of guys out there. I figure the right one for me wouldn't be bothered by my knowing what I wanted out of life."

I couldn't help but stare into her bright blue eyes, and a gentle smile broke across my face. She became shy again and looked down as she blushed.

"Something tells me you don't mind my demeanor," she said.

I shook my head. "Not one bit. I'm used to strong women."

Her eyes began to water, and I knit my brow together in concern. "Thank you for that," she said. "It's hard to find a man who isn't intimidated... You're talking about your mother, ain't ya'?"

I nodded. "I sure am. She is the toughest one in the family. She used to fight the forest fires in California until my father got transferred for his trucking job to New York. We moved to Saratoga Springs because my Mom thought it was a good place to raise us. She still worked too, but she needed a job that wouldn't take her away from home six months out of the year. She decided to work as a welder, and she made decent money."

Christina looked at me with admiration in her eyes. "Your mama sounds like an amazing woman."

"She is." Then I added nonchalantly. "My Dad's alright too." That made her laugh.

Our food eventually arrived, and we spent most of the meal eating in silence. Christina had good table manners, but she ate quickly as though she couldn't shuffle enough food in. She caught me staring at her and nearly laughed the food out of her mouth. She took a few gulps of her wine.

"Sorry, I am just *starving*," she said. "I'm usually much more ladylike than this, I promise."

I got a good chuckle out of her embarrassment. "It's good. I prefer it." I gave her one of my meatballs. "Try it with their sauce. It's the best."

We finished our meals, and she got her tiramisu to go as she wanted. At her insistence, we split the bill in half, and we both left a tip before leaving. "Do you want me to walk you to your car?" I offered.

"Yes, please," she said in a perky tone.

It was silent as we walked outside. The cool spring air felt nice as I zipped up my jacket, and I could smell the promise of rain in the night sky.

"Thank you for everything," she said. "I had a great time."

"You're welcome. I hope to do it again."

She giggled. "Me too. I really did enjoy myself."

"And I promise to figure myself out." We made it to her car, and I faced her. I gripped my hand that was hiding in my jacket pocket into a fist out of pure nervousness. "Because I wish to keep seeing you for however long you'll have me."

A small smile broke across her face. "I'll keep having you."

I tried not to let the relief show on my face, but Christina's knowing grin told me I had failed. "Oh, good. I was hoping you wouldn't find what I said too cheesy."

She tilted her head back as she laughed. "It was, but it worked." We fell silent, and the way she chewed on her lip as she stared up at me, drove me crazy. I grabbed ahold of her hand and leaned in slowly to place my lips on top of hers. When we parted, she let out a small giggle. "I never kissed on a first date before." Her face beat red again.

I grazed my lips across her cheek. "Goodnight, Christina. Thank you for tonight."

I watched her as she left in her car, and we waved at one another before she turned onto the busy road. That night I drove home with the biggest smile on my face.

I totally nailed it.

At work the following morning, I went to give Hank his breakfast. He didn't even bother to say hello. He went straight to, "So did you fuck her?" Hearing an older man with a raspy voice talk about sex was a little jarring, but it still made me laugh.

"I don't kiss and tell, sir." I placed the tray on top of his lap.

"Normally I'd respect that but seeing as I haven't gotten any action in the past ten years, I'm craving for somethin'."

"We kissed," said Christina. I turned my head around, and there she was standing at the doorway. She walked in and handed me a piece of paper. "This is for you. You forgot to do medicine check." She playfully tickled her fingers under my chin before leaving.

I turned my attention back to Hank, whose head was cocked out as he watched her walk away. "She's got a nice ass."

"Hank," I said sternly.

"Sorry. That's your girl."

I gave a wry smile as I opened Hank's pudding cup for him. "She isn't mine. She's her own woman. I'm just lucky to be involved in her life, that's all."

"You've been single a long time, huh?"

"So, have you, sir," I said. I could hear Hank's cackle as I went down the hall to attend to my other patients. Monica caught my eye when she came walking past me pushing Camille in her wheelchair, and the weight of my other world I lived in crushed my shoulders. There was still that issue of seeing dead people in my dreams I needed to attend to, and I had to do it sooner rather than later if I wanted any chance at a solid and *normal* relationship with Christina.

On my way home from work, my father called me. Thinking it was an emergency about my mother, I answered it and put it on speaker. "Hi, Dad," I said. "Everything alright?"

"Everything is fine," my father said in an upbeat tone. "I was just calling to ask for some of your help on something."

"Of course. What is it?"

"Your mother has twice as many doctor's appointments now. During her last visit, they needed to draw her blood, and they found she is low on vitamins and getting dehydrated easily. They want her to come in weekly now to get transfusions done. That's a lot of driving for us. I was wondering if it'd be okay to take you up on your offer for us to move in. We'd still keep the cabin for you kids to have, but we need to be closer to her doctors. I can't keep going back and forth, and if there are emergencies, it will be best for her to be near a hospital."

"I completely agree." I was elated that my parents were finally going to move in. My body pressed firmly against the seatbelt as I nearly jumped up out of my seat. I calmly situated myself.

"Okay, I want to move her in slowly rather than too fast," he said. "It may be too much for her. This way, it'll give her time to get used to the situation."

"Of course, of course." I gripped tightly to the steering wheel as a smile stretched across my face. I tried my best to contain myself. The thought of Lavinia and the nightmares I'd been having instantly caused my stomach to drop. I wasn't sure if ghosts existed, but whatever was going on, I didn't want my mother to be a victim to it. She would be the most susceptible.

"I'll slowly be bringing things over the next few weeks. Is that okay?"

I blinked and came back to reality. "Yes. That's more than fine. I'll give you a key. You can take the master bedroom. I'll move my things out of there."

"You don't have to do all that."

"I know, but I want to. It'll be better for Mom that way."

"Alright, thanks, son. I'll talk to you soon." With that, he hung up.

For the rest of the week, I spent time clearing out my bedroom, which wasn't hard to do, considering I didn't have many things anyway. I couldn't stand clutter, so I never kept anything that I didn't have use for.

During that week, I also read the papers in the box that Monica had given me. I saw on one of the newspaper articles that Dr. Ransteen fired every single nurse and staff worker there. People wondered how he'd upkeep the facility without the proper staff. He quoted saying, "I will only take in the gravest of cases and will see to them myself. I will only take in a few at a time that have little to no family. This work I am doing is of the most importance and must be attended to in a manner that only I can do perfectly. Even the smallest defect can render my entire work obsolete. We are working on cures here."

One of the notes that Dr. Ransteen wrote caught my eye, which said, "Surgery scheduled for Paulton Edwards the fifteenth at three o'clock." After that, I couldn't find any more information about this patient. It was as though he disappeared completely. In fact, there were many patients that went missing after a reported surgery. Yet, there was no information on why.

Saturday rolled around, and the last thing I needed to do was move my bed into the next bedroom. I decided to wait until my father could help me with the heavy lifting. As I hung up the last of my clothes in my new closet, I heard a knock at my door, followed by a doorbell ring. I went downstairs and opened it to find Monica standing there.

"You have a bad habit of coming over without calling first," I joked.

"Sorry, it's how I am. I picked it up from my family. We tend to make ourselves at home. May I come in?" Monica walked past me without bothering to wait for me to say it was okay. It was a little annoying considering it was typically customary to wait for a response, but I didn't want to be rude towards her either even though she was the barging into *my* home. I closed the door, and I noticed how she rubbed her hands together and popped her fingers as she stood there, surveying the inside of my house. It must've been hard to be in the same home that your sister died in not knowing what entirely happened.

"I had a dream about my sister. That's why I'm here," she said. "She didn't say anything, but I woke up knowing I had to see you. Did you read over the paperwork yet?"

I ran my fingers through my hair and chuckled nervously as though she were a teacher asking if I finished my homework. "Yes, a little bit, but I was caught up with moving in my parents."

She snapped her head around to face me. Her eyes wide and mouth agape. "What? They're moving *here*?"

"Yeah. I've told you about my plans for my Mom moving in. Why is it such a surprise?"

"Do you really think that's safe for them? Especially for your mother?"

I shrugged as I put my hands in my pockets. "You're being superstitious."

"I would be more so if I were you after having dreams about someone I didn't know and later finding they were actually real."

"It's just illogical to buy into the paranormal."

"I disagree. I'd say it's illogical not to after what you've been through. It's no different than a religious person, not seeing the facts of evolution and forcing themselves to only see creationism."

As far-fetched that was, she had a point, and I decided to drop it. She didn't come here to argue. Changing the subject, I said, "I read his notes of the numerous surgeries he did. After the surgeries, any further information about them disappeared. He doesn't report them missing or dead. He stops writing prescriptions about them and any other updates."

"Yes, I noticed the same, and so did Lavinia when she found these notes. That's what drove her to investigate." Monica looked at all the papers that were neatly stacked around my kitchen table, where I had left them. I took it upon myself to organize them by date and by category: prescriptions, newspaper articles, photos, and so on. "My theory," she said. "Is that he kept them here and didn't want people to know what he was doing."

"Or maybe he was overworked with handling all the patients himself, so he didn't have time to take the notes."

"He only took in 5 at a time."

"At a time? Then what happened to those five patients that went missing?"

She shrugged. "Lavinia never said." Monica rifled through my newspaper pile and took out a photocopy of an older article from the early nineteen-hundreds. "Here is something where he mentions adding more patients. He says here that he'll be taking in more because he hired new nurses, but he never named them. He had no other nurses or staff members logged into his books at all."

"Maybe they were paid under the table."

Monica shook her head. "I think he was lying."

"But why?"

She bit on her thumbnail. "To not raise suspicion, I suppose. It'd be suspicious to add more patients without hiring more staff members, wouldn't it? I think something happened to those first five patients, and then he took in another five to replace them. You'll notice he kept taking in five at a time."

Suddenly, I heard clear footsteps coming from upstairs. They sounded heavy and took long, slow strides. Monica tilted her head up as she listened too.

"Is there someone here?" she asked. I shook my head slowly. It was happening again, and I swallowed hard as fear began to swarm in my core. It wasn't necessarily fear of ghosts or anything paranormal, but fear at the fact that the noises started up again and may not go away this time.

Monica sprang into action by running out to her car. The footsteps continued, but it felt like they were only staying in one area in the hallway by the top of the stairs.

My arms shook as I walked into the kitchen to look up at the top floor. The angle I stood at allowed me to look up into the hallway from the bottom floor, and my heart raced. Part of me wanted to run and hide and not look. I fought past those feelings and willed my eyes to inspect.

Nothing.

No one was there, but I could still hear the thumping of the footsteps. The hair on the back of my neck rose, and I could have sworn someone up there was staring right at me.

Just then, Monica came back in, holding a rectangular-shaped device. It was gray and had a small bulb at one end that Monica had pointed out towards the room. On top of the device was a chart with a needle that moved slightly. "This is called an electromagnetic field sensor or EMF sensor," said Monica. "EMF is the type of energy the ghosts are made of, in theory. The more EMF detected, the higher the needle will go, and the light comes on. The only problem is the electrical wiring in the house can be detected as well, so it's far from perfect."

The doubt was thick in my tone. "How can you tell the difference between what a spirit is and what is just the wiring in the house?"

"That's why we test out the room to see where the device points where the high voltage is. If it's a spirit, it'll give a high reading and then shut off for no reason. If it's the electrical wiring, the meter usually stays at a steady level the entire time. If we point it at a wall or near a place that could have an electrical source, the meter will stay steady at a high reading the whole time until we pull it away from that source. That's how we'll know if it's electrical wiring or not. With spirit, there is no source. It'll go off in the middle of a room as if an electric wire were dangling right there in front of it."

I raised an eyebrow. "Okay." I did not believe in any of this hogwash, but I followed her anyway. Monica held the device in her long, thin fingers as she went up the steps. She pointed it towards the hallway in the direction that we heard the footsteps, and it went off with the needle at the highest point. The little bulb turned red, and then in a snap, the needle went back down to zero. She went down the hall, putting the device up against the walls.

"What are you doing?" I asked.

"Checking to see if it was the electrical wiring in the walls that caused that reading." She reached her arm up towards the ceiling near one of the lights that were turned off. "Nope. Nothing. It's completely dead, so it wasn't any voltage." She checked the bedrooms leading up to the master bedroom, and the EMF didn't go off at all. Finally, she went into the master bedroom, and the second she took a step in, the needle darted to the highest point, and the bulb went red. "Do you sleep here often?" she asked.

"Yes, I'm moving out of it currently so my parents could sleep in here instead." I wasn't sure why I added that last part. "This is where I get the bulk of my dreams and visions."

She looked over at me with a knowing look in her eyes. She walked along the walls, and the EMF was flat. She reached up towards the ceiling fan and nothing. She walked towards the middle of the room, and the EMF went off again near where I was standing. She followed it, and the meter stayed steady at the highest reading. A sudden cold spot took over the left half of my body, and goosebumps ran down my left arm. The EMF continued to go off right next to me, but when my cold spot vanished, the EMF turned to zero. I got a chill for an entirely different reason, and my shoulders shook as the fear dripped down my spine like melting ice.

"Is there any other place in the house that you had a lot of activity in?" she asked me.

I thought of the strange vision of Dr. Ransteen, and the time Lavinia appeared in front of me. "The basement," I answered.

We left down there, and when she reached the bottom floor, the EMF went off again. "I'm going to try to catch an EVP," Monica said as she put the device in her pocket.

I was thoroughly confused. "A what?"

"Electronic voice phenomena. I have a device that can pick up the voices of spirits."

I couldn't help but laugh. I didn't mean to be rude, but this was just getting ridiculous. Monica's lip pouted as she glowered at me. I immediately shut my mouth and apologized. She took out a black rectangular-shaped device that reminded me of a basic radio, but it had a lot more buttons on it.

"I just find this all too hard to believe," I said. I pointed at it. "You could be picking up radio waves on that thing."

"And if I'm not?" she asked.

I shrugged. "There's no proof."

"I have plenty," she said. She pushed the recording button, and then another button on the side of the device. Then she began asking questions. "Who is here?" She paused. "Why are you here?"

There's silence.

"Why are you contacting Ted? Is it because he lives here?"

Still no answer.

I shook my head as I sighed. This was utterly absurd. *"Trapped."*

It was a jumble of voices that spoke as though it were a loud group answering all at once. My blood ran cold, and Monica turned towards me—Her face ashen. "H-how are you trapped?" she asked. Her hand shook as she held the device. She kept asking, but she never got an answer.

We waited for another response. I wasn't even sure I wanted anyone to answer. My chest sunk in from the anticipation and the fear of what may or may not happen. I let out a breath of relief when Monica turned off the device.

I decided to break the silence. "I've had visions of Dr. Ransteen." It felt like I was confessing something, and I swallowed hard as I waited for her response.

"What do you mean?" Monica's voice sounded so far away. She looked defeated.

"It was of him doing some kind of ritual in the basement, and he was... Giving his soul away to something in order to live longer? I have no idea. There were these strange symbols he wrote on the floor in a circle." I pointed to the surrounding area.

Her eyes sparked. "Can you draw these symbols for me? What did he say exactly?"

"Yeah, I can. He said something about a Beast of Eternal Life."

Her chest rose up and down erratically as she nodded. "Okay, okay. We can figure this out. This leads us somewhere."

"But it was just a dream," I said.

"Nothing is ever just a dream," she said as she left up the stairs.

One of the symbols that stuck out to me the most was the U shaped one whose ends curved outwards. It had two lines above it and one below it. I sketched it for Monica and handed her the paper. She furrowed her brow as she studied it. "I'll be back with more information about this later," she said. "I need to research. You can keep the EVP device. Maybe you can catch something. I've had more luck here than anywhere else with it." With that, she left out the front door in a rush.

On Sunday, I sat at the kitchen table, reading over the papers Lavinia had left behind. I wanted to read over everything just in case I overlooked something that could link the missing patients to an answer. There was nothing.

The EVP recorder that I left on the kitchen table caught my eye. I knew it was silly, but perhaps it could give me some clues on where to proceed in this investigation I happened to fall into. I was at a dead end, and I wanted more than anything for these visions to stop.

I grabbed the recorder and headed down towards the basement since that was the place Monica and I heard the voices. Once I started the device, I couldn't seem to open my mouth to ask anything. When I did, I immediately started laughing at myself. I had never felt sillier in my life. If anyone were watching, they'd find me insane and think I was grasping at straws for answers rather than perfectly sane solutions. Still, part of me wanted to test out the device and see if it was radio waves or not. If they could answer my questions intelligently, then that'd be too much of a coincidence for it to be radio waves picking up random words that had no relevance.

I was about to ask a question when a menacing growl startled me. All blood drained from my face. It didn't sound like any animal I knew of, and I grew up in the woods. I knew a bear's growl from a mountain lion. I could tell if a wolf was nearby just by how fresh the paw prints were. This was not something I was used to hearing. It was deep and low, and it took on a sinister tone.

Whatever it was, it snarled again and made the volume bars on the screen of the recorder go up. My muscles tightened, and I turned in every direction to see if there was an animal hiding. I had an inkling that there was something behind me ready to grab me at any moment. I heard it again, but this time it sounded as though it were saying something. It was a deep male voice, but it sounded so inhuman. It made chills run down my spine. Whatever it was, I didn't want to wait to find out in case it was some rabid animal, so I quickly ran up the stairs and closed the door. I backed away from it, and the palpitations in my chest as I feared that something might slam that door open and leap on top of me.

My whole body shook as I took a seat at the kitchen table, making sure to face towards the basement door in case someone or something decided to open it. I noticed the EVP device had a playback button, and I decided to play it. The first thing that played was Monica's voice when she was asking the questions the day before.

I fast-forwarded it to when I heard the growl. You could hear my panicked breathing through the recording, and that was when I heard the burly voice speak. I played it over and over to try and catch what it said, but it was as though it were speaking in another language. The voice was muffled a bit like a bad radio connection. I rewound it and replayed it numerous times writing down each letter I heard. It took several minutes, but I eventually came up with the words Bestia de Vita Aeterna.

I put the recorder away. That had to be Spanish or Italian. It was getting late, and I decided to go to bed earlier that night since I had work in the morning. I went into the living room, making sure to keep my body facing the basement door just in case. I found the crucifix my mother gave me, and even though I felt ridiculous holding it, it did give me some comfort, which was the point of having it.

I gingerly stepped out of the living room, making sure to give a wide berth between me and the basement door. I stomped up the steps itching put as much distance between me and the eerie room below. When I closed my bedroom door, I finally took a breath of relief.

That night, I had an atrocious nightmare of an invisible being snarling around me. However, I couldn't find it. I sat up in bed and clenched the blankets into my fists. I scanned the room, but I could not find anything. I bit down hard, causing my jaw muscles to ache. My heart fluttered frantically—anticipating another sound.

The sound of sharp nails scratching against the hollow floorboards underneath my bed made me jump into a panic. I threw the blankets off of me and leaped onto my mattress. Whatever it was, I wanted to be ready to fight it.

My body wobbled back and forth as I found my balance on the bed. I peered over the edge of it as the scratching continued. It sounded like several daggers digging into the floor.

I took a step closer to the edge, and the scratching suddenly ceased. I held my breath waiting for another sound. I took a second step, and a black mass came rushing out from underneath the bed. Before I could react, I was pinned onto my back. I couldn't move. I couldn't even breathe. It was that same black mass as before choking me—Crushing my lungs causing me to cough. There was no way I could fight it, and my eyes bulged out as I stared into the black abyss. My heart was beating so hard against my chest I felt it might burst. I struggled to move to break free so that I could run but to no avail.

I felt the flesh of my back rip open, and a fire burned in its place. I managed to yell out, and that's when the dark mass suddenly vanished. I shot awake in bed in a cold sweat. I took deep breaths thankful for each one. I moved my arms, but they felt numb as though I wasn't fully attached to them. Then I patted my mattress, and the sweat dampened my sheets.

It was just a dream. I sighed and lied back down in bed. Now more than ever, I *had* to stop these dreams.

In the morning, I took a shower before leaving to work. When I turned my back to the water, a shot of piercing fire throbbed on the side of my back. I quickly turned off the water and stepped out of the shower. I faced the mirror and turned my body to check my back, and there plain as day were three slash marks that ran from the middle of my back and around my waist to my hip. It was fresh, and I touched it gingerly. I winced at the dull ache from where my finger had brushed it.

My stomach churned, and nausea stirred in my lower abdomen. I looked over to my bed and took long strides towards it before ripping off the covers. A dry, small pool of blood soaked my sheets. I blinked hoping it was all a hallucination that would suddenly vanish. I clutched the blankets in my hand unaware of how hard I was gripping them until the joints in my fingers ached. I dropped them and took a step back from the bed as though it were the plague. I gasped for air realizing I forgotten to breathe. There was no way this was happening.

Chapter Seven
The Man in the Beat-up Truck

I was careful not to twist my body too much while at work. I wrapped up my injury in some gauze and medical tape to keep it in place after applying rubbing alcohol and Neosporin. I couldn't bend over much without the searing pain coursing through my body. It made my movements very constricted.

Before work, I had researched what Bestia de Vita Aeterna meant because clearly, it could lead to what attacked me. What I found out made me excited to speak with Monica at work because it could help us find out more about the mystery of what happened to her sister. And then, hopefully, put an end to the nightmares.

I went to Mrs. Sal's room to give her, her lunch. I saw her lying down in bed with a damp towel over her forehead and a bundle of pills on her nightstand. Her mouth was agape as she attempted to breathe. Her breathing sounded forceful and raspy like something was blocking her lungs from opening. She turned her head towards me as I entered, and her wrinkled arm barely lifted itself out towards me. Her old body made her skin shrunken in, and as a result, her veins poked out.

Shoving the bottles of pills out of the way, I set down her tray of food on her nightstand. I checked her forehead, and she was burning up. "When was the last time you took your medicine?" I asked.

"An…" She took a deep breath, and it sounded labored. "Hour ago."

I pressed my lips together and frowned. "Okay." I took her towel and ran it under cool water to place over her forehead. I patted her arm, and I could feel how frail it was. Her skin was soft, but I could feel her bones. "I'll be right back," I said.

I walked out of the room and went to Christina, who was at the front desk, "We have an emergency with Mrs. Sal. We need to call an ambulance."

Christina's brow knit together, and her tone was soft with concern. "What's wrong?"

My voice was grave. "She is *very* ill. She needs to go to the hospital."

Christina sat up in her seat and nodded. She immediately dialed the emergency number. I went back towards Mrs. Sal's room, who looked worse within minutes of my leaving. I sat by her. "You are going to the hospital," I said.

If she had the strength, she would've sassed me, but instead, her tone came out dull and lacked life. "Why, boy? What's going on?"

"You're not doing well. The medicine isn't working." I didn't want her to be scared, so I decided to try a joke. "So, you need to go where they got the good stuff. They can hook you up."

She smiled, but it faltered. She began to cough, and her body convulsed with each one. Her breathing shook even more, and it was as though she didn't have the strength to force out the phlegm from within her throat.

I put my hand on her shoulder, and she relaxed. "I'll stay with you the whole time until they come," I said.

Her eyes watered as she smiled. Her hand trembled as she went to put it on top of mine. The hospital was only a few minutes away, so they'd be here quickly. "Tell me a story," she said.

I thought for a minute. "There is one story my mother used to tell me. She learned it from a Native American who lived near us. It's the story of a girl and a snake. There was once a tree at the top of a hill in a village where the little girl lived. Every day she'd go to the top of the hill to sit underneath the tree, and one day she came across a snake who asked for her help to bring him down the hill where it'd be warmer for him. She told him, 'No. You're a snake. You'll bite me.' The snake promised he wouldn't bite her. He said, 'I need your help. I promise I won't bite. Get me down to safety, and you will see.' So, with warmth in her heart, she picked up the snake and brought him down the hill. She put him down, and he uncurled himself as his body warmed up under the sun. After feeling better, he bit the girl. The girl grabbed her hand where she was bitten and said, 'Ouch! You bit me! You promised you wouldn't. How could you?' And the snake said, 'Ah, but you knew what I was.'"

"That is a depressin' ass story," said Mrs. Sal.

I let out a chuckle. "I suppose so, but the moral of the story is to listen to your instincts and not be gullible."

"I could have learned from that." Her lips fit into a tight line. "I used to be a singer; you know. I was a backup vocalist back in the day, and I had quite the voice." She raised her eyebrows and looked at me from the corner of her eye. "I went on tour too with a few different bands. I wanted to be a lead vocalist, but being black, that was hard to accomplish in a white man's industry. This was the 1950s, and we were making our strides in the industry, but you had to be lucky. I trusted a man to get me there. I knew in my gut I couldn't trust him, but he said such sweet things to me as that snake did to that girl. He promised me a stage and my name in lights. I figured he was my best shot. He was a white man, so he could get me in through the door. However, he ended up burnin' me in the end and left me there without a penny to my name. I had left my family behind to pursue this dream only to find out the man didn't have the reputation he fooled me into thinking. Hm! So, I went back home and ended up becoming a dry cleaner. So much for my life."

I frowned. "Did you ever find your happiness? It couldn't have been all bad."

She looked at me. Her eyes were glossy. "It wasn't. I met myself a good man, and we had a couple of kids." She smiled. "Those were the best years of my life. I sang to those kids and boy did they love it. I found a whole new audience I'd love to perform in front of. Nobody else deserved to hear my voice. Only the people I cared about."

I nodded. "That's good for you. Your talents are special, and they should be saved for people that are special enough to share them with."

"That's what my experiences taught me." She furrowed her brow. "I don't know why I told you this. I suppose this is my last chance to tell my story."

I gripped onto her frail fingers. They were so thin in my muscular hand. "No, it's not."

Her sass came back. "Boy, I'm old. Do not lie to me to make me feel better." Her voice softened, and she smiled at me. "But thank you for keeping me company before they come."

I stayed with her until the EMTs came to take her to the hospital. I held her hand as they carried her on the stretcher all the way to the ambulance. I stood there as they drove away. A lump formed in my throat, and I tried to swallow it down before any tears could fall.

Towards the end of my shift, I bumped into Monica. She had just started her shift since she usually worked nights. Seeing her reminded me of my dream and the scratch marks, which made all life drain from my face. "What's wrong?" she asked.

I opened my mouth to speak, but I struggled to find the words.

"Did something happen?" she asked.

All I could manage was a nod.

"What is it?" she implored.

"I heard a voice on the EVP last night."

Her eyes widened, and she pulled me off to the side of the hallway. "What did it say?"

"I researched what it said before work, and I found out it was Latin for Beast of Eternal Life." I closed my mouth, debating whether to tell her about my scratch marks. I eventually decided against it. "Also, I found something that

193

could help lead us to what the symbols mean. There's a book that is all black, and I recognized the symbols on the cover to the few that Dr. Ransteen drew on the ground. I think that book has something to do with this. We need to find that book."

Monica chewed on her pencil. "I'll have to research that. I'll get back to you."

I looked over Monica's shoulder and noticed Christina was staring right at us from behind her desk in the lobby area. She immediately looked down when I caught her and pretended to work on the computer.

Monica noticed I was staring off towards the lobby and turned around to see Christina. She looked back at me with a grimace on her face. "I'll talk to you later."

When my shift was over, I grabbed my backpack out of my locker and went to find Christina, who was sitting behind the front desk. "I'll call you tonight, okay?" I said. "Maybe we can plan something for later this week. I must build a walkway for my Mom that leads up to the front porch. *That* sounds like a fun date, right?"

Christina giggled. "Totally exciting." With all sincerity, she said, "I'd love to help you with that. We can order dinner afterward."

"That sounds perfect." The fact that she was willing to help me with my parents' situation made my feelings for her deepen. She wanted to do more than just go on fun dates. She wanted to actually spend time with me no matter what it was. It showed her dedication. After all my years of dating, it was rare to find someone like that.

"Um, so you and Monica…" Christina trailed off.
"What about her?"

Christina bit her bottom lip as if she were debating what to say next. After a few seconds, she shook her head and said, "Never mind."

I didn't know if I should worry about that or not. She knows about Monica's connection to my house. "Monica is just asking about the house. How it's working out for me." I know if I say anything more, I will be diving into a hole I can't get out of.

"It's okay," she said while looking into my eyes. "We're all friends here, we look out for one another," she smiles. "I know you would do the same for me," as if she could read my mind. I leave while smiling back.

The rest of the workweek passed by without any paranormal activity, and I was grateful for it. The injury along the side of my back seemed to be getting better. I made sure to put medicine on it every night. I didn't know what to make of it, but I refused to let the thought of some strange shadow creature causing this to seep into my mind.

I made plans with Christina to come over that Saturday, and she arrived with a few beers and some delicious sub sandwiches in tow. "I brought us some fuel," she said as she entered my home. She plopped her things down on the kitchen table. I marveled at the way she was dressed: she wore well-fitted jeans that complemented her thighs and hips. She wore a loose collared shirt that the front half was tucked into the jeans. Her hair was up in a ponytail, and I loved how frizzy and curly it was. She turned to me and put a hand on her hip. "What?" she asked.

I grinned. "You look nice."

A smile adorned her face. "Thank you, Teddy." She eyed me up and down with a flirtatious look in her eye as she took out a couple of beers from the case. "You don't look too bad yourself."

It was good that Christina was there because I was going to need someone to hold down the wooden boards as I nailed them together. I also needed to sand down the wooden planks first, which Christina was willing to do. What would have taken me all day to do, it only took a few hours with her help. Plus, I was having fun while doing it.

After we were finished hammering the last nail in, Christina sat up and put her hands on her hips. "I'd say we did a pretty good job. Lunch break?"

I wiped the dirt off my jeans and followed her inside. Christina prepared the sandwiches by adding the mustard and mayonnaise and handed me a plate. It was the first time I ever shared a meal in my own home with a girl I liked. Christina had moved the chair closer to me, so we could eat right next to each other. "You have a nice house," she commented.

I nodded my head, my mouth full of food. "Thank you."

She giggled and used her napkin to wipe the corner of my mouth. "You got some mustard there."

I swallowed. "Thanks." Without thinking, I placed my hand gently on top of hers.

She stopped mid-chew and met my eyes. Her cheeks were puffed out from the food that was inside, and it made me chuckle. I leaned over to kiss her cheek, which made her turn bright pink.

After we finished lunch, we sat on the couch to watch some television. We didn't go out all day, and I appreciated that even though we weren't doing much, it was still fun. She laid her head on my shoulder as the rest of her body furled up against mine. I was unsure of what move to make next, and my palms began to sweat.

I thought that once a person got old enough, they'd get over their nerves and make a move, but I was still that shy teenage boy unaware of whether or not the girl wanted to kiss me after the school dance. I think it was because I genuinely cared about Christina, and I didn't want to fuck anything up. One wrong move, and she'd be out of my life.

I took a small risk and stroked my hand up and down her arm. She responded by nuzzling her head up against my arm. After finishing a few episodes, it started to get dark, and Christina sat up and said, "I have to get going. I have to work a shift on Sunday morning." She gave me a crooked smile to show her disappointment. I walked her to the door, and she paused on her way out. "I had a lot of fun today. We should do more of this," she said. She stood up on her tiptoes to plant a kiss on my lips. "I'll see you soon, okay?"

I nodded, my head swooning from the contact. "I'll call you." I watched her as she got into her car to make sure she made it safely before closing my front door. Other girls I dated would've stayed the night, and we would've ended up having sex. But I got the feeling Christina was different. Perhaps it was because she was a country girl, but I got the sense that she was old-fashioned. I smirked. I liked that about her.

The following day, Monica called me while I was at home eating lunch. "Ted! I figured it out. I found the book, and I'm on my way over," she exclaimed.

I nearly choked on my soup. "You mean you found that obscure black book?"

"I believe so. It had a spell in it similar to the one you saw with the Beast of Eternal Life. I'm heading over right now. I drove to the city to find it in an old bookstore. The people there were highly unusual, and I stuck out like a sore thumb. Whenever I asked people about it, they gave me this weird look like I was a freak. That is a *whole* other story. Anyway, I'll be there in a few." She hung up abruptly. In a way, Monica reminded me of Scarlett in how she just lets herself in and doesn't bother to ask. It was something I was used to, so it didn't bother me too much.

I finished up my soup and waited for Monica's arrival. I heard the slamming of a car door from outside before the knocks came to my door. When I opened it, she gave me a small smile that seemed rather strained.

"Are you okay?" I asked.

She slowly nodded, but that grim expression on her face lingered. She pointed to the wooden ramp behind her. "What's that?" she asked.

"It's for my Mom," I said.

"Oh…" She looked down briefly. "That's right. I forgot May I come in?" She walked past me without bothering to wait for my response. I noticed she had a rather large book in her hand. The cover of it was licorice black. It was the blackest color I had ever seen. It seemed almost unreal, and I went to touch it, half expecting my hand to go through it. The appearance made it look like it was a portal—A gateway to another dimension. The silver symbols etched into the cover is what gave away that illusion.

She set it on the table and stood there, staring off into space.

"Monica?" I called out. "You there?"

She blinked, and then said in a faraway voice that sounded almost robotic, "I found a way to reverse the spell."

My brow furrowed. "What spell?" *We're getting into spells now?*

She didn't respond to my question at all. Instead, she continued to gaze off into the distance.

"Are you okay?" I asked.

She looked up at me, but her eyes weren't staring at me. They were looking in my direction, but they seemed to be somewhere else. She blinked again, and she finally became fully present. "Yeah. Why?"

"You seem out of it today." I reached my arm out to gesture her to take a seat making sure to stand close to her in case she fell.

She rubbed her forehead as she took a seat. "Yeah, sorry about that. It's been a long day. You wouldn't believe the nightmares I've been having."

"I think I can imagine."

She grimaced. "I bet you can." She stared off into space again. "I feel like something dark is following me, and I can't say why I feel this way. It sounds crazy. Maybe this is what my sister felt like towards the end."

"Was she spacey like this?"

"Yeah." she nodded her head and kept saying "yeah" over and over in a whisper. She shook her head. "She also kept looking over her shoulder like something was following her. We all thought she was just stressed."

"I know that all too well."

She took a deep breath and stared down at the book. "But I found it, and we're that much closer. The spell I was talking about is from this book." She opened it up to one of

199

the last pages, and I saw that same dragon-like creature again from my vision. It snaked across the page, and on the page next to it was Latin. "I had to translate it, but pretty much the gist of it is selling your soul to this being in order to live forever, but there's a catch. You can't stay in one body forever. It'll eventually die, but this beast will make you powerful enough so that you can possess bodies."

"Possess?"

"Yeah, like in those scary movies where the demon takes over some devout Christian girl's body?"

I nodded my head. "Right."

"This beast uses souls to make him stronger, right? So, the deal is this person who made this agreement with this demon must give it souls, so essentially killing people and trapping their spirits."

I was so utterly dumbfounded. I had no idea whether to laugh or actually believe it and be scared. "How does someone trap souls?"

"It can be done anywhere from my understanding," said Monica as she flipped the page. "This is where it explains how to trap souls. You must do the markup, which are the three main symbols used to create the barrier that traps the souls in one place. You must use the victims' ashes to trap the souls while keeping their bones on the property nearby. Wherever you place the ashes, you draw these symbols. You could place them in a box, for instance, but as long as they have these symbols, the demon can gain access to the souls."

"What are the three symbols?"

Monica pointed at the aged paper with the smeared black ink. One of the symbols was made of two straight lines that crossed over one another with a U-shaped curve at each end of the two lines. The second symbol was the same as the previous one, but it had an additional line that ran through the middle with an isosceles triangle at the end. On either side of the triangle were two circles with lines between each. The last symbol was three curved lines that overlapped one another with an arrow in the middle. "You have to find the ashes and destroy the symbols to free the souls," she said.

I scrunched my face in confusion. "None of this makes sense. You're saying the soul is attached to the body and that's how you preserve the soul?"

Monica shook her head. "You have to draw the circle of Capture first. Wherever you are burning the bodies, you must draw the circle." She pointed to a drawn picture below the three symbols. There were two circles with one bigger than the other. In between the two circles were more satanic-like figures. "This traps the souls from leaving their bodies. You must burn them right away or burn them alive is better. Killing them right before you put them in the fire is best. It traps the soul within the ashes, and then you place those ashes in whatever place you want. You could leave them in the fire pit if you want. If they stay in there, the Beast of Eternal Life will have their souls."

I sat back in my seat and let out a big breath. "Okay, this is too much for me. This is insane, Monica."

"I know, I know it is, but it's hard to deny. I think…" She paused. "I think Howard didn't kill my sister. I think Dr. Ransteen possessed Howard's body and killed her because she was going to find a way to break the curse and free those souls and thereby trapping *him*."

I rubbed my face. "This is unreal." I didn't know whether to commit Monica or myself for listening to this crap.

"I know it is, but it has to be real. Howard just randomly killing my sister doesn't make sense, and he went missing. They can't find him anywhere!"

"Why not just possess your sister then, huh? Why Howard? If she was the one that knew all the secrets, then why not just take over *her* body?"

"Not all bodies are easily possessed. I think Lavinia was too strong-willed of a soul. She was powerful all on her own, which makes sense. She had a very strong personality and was tough. Towards the end of her life, she was acting strange a bit. She'd have massive personality changes and had lots of bruises on her. After that, she was super paranoid. I think Dr. Ransteen tried to possess her but couldn't, and maybe that's what triggered her into researching this further because she knew something bigger was going on."

There had to be a logical explanation, and I think I found it. I tried to word this carefully for Monica, so I trod lightly and spoke slowly. "Don't you think the bruising and the strange behavior could be due to Howard abusing her?"

She rolled her eyes and sighed as if she had heard this all before. "I thought about that, but I don't feel it was a coincidence that she was researching about Dr. Ransteen, who happened to be into this type of occult stuff, and then Howard randomly kills her out of the blue. That's too coincidental in my book."

"It seems highly unlikely." I thought back to my own experiences and the scratches I woke up with. "But it's probable." I internally kicked myself for almost believing for even half a second that this was probably real. It wasn't, and it couldn't be. My stress was going too far. Maybe I was unhappy in my life, and with the house I bought, so this was just some odd way of me coping with that. That's why some people get into conspiracy theories: because they need to believe in something and get heavily engrossed in it to escape their own reality.

Deep in thought, I hadn't noticed Monica glaring at something out the window. Perplexed, I followed her gaze to find a beat-up truck idling right outside my home. There was a man inside, but I couldn't get a good look at him.

"Do you know who that is?" Monica asked with an apparent strain in her voice. She began to pull at her fingers, nervously. "He's been there a while and staring right at us through the window. He was there even when I first arrived." The worry seeped into her voice. "I think he may have followed me from New York City."

The color of the beat-up truck with the faded blue and light rust forming on the sides reminded me of the same vehicle I saw driving by my parents' property. Whoever was inside the truck stared straight ahead. From what I could see, he had a long beard.

My main concern was for Monica's safety. I didn't want her to drive home alone with this man right outside my home. "Let me go check it out and see what his deal is," I said. Perhaps I could scare him off.

I walked out the front door and bee-lined straight towards him, but then he shifted his gears and slowly drove off. I stood there in the middle of the road with a sense of bewilderment.

"I think that was Dr. Ransteen," said Monica right behind me. Her voice shook with fear.

I turned around and headed back to the house. "No. Just some creep."

"We need to find Dr. Ransteen in Howard's body."

"I agree." I didn't tell her what I really thought, though. I was unsure if it'd hurt her feelings that I doubted her. I thought of finding Lavinia's killer, whom I believe was Howard. I believe Howard was an abusive boyfriend, and he killed Lavinia during one of his rages. I also thought there was a connection between Howard and the missing people because shortly after Lavinia's death was when people started to go missing. If my memory served me right, Lavinia died eight years ago, and that was right around the time that the first mentally ill person went missing.

Monica stayed for a bit longer with me until we both felt it was safe for her to drive home. "I'm leaving the book with you," she said. "You can read over it if you'd like." When she left out the door, I watched to make sure she made it to her car safely.

The following Monday, I noticed Christina wasn't at her post. She must've had the day off, and I had to admit that I was a bit bummed that she wasn't at work. Instead, the other front desk secretary filled her space. I was looking forward to that heart-fluttering feeling Christina always gave me, but instead, Stacey greeted me. Whom, to be quite honest, I didn't get along with. She always snarled at me, and I had no idea what I did to her. Maybe it was because one year during Christmas we did White Elephant, and I got her socks. Okay, I had forgotten to get her a gift and ended up grabbing the first thing I could find. It turned out I got her a pack of large male socks, and I didn't know she had big feet. She thought I was making a jab at her insecurity. Everyone found it hysterical. Well, everyone except for her.

Monica arrived at work, and she fumbled with her hands in that way she did whenever she was nervous. She looked over her shoulder once she entered through the building's front entrance, and then picked up her pace as she went into the break room. Concerned, I followed her. "What's going on?" I asked.

She put her gloves into her purse. "That man followed me again. I'm late because I was scared to leave my house. He was out there *all* night and this morning."

My heart clenched, and my stomach churned, making me regret having that burrito for breakfast. "Is he still here?"

She put her purse into her locker. "No, but I'm scared to go home."

"We need to call the cops."

She closed her locker. "Stalking isn't a crime, Ted."

"It should be. Let me follow you home tonight. I'd feel better about it."

Monica gave me a small smile. "You're a good man, Ted. Thank you."

My day at work was normal. The usual daylight wasn't breaking through the windows due to the weather. It always put me in a strange funk whenever we had the fluorescent lights on during an overcast day. It tricked me into thinking I was working a night shift because of how dark the sky was. I noticed that Mrs. Sal still hadn't returned from the hospital, and I made sure to fix her bedding and to dust her things. She always liked to keep things tidy, and I wanted her to return to a clean room.

After work, as promised, I followed Monica home in my truck. As I was driving, I got a call from Christina. "What are you up to tonight, Ted?" she asked.

I had it on speaker and answered, "I just got off and following Monica home.

"Oh." Christina sounded surprised. "Is everything alright?"

"She said a man has been following her since yesterday, and he stayed outside her home all day. I decided to see her home just in case he follows her again today."

Christina gasped. "Oh, my goodness! Has she called the cops?"

"I told her to, but she doesn't seem to think they can do anything."

"I still would. Maybe they could keep an eye on her for safety."

I shrugged. "Perhaps… Maybe we could do something later tonight if you want."

I could hear the smile in her voice. "Yes, I'd like that."

"Okay, I'll surprise you. Dress nicely because I'm taking you out."

I heard her giggle, and it made my heart stop. "Okay, Teddy. See you soon."

I sat in my truck as I watched Monica park her car. She waved at me as she entered her building. I waved back before turning my truck around and headed home. Nobody followed her home, and I was relieved thinking perhaps the man would leave her alone.

As I turned into my neighborhood, I drove past the same beat-up truck. We made brief eye contact as he drove past. His eyes were dark and piercing. It made a chill run down my spine, causing my body to convulse involuntarily. Seeing him confirmed my suspicions that it was the same man from the mountains. I'd recognize those eyes anywhere. I took a sharp intake of breath as he passed me, and he turned to go towards the highway.

When I parked, and I noticed my screen door was wide open. I threw open my car door and slammed it shut behind me forgetting to lock it. I took large strides up the walkway to my porch. I turned the front door's knob to see if it was locked or not. It wasn't. My heartbeat became erratic, and I chastised myself for leaving my home unlocked. However, I could have sworn I locked it that morning.

I held on tightly to my keys with each key sticking out between my fingers as a makeshift weapon in case there was someone inside. I braced myself for what could be behind the door and threw it open. It slammed against the wall, and the momentum caused it to swing back towards me. Nothing was there in the living room or kitchen, and I gingerly stepped inside before closing my front door.

Tentatively, I stepped into the living room to check if my television was there. It was. I took careful steps upstairs, but despite my best efforts, each step still creaked beneath my sneakers. And I cursed the aged wood. I backed up against the wall as I threw open each bedroom door and poked my head in to check if anyone was in there. I had my weapon held up in my clenched fist, ready to attack.

I noticed nothing of value was missing in my bedroom, and I lowered my weapon. Perhaps I did just leave the front door unlocked today. As I went downstairs, I noticed the book Monica had left me was missing from the kitchen table. A horrifying thought dawned on me, and I scurried down the basement stairs where I had placed the box full of Lavinia's notes. I misstepped and nearly tumbled down the stairs. Gripping onto the handrails, I broke my fall.

Once I got down to the basement floor, I saw the storage room door was wide open, and the items inside were tossed over and thrown about. Whoever was down there was looking for something in a panic. The old hospital beds were toppled over. The boxes were dumped out with all its contents strewed across the floor. The metal cabinets in the far back that I never searched through were pried open. At the opening of the cabinets, there were large dents where someone must've used a crowbar to force the drawers open. Whatever was once inside those cabinets was now gone. I also noticed Lavinia's box with her notes were missing as well.

Maybe there was some truth to what Monica was saying. The thought of a stranger in this home—a possessed stranger—made me clench my fists so tightly my nails dug into my flesh. I stomped up the stairs to find my phone. Even though the robbery was under strange circumstances, any sane person would call the police to report a robbery. I needed to *at least* act as a sane person would. It doesn't matter that this could be some demon related activity. I had things stolen from me, and therefore, calling the authorities was the perfect reaction. Maybe they would even be able to track down this person for me, and we could finally get Howard behind bars. I still wasn't sure if Howard was, in fact, Howard or Dr. Ransteen. I shook my head of the crazy thought as I dialed 9-1-1.

The police arrived almost an hour later, and they took a seat at my kitchen table as they took note of the situation. "What did they steal?" asked the officer.

"Just papers," I said. I didn't want to say what the papers were.

The officer looked up from his notepad with his eyebrows raised. "Papers? What kind of papers?"

I kept adjusting myself in my seat nervously. "They were copies of old newspaper clippings, photos, and notes from the early nineteen-hundreds."

Both officers eyed one another. "So, these were some kind of historical artifacts?"

I cleared my throat. "It's more like research."

"And this person took your research?" The tone in the one officer's voice gave away that he was thoroughly confused, and a bit irritated by my unwillingness to share the full story outright.

I sighed instantly regretting that I had called them. "Yes. A friend of mine and I were researching this house when these were stolen."

"Were you planning on publishing these anywhere? Do you work as a journalist? Maybe it could have been a competitor that wanted to get their hands on the story."

Filing a report was exhausting. There were too many questions. I looked down at my folded hands. "No, nothing like that. It was general curiosity about the history of my house." I had no idea why I didn't just tell them the truth. I could have at least told them I was researching someone's killer and told them I thought this killer took them. However, I feared sounding insane.

The officer chuckled. "Well, I bet it is one interesting house if some stranger came in to take all your information. Maybe it could have been your friend. Does he have access to your house?"

"No, *she* doesn't. I think I saw the perpetrator drive out of my neighborhood."

This made one of the officers sit forward in his seat while the other eyed me suspiciously. "Why do you think it was this person? What did they look like?"

"The reason why I suspect him is because he's been parked outside my house before, and he's been following my friend home too."

The officers exchanged glances. "So, this man has been following you?"

I gave a nod. "That is correct."

"Can you give us his description and details about the type of vehicle he drives? Do you know his license plate number?"

I told them what the truck looked like, and how I saw it near the mountains where my parents lived. They wrote everything down and then said, "We'll keep our eyes peeled, but most often stolen items are not returned to the owners. We make no promises on that, but we will try to find this guy."

I thanked them for their time, and they left.

It was so late, and a lot had happened. I nearly forgot about Christina. I fumbled through my pockets searching for my phone to call her. When she answered, she did not sound at all pleased. "Hi, Ted." She sounded monotone and exhausted.

Ted. Just Ted. Not Teddy or anything else. I chastised myself for not remembering sooner. "I am so sorry. When I got home from work, someone had broken in, and I had to call the police. They just left."

Her voice perked up a bit, but I could hear the faint sounds of disbelief. "Are you okay?"

"Yes, I'm fine. I saw the guy when he drove out."

"I'm glad you're safe. It seems a lot has been happening to you lately." And there it was. That tone matched exactly to what she was thinking. She believed I was making it up, and I didn't entirely blame her.

"I know it sounds like I keep coming up with one excuse after another." I laughed lightly as I ran my fingers through my hair. "I guess we chose the worst timing for us to start this up." I meant that as a joke, but her silence made me instantly regret my practice at humor. I wanted to say I was sorry, but I forced that apology down my throat. She didn't want to hear that again. All I wanted was to be with her.

"I gotta go, Ted." Her voice was flat, and the sound of it crushed my hopes.

"Okay." I wasn't about to force her into not giving up on me. I had to *show* her and not tell her, and that's what I set out to do the following day at work.

I had a hard time sleeping that night knowing a man had successfully broken into my home, and it enraged me that he was keeping me up. I didn't want him to have that kind of control over me, but there I was getting up every hour to inspect the front door to make sure it was still locked. I kicked myself for being so paranoid, but I did have every right to be. Still, it didn't help ease my fury any less.

The following morning, I was exhausted, but I had to get up to prepare something special for Christina as an apology. After I had clocked in, I approached her at her desk. She greeted me only with that pleasant smile she showed to passersby. It was my first time being on the receiving end of it, and I hated how quickly she pulled back from me. At first, I wanted to blame her for being fickle, but she had every reason to be that way. I hadn't exactly been the most present with her.

"When is your lunch?" I asked. "I was wondering if you wanted to go out to lunch with me today." I chewed on the inside of my cheek dreading the next words she'd say.

She swiveled in her chair a bit. "I don't know. We won't have much time."

"I brought us lunch."

She looked up at me a bit surprised.

"You said how much you like chicken with rosemary, and I decided to cook is some to enjoy during lunch today. We can eat outside on the park benches."

A small smile broke across her face, and her cheeks began to turn a light shade of pink. "That was very sweet of you, Ted."

"Would you join me?" I didn't want to come off as desperate, but I supposed I was. She was the first girl I ever genuinely liked. Every other girl in the past was just to fill time or to cure my loneliness.

"Will you tell me what's really going on while we eat?"

A battle ensued inside me. Dare I tell her and risk her finding me crazy? Or do I not tell her and risk her breaking things off with me? Either way, I'd lose because she wouldn't want to continue dating me. "It's hard for me to talk about. It's... Not what you think."

She pursed her lips together. "Then tell me what it is I should be thinking?"

I opened my mouth to speak, but I couldn't think of an excuse. "I... I just need time."

Whatever happiness she had at speaking to me was now gone. Her eyes turned cold, and the sight of it made my heart plummet. She turned in her chair to face her computer screen. With an aloof manner, she said, "Take all the time you need, Ted."

"Christina," I began.

She motioned with her eyes towards the hall where the patient rooms were. "Don't you have patients to take care of?"

I bit down and swallowed. I drummed my fingers on the counter before turning on my heels to leave. She was done talking to me. With a cesspool of grief bubbling in my core, I went to see if Mrs. Sal returned from the hospital. When I went into her room, all her belongings were cleared out. I knit my brow together as my eyes scanned the empty room. The bed was neatly made as though nobody had been there in the first place—As if Mrs. Sal hadn't spent the last five years there. Her tiny glass figurines were now gone. I grabbed one of the nearby nurses. "What happened to Mrs. Sal?" I asked.

He just shrugged. "Don't know, man. Ask one of the other nurses."

I went down the hall searching for the nurse on duty for the day but couldn't find one. I turned around and headed towards the front and saw a nurse standing there with his clipboard talking to Christina. However, it was the nurse I couldn't stand.

Nurse Brooks always intimidated me a bit only because he was technically my boss, but he wasn't a very friendly one. It didn't make my job any easier. The nurses worked in different shifts, and whenever Brooks was there, it made my day a living hell.

I approached him and stood there quietly waiting for him to finish his conversation. I learned not to stand too closely as I waited. I got written up for that before. I also got written up for waiting for him for too long. He had told me, "You should have gone back to work and come find me when I was free." I figured waiting one minute was enough. If after that, he still wasn't ready, I learned to walk away. So far in the past, it worked.

I had ten seconds left of waiting before I had to leave when he finally turned his attention to me. "What do you want?" he asked in a dull tone.

"I was wondering about the status of Mrs. Sal."

"Who?" He squinted his eyes at me.

"Mrs. Aaliyah Sal."

He still looked utterly confused, but it was mixed with his perpetual anger. I decided to jog his memory. "She had gotten ill, and I called for an ambulance—."

He cut me off with the wave of his hand. "I don't need a history lesson on my patients. Why are you worried about someone that is no longer here when you have plenty of patients that *are* here in need of your attention?"

I held my tongue. I bit down on it, so I wouldn't be tempted to raise my voice at him. I badly wanted to call him a dick. All I could muster was a nod of my head, and I turned to leave.

I went to work checking on my other patients and tending to their every need. To me, it felt like Brooks did the bare minimum like many of the other nurses here, and it bothered me. I expected the others within my same position to only do the bare minimum, but I held a nurse up to a higher esteem. He should take better care of his patients. He should at least show he cared, but he always just shoved pills down their throats at every tiny complaint. "Here take this," he'd said nonchalantly to them. He prescribed medicine like a coke dealer needing to push for more sales. Half of these residents didn't need to be on nearly as many drugs as he had them on. It disgusted me.

By lunchtime, I was exhausted from running back and forth down the halls and literally running with one of the patients, Mr. Tuck. He liked to have a running buddy, and I chose to go with him in case he needed help at any point. Plus, it made me get some exercise in as well.

I walked past the front desk where Christina was on my way to the break room to clock out for lunch. Christina stood up and quickly made her way over to me. She looked down the hall apprehensively as if she was worried someone might see her. Probably Nurse Brooks. He hated it when you weren't in your designated spot. I was surprised she wanted to be near me. Once she approached me, she whispered, "She passed."

At first, I didn't know what she was talking about.

"Mrs. Sal. She passed away in the hospital," said Christina.

My world stopped for a split second.

215

Gone.

Just like that. I hadn't realized my mouth was open in shock until Christina put a hand on my back. The physical contact snapped me back to life. At first, I was in disbelief, but then a weight fell onto my heart, and I had to blink away the tears.

"Let's talk about it over lunch," she offered. She guided me to the break room, and if it weren't for hearing about Mrs. Sal's death, I would have been genuinely excited at Christina wanting to eat with me.

I warmed up the chicken for us, and we went outside to the back of the SNF, where we had a few windy walkways, trees, park benches, and picnic tables for the residents. It was where Mr. Tuck and I had run earlier. A few trees were placed sporadically across the well-trimmed grass. Some of the residents enjoyed planting flowers around the area. It was a nice way to make them feel like they were more at home.

"I'm sorry to hear about Mrs. Sal," said Christina. She was the first to speak after several minutes of silence.

I sighed. "She was a patient… But I care about my patients."

She gave me a soft smile, and her eye twinkled with something I was unfamiliar with. Admiration? It made me uncomfortable. "I know you do." She reached her hand out to grab mine.

I grimaced. "Thanks." I let out another deep breath. "I'll be fine eventually. I just have to get over the first initial shock of it is all."

"Understandable."

I watched her as she ate her lunch. The way her hair was pulled back but that one small strand that always fell in front of her face made me smile. I found it endearing. She always tried to tuck it behind her ear, but it was too short for that, and it'd creep itself back in front of her eyes after some time. I reached my hand out and took the strand to place it behind her ear. My heart fluttered as she looked into my eyes. I decided I need to tell her the truth.

"I'll tell you what's been going on." I nervously rubbed my hands together.

She placed her fork down and pushed aside her dish.

"You know how the home I moved into is the same place Monica's sister died at?"

Christina nodded as she took a sip of water.

"Well, I've been getting dreams about her sister ever since I moved into that house."

Christina furrowed her brow and tilted her head to one side.

"I know it sounds crazy, and I don't know if I fully believe in any of it." I sucked in a breath as I contemplated telling her the whole truth. I decided with just leaving it as having dreams about Lavinia. She didn't need to know about the shadows attacking me. "I told Monica about it that day we ran into each other at the Farmer's Market. I wanted to know what Lavinia looked like to see if I was truly seeing her in my dreams."

"And?" Christina seemed thoroughly perplexed and interested, which I wasn't expecting.

"Turns out I was right. That led to Monica coming over because she thought maybe we could figure out what happened to her sister together. You know, they never found her killer."

Christina nodded. "Yes, I heard."

"Well, ever since then, strange things have been happening. We've been..." I thought carefully of how to word this. "Collecting evidence about her murder." Not the whole truth, but it was good enough for now. Perhaps one day I'd tell her everything. "And that's when a man in an old truck started following Monica around."

Christina's eyes widened, and her mouth fell open a bit.

"And that same man broke into my home and stole the evidence from my house."

Christina blinked. Her eyes still wide. "Oh, my Lord." She was talking more to herself than to me, and I let her sit there as she thought this through. Finally, she met my eyes and said, "How do you know? I mean, it all sounds pretty far-fetched to me."

Yeah, imagine if I were to tell you about the ghosts. "I know it does, but you wanted me to tell you, and there it is."

Christina held her chin in her hand as she mulled this over. I was so nervous about her reaction that my stomach churned and made me regret eating that chicken. "So, you think Howard is the one that's been stalking you guys?" Christina finally asked.

I shrugged. "I don't know for sure, but that's my best guess. Who else could it be?"

"And why would he know to stalk you in the first place?"

"That's where I'm confused too," I confessed. "I am the first person to have moved into that house since the crime."

"Maybe he found out and decided to make sure you didn't find anythin' out? But that still doesn't make much sense." Her forehead puckered.

"I know, but it's just an assumption," I said.

"Only the evidence got stolen?"

My lips spread into a tight line. "Yes. The person didn't take my television or anything else."

"That's so odd and much creepier than a typical robbery." She reached her hand out to me. "Maybe stop researching it? I don't want anything happening to you, Teddy."

I let out a breath of relief, and I couldn't help but smile; However, it was not because of Christina's gesture. It was because she believed me, and that brought me a wave of ease. But I couldn't help but be nagged by a feeling that my home being broken into was the least of my worries. The worst was yet to come.

Chapter Eight
Monica's Fate

Throughout the week, I noticed how Monica wasn't there. I didn't think much of it at first. However, it wasn't like her to be gone for almost an entire week. Finally, Nurse Brooks approached me and asked, "Have you seen or heard from Monica lately? I've been asking everyone, and I've been trying to call her because she's been missing work."

My muscles tensed, and an uneasy rumble shook lower abdomen. "She's missing?"

Brooks had his hands inside the pockets of his white jacket. "I assume so unless she decided she no longer wishes to work here and didn't bother to tell anyone." He turned to walk away, and I rushed over to my locker room to find my phone to call her. With each ring, my body shifted from side to side with apprehension. As a few more seconds ringed by, I began pacing around the break room. Her voicemail picked up, and I left a message. "It's Ted. Call me back as soon as you can." I decided to call again, but I got the same result. I texted her, asking where she was before going back to work.

The following day, a man in a suit that was accompanied by a police officer was in the main lobby at the SNF talking to a couple of nurses. I passed by Christina's desk on my way to the break room. "What's going on?" I asked.

Christina's lip quivered. "Monica was reported missing by her family, and the police are here to figure out if anyone knows anything."

My muscles went rigid as I looked over my shoulder at the cops.

"You should talk to them about what you know," said Christina. "I think there's a connection." Christina's face was completely white, and her lips were transfixed into a grim line.

I shifted my backpack onto my other shoulder. "I will." I went to the break room and clocked in. Once I went back to the lobby, the detective and the cop were done questioning my other two coworkers and started to make their way over to me. They began by holding up a photo of Monica. It appeared to be a profile picture of her from one of her social media accounts. She had flowers in her hair, which seemed vibrant against her midnight black hair. She always gave a small smile in her pictures and never showed her teeth.

"Hello. I'm Detective Waterson. Do you know this woman?" the detective asked.

I nodded my head. The cop who was standing beside the detective looked familiar. I recognized him by his mustache. He was the same cop that came to my home when I thought I heard a gunshot. I was becoming much too familiar with the police these days. "Yes, that's Monica," I said.

"She was reported missing. Apparently, her family hasn't heard from her all week. Have you heard anything from her recently?"

I was finding it hard to answer, and the blood drained from my face. My eyes shifted around the room.

"You okay?" he asked.

"I... We've been spending time together, and the last time I saw her was when I drove her home from work because she told me someone was following her."

This sparked Waterson's interest, and he along with the mustached cop, exchanged a glance at one another. "What did she say about this person?" asked the detective.

"It's the same man who waited outside my house."

Waterson stared at me with curiosity. "Is he related to both of you in some way?"

I rubbed my sweaty palms on my bottom scrubs. "He mostly just followed her. That's why he was outside my house because she was there, I'm assuming."

"Did you get a good look at him?"

"He had a long beard." I gestured with my hands the shape and length of it, and the police took notes. "He wore a beanie. His hair was long and unkempt, and his eyes were blue, I believe."

Waterson finished up his notes. "And his vehicle?"

"A blue colored beat-up truck."

"Do you happen to know the license plate number?"

I took a deep sigh. "Unfortunately, no."

"Would you be willing to come down to the station for a composite sketch?"

Finally, the mustached cop got a good look at me and pointed at me with his pen. "You were that guy that called about the gunshot, weren't you?"

My cheeks warmed from embarrassment, and I put my hands in my pockets. "Yeah, that was me."

"You also reported a burglary earlier, didn't you?" he asked.

"I did."

Waterson looked at his partner, wide-eyed. "You seem to be needing our help a lot lately," said Waterson.

My palms became sweaty, and I was thankful that I was able to hide them, or they'd see them trembling. "Yeah. It's been a weird time."

Waterson looked me up and down with a suspiciously. "Alright, well come down after your shift."

After an anxiety-filled day at work, I went to the police station to give the composite sketch. I was guided to an all-cemented room that had a two-way mirror to my left and a metal table with some chairs. The artist came in, and I described to him to the best of my ability what the man looked like. However, the sketch was the least of my worries. After the artist left, detective Waterson along with the mustached cop, entered the room and told me to stay seated.

I tapped my finger on the table as they took their seats across from me. I had never been in a situation like this before, and it suddenly felt like I was the suspect. "What else do you know?" asked Waterson. "I read over the robbery report, and it says that a man in a similar truck was the one that robbed your home. Is that correct?"

Sweat beat down the side of my head. "I suspect it was him since he was there when Monica was at my house last."

Waterson glowered. "And you didn't think to call the police when you heard a man was following your friend?"

"I figured that was something Monica should be doing. I offered to give her a ride home when she came to work last week saying someone was following her."

Waterson puckered out his lip as he continued to glare at me. "And you just so happened to be that nice of a guy."

Shit. They suspected me of something.

"According to the others we interviewed, nobody else saw her that day you followed her home." Waterson pointed at me. "You were the last one to see her alive."

Double shit.

This looked bad, and my knee began to shake. "She seemed uneasy when I last saw her, but no truck followed her home that day, so I figured she was fine. That was the day I got robbed."

Waterson leaned back in his chair. "So, he went after you instead of Monica. Why?" He didn't sound like he believed me in the slightest.

"We…" I struggled to finish the sentence because I knew this would open a whole new can of worms, but I had to if it led to Monica's safe return. "We were researching for who killed her sister. We had reason to suspect that Howard was nearby." I left out the part about demons because that was really Monica's idea and not mine. "And during the robbery, the man took only the evidence we had accumulated."

225

Waterson furrowed his brow. "According to the report filed, it said it was evidence about the home you lived in and not a murder."

"I know. I just didn't want to confess to what we were really doing."

Waterson placed crossed his arms as he continued to lean back in his chair. The tone he took on was like that of a father who had their child cornered in a lie and was about to solve the mystery of who broke the vase. "Why?"

"Because it would have led to more questions, and at the time it was just a robbery, and Monica wasn't missing. At least I didn't know she was. I know that was wrong of me, but how would knowing about what we were researching lead to the police finding the robber?"

"It could have. You never know."

"Her sister had been researching about the home before she died, and we thought that somehow it might lead to how and why she was killed."

"How?" I noticed Waterson had the same habit of tapping his finger like me.

I shrugged. "I don't know, but it got stolen, so we had to have been on the right track."

Waterson nodded and smirked. "That's true. You'll need to tell me everything you know so that we can be on the lookout. You said this man lives up near the mountains?"

"Yeah, I saw him up there once before all this started."

"What were you doing up in the mountains?"

"My parents live there."

Waterson grins at me. "It's a small world, isn't it?"

I let out a laugh, and that was the first time in a while, I had laughed. It was as though that laugh allowed me to let go of all the stress that had been twisting the muscles around my stomach.

I broke down everything since the beginning, and I started with when Monica first approached me after I confessed about my dreams. The dreams made them raise an eyebrow, which led to complete disbelief when I eventually brought up Monica's theory.

"She thought Howard was possessed by Dr. Ransteen and killed Lavinia to continue his work," I said. I rolled my eyes along with them. "I thought Howard was just abusive, and perhaps he took the evidence for some reason. Maybe there was something in there that could condemn him or show where he was at now. Or maybe it was his way of having that last control over her? I have no clue what he'd have to gain from that."

"But you saw this man, and did he look like Howard?" asked Waterson.

I looked down at the table as I rifled through my memory. I pressed my lips together. "You know, I can't say for sure because he had so much facial hair and looked so different from the last photo ever shown of Howard."

"But it's a possibility. He could have grown out his hair."

"That is true, but I still wouldn't know."

Waterson tapped his finger on the table. "Okay, thank you for your information. Stay close by in case we need to come into contact with you again."

As I went back to my vehicle, I thought about the man in the beat-up truck up in the mountains. I had an

227

inkling that he lived up there. Where else could he be? The mountains were away from civilization, and he needed a place to hide. A shiver ran down my spine. If he knew about us researching him and knew to steal the box, was it so far-fetched that he'd know where my parents were? My sister? I jumped into the truck and sped off out of the parking lot towards my parents' place. I just needed to see if they were safe and get them as far away from there as quickly as possible. They were already planning on moving out. If I could just convince my father to do it sooner, then maybe they would be safer.

I sped up the mountain and nearly spun out as I turned around a cliff side. I turned my wheel urgently in the opposite direction. Smoke rose from my back tires as I pressed on the brakes. My truck turned abruptly and then stopped. I rested my forehead against the wheel and took deep breaths. My truck's front tires were barely hanging off the cliff. After my heart rate slowed down and my hands stopped trembling, I turned back onto the road.

I arrived at my parents' home and didn't even bother to close the truck door as I ran up the porch. I opened the front door and saw my father taping up a box while my mother sat on her Lazy Boy chair with her head cocked back, mouth open, and drool dripping out as she quietly snored. I smiled out of relief and placed my hands on my knees to catch my breath.

"Oh, hey there, son. I wasn't expecting you," said my father. He looked over at me with his head tilted to one side. He pushed his glasses back up. "Are you okay?"

I took a breath and stood up straight. "I am now." I didn't want to alarm my father, so I didn't say anything about why I was there.

My father chuckled. "Well, good. Help me with these boxes, will ya'?"

I went to work, helping my Dad take down some books off the shelf.

"We'll keep some of them here. We're just taking the books Mom is working on. She starts one and then forgets she's reading it and then reads another."

There were a total of fifteen unfinished books that I packed away into the box, and it just served as a stark reminder of her ailment. I worked fast as I wrapped up some of my parents' dishes in old newspapers. I wanted to get as much done as soon as I could because then they could move in.

My father noticed and asked, "In a rush?"

"I just want to get you guys closer sooner." I paused. "You know, for Mom."

"Uh-huh." My father eyed me, suspiciously.

I saw the trash was full and offered to take it out. I went out towards the dumpster that sat at the edge of the property when a strange odor overpowered my nose. It smelt like an odd mixture of Sulfur, burning hair, a strangely sweet aroma, and a charcoal-like scent. The horrid and confusing combination made me cover my mouth with my hand. I dumped the trash into the dumpster, and that's when I saw that further up the mountain to my left, there was smoke rising between the trees.

I knew it had to be Howard. It just *had* to be. This was my chance to find Monica and to send this man to jail. I ran back to my truck and hopped in. I took off up the road using the rising smoke as my compass. It eventually led to a dirt road that was off the main one. I decided to park my truck on the side of the road and follow the dirt path into the woods so as not to be detected. All the while, my heart pounded in my ears. I crouched down and paid careful attention to where I stepped so as not make too much noise.

I walked among the trees hiding behind their trunks as I made my way slowly towards the property. The road winded up along the mountain, and my knees ached from overuse as I climbed up at a steep incline. I finally came to the end of the road when I saw a large cabin with a truck parked outside it. I recognized the beat-up blue truck. Through the windows of the truck, I recognized the same barrier gate to block the back seats from the front seats. On the back of the window was smeared blood.

The cabin had moss growing up one side of it, and the shingle wood roof was so old it looked like it was about to cave in. The home didn't appear to be very large. Two windows sat on either side of the front door, and the panes were painted a dark green. I saw through one window on the side of the house there was a kitchen and living room. At the corner of the living room was a large bed.

I decided to follow the smoke, but it was on the other side of the property, which meant I had to cross through an opening to get to the trees on the other side of the clearing. I took a step out and looked both ways before sprinting across the clearing. Camouflaged once again, I followed the smoke. The stench of rotting flesh made my eyes water. I gagged as I covered my mouth with the sleeve of my jacket.

There was that bearded man again standing in front of the pit. He was holding the black spellbook that was stolen from my home as he chanted in what I recognized to be Latin. His voice was deep and solemn, and I couldn't help but find it fitting to what he was doing. Against the wall of the cabin were tools hanging up with a perched metal sheet that provided cover from the weather. One of the tools was an ax that was drenched in blood. I could see the handprints of its owner all over the handle. My stomach churned.

The man stood in front of a makeshift fire pit made up of stone marble, which I found odd. The marble appeared to be much too extravagant to be used around a firepit. I noticed more of those satanic symbols engraved into the marble. One of the symbols I recognized as the cursive U that curved outwards with one short line underneath and two on top. The pit was filled with embers that were being re-burned.

In the fire, I could see plain as day Monica's ankle. How I knew it was hers was because of the tattoo of Lavinia's name along with the dates of her birth and death. I bent over and heaved. I stumbled back as my chest caved in and out. The man stopped chanting and stared towards my direction. My eyes widened in pure terror. Without giving it a second thought, I took off sprinting back to my truck.

My lungs ached from the cold air by the time I made it to my truck and sped off. All the while, I clenched tightly to the steering wheel and looked expectantly through the rearview mirror anticipating the man to race after me.

Once I reached my parents' property, I slammed the door shut and peered over my shoulder convinced the man had followed me even though nobody was there. Once inside, I could finally take a deep breath.

"You alright, son?" asked my father. He approached me slowly and had his arm reached out towards me. My mother was awake and had her head tilted to one side in question. She had that far off gaze again.

I took a step back from my father and waved my hand to dismiss his gesture. I didn't know where to begin on what happened. My father wouldn't understand any of it since he wouldn't know the people involved or the stakes. "S-s-someone is dead." I blurted out. "My friend. Dead." I pointed out the direction where I saw the atrocity. "She was… She was burned." I was at a loss for words, and my breath became labored. I couldn't find enough oxygen. My chest was constricted. "She…"

"Why don't you take a seat," said my father. He guided me towards the couch, and I sat down beside my mother who asked, "What is going on? Who is this man?" She lowered her head to see into my downcast eyes. "Are you okay, sir? Do we need to call the police?" she asked.

I couldn't handle my own mother's lack of remembrance of me at that moment. I ran my fingers through my hair. My breathing was still labored. It felt like a brick wall prevented me from sucking in enough oxygen to fill my lungs. They just came out in short, quick bursts.

My father handed me a paper bag. "Breathe through this. It'll help. Put your head between your knees," he said. I did as he said, but nothing improved after a few minutes. "Just give it time," he said.

Slowly, the muscles in my chest loosened, and with that so did my short breaths. I could finally fill my lungs fully, and it was the greatest relief I had ever known. "I thought I was having a heart attack," I said.

My father smirked, but it was crooked with concern. "No, just a panic attack. Your Mom used to get them all the time at the beginning of her Alzheimer's diagnosis." He paused for a few seconds. I could feel his eyes analyzing me to make sure I was mentally okay. It made me cringe. "Do you want to tell me what's going on?"

I took a deep breath. "Yes. We need to call the police. I had a friend who went missing, and I found her dead."

My father's eyes widened, and my mother covered her mouth with her hand. She murmured, "Oh my."

My father looked at me with both shock and concern. "Are you sure you saw this?"

Ripping my fingers from my hair, I exclaimed, "Yes! I know what I saw! He was burning her body! I saw her tattoo!"

My father gestured with his hand for me to relax. "Okay, okay. I just want to get the full story before we go calling the cops. Are you sure it wasn't something you wanted to see because you are still in grief over your friend going missing? Someone burning bodies out here is highly unlikely, son. Could it be you saw something you didn't quite understand and mistook it for your friend because you are stressed over her missing?"

I knew my father was only trying to help, but it angered me further. I shot up from the couch. "I know what I saw! It was her!"

"We should trust him," said my mother. "He obviously looks upset enough. We should call the cops just in case."

My father looked between the both of us and sighed. "It just seems unlikely like something from a movie."

"If I were to have a child, I'd want someone to call if they thought they saw my kid dead," my mother said.

I frowned, and I felt like I was punched in the gut by my mother's comment. She couldn't remember me. It was as though she had more bad days than good nowadays. I met my father's eyes, and he had the same grim expression. We both knew we'd lose her sooner rather than later.

"I just think maybe you saw a man who finished hunting and was cooking his meal. I think your stress made you hallucinate. It's not the first time," my father said. "Stress and misunderstandings can make your brain jump to some strange conclusions to fill the gaps. That's all." He grabbed his cell phone and handed it to me as he shrugged. "But if you feel this is best, then…" He sighed. "Use my phone. My plan has a bit better reception out here."

After I dialed 9-1-1 and gave them the information, we sat around the cabin in total silence awaiting some type of call back or for a police car to come rolling up. My father made us some tea, and I decided to make conversation with my mother, who seemed oblivious to what was going on. "How are you feeling today?" I asked.

She pulled some lint off her blanket. It was an old orange blanket that had been crocheted by my grandmother years ago. My sister and I used that blanket to build many forts in the past. Nowadays, it was gnarled, thinning, and becoming untangled from its knitted knots. I couldn't help but find the similarities in both the blanket and my mother. "I am fine," she said casually. "I had soup today."

I gave her a small smile. "Was it any good?"

She lifted a shoulder. "I suppose. It was old soup. I hated the crackers, but the man who fed it to me was nice enough."

"You mean my Dad?"

She looked at me wide-eyed. "That's your father? He takes care of me."

I chuckled a bit. "I know he does."

She stared out the window that was passed my shoulder. Her eyes seemed so far away.

I followed her gaze and then looked back at her. "What are you looking at?"

"I sometimes go for walks. I get lost." Her voice was distant.

"Why is that?"

She finally looked back at me. "I'm looking for something."

"What are you looking for?" I was genuinely curious as to what she'd say.

Her voice was small. "I don't know." She looked down, and then her eyes brightened again when she peered up at me. It was as if the lights turned back on inside her head. "Teddy! It's you."

A huge grin broke across my face. "Hi, Mom."

Right then, the blaring red and blue lights of a police car came rolling up towards the cabin. My father and I stepped out of the cabin as two officers approached us. Both had fiercely grim expressions on their face. One of them had all color drained from their face. The main officer tipped his hat towards us and had his thumbs hooked to his belt. "Good evening," he said.

"Did you find anything?" I asked.

"Oh yeah, we did." he said. "Thank you for calling when you did. Now guide me through how you stumbled upon this man's property. Why were you there?"

I gave the cop my entire story of what I told Detective Watterson, and then led up to when I was on the property. "When I saw her ankle with the tattoo, I ran for it. He saw me, but I don't think he saw me. I came straight here and called the police."

The cop nodded. The other officer was still entirely pale, and his cheeks were turning a bit green. "Well, we found human remains and a shed with surgical tables and supplies. That's all we can say for now, but there was no man on the property. He must have left when you saw him. We will send out a report to be on the lookout for him."

All hope instantly dwindled when I heard he was gone. He'd come after me next, and I knew it. My stomach knotted up, and my heart dropped. "Thank you for checking it out," I said.

The officer nodded his head. "Thank *you* for reporting it. Lord knows how long that man has been there doing that. We'll find him." The two officers headed back to their cars and drove off. Once they were gone, my father placed his hand on my shoulder. "You should stay here tonight, son," he said in a somber tone. I agreed. There was no way in hell I could go home alone now. That man was on the run again.

In the early morning, my father shook me awake. The sudden jolt as I was ripped from my dreams made me ill-prepared for what he said next. I couldn't quite catch it, and I asked him to speak again. "Your mother is missing," he said hysterically.

My blood ran cold. "What do you mean? Did you go looking for her?"

"I did. She's gone. I can't find her anywhere."

"Did you call the police?" My adrenaline was pumping as I jumped from the couch still blinking the dreams away.

"Not yet. I can't find her anywhere on the property. She must have gotten up in the middle of the night or something."

I threw on my sneakers and didn't bother even to tie them as I ran out the front door. The fresh morning air hit my face, and it sent a chill through me. I zipped up my jacket as I looked at the ground searching for any footprints. Minuscule drops of water from the mist in the air covered my face, and the gray clouds filled with rain slowly began to overcast the sky.

I dug through the metal cabinets in the shed and found an industrial flashlight. I ran off into the woods in the same direction I had seen her wander off before. The overcast sky didn't provide nearly enough light as I ran deeper amongst the trees. I shined my flashlight against the dark trunks and branches that stretched out like spider webs weaving themselves endlessly in the empty space.

The sounds of my feet crunching on the ground along with my heavy breathing was all that accompanied me. I stepped in deep mud and looked down. There were bare footprints that headed in one direction. My heart rate picked up as I followed them. Further up, I noticed boot prints

237

approaching my mother's trail and following close beside her. I picked up my pace in a panic. I hoped it was an officer or a neighbor that had taken her to safety. Ahead, I saw a small light that broke out among the dark abyss. I followed it and found myself at a road where the mudded prints continued.

They disappeared where there were tire tracks. The tracks took off from the side of the road, and I could see the mudded tracks head down the road towards town. Despite the cold, my palms began to sweat. I decided to follow the road and took out my cell phone from my pocket to call my father and let him know I had a lead, but the phone line went dead. I ground my teeth together as I tossed it back into my pocket.

The sky had gotten progressively darker, and thunder roared in the distance. Small droplets of water fell, and I picked up my pace, so I wouldn't lose the tracks in the rain. I hiked down the side of the road for several minutes. As the rain beat down harder, I pulled up my hood and started to jog. My lungs felt weak by the time I found tracks similar to the ones up the road. They were off the side of the street in the mud, and there appeared to have been some type of scuffle that took place with my Mom's bare feet and the mysterious person's boot prints.

My heart dropped. This happened right outside my parents' property. That meant my mother tried to get out, but this person wouldn't let her and forced her back in. I tightened my grip around the flashlight and bit down until the muscles in my jaw ached. The tracks went off from the side of the road towards town. My gut told me what and who it was, and I decided to follow that feeling. At this point in my life, I had to because my mother's life was at stake. I'd give into whatever superstitions for her.

I ran back towards my truck, where I saw my father on the phone with whom I assumed was the police. I threw my truck into drive and sped off without even bothering to tell him where I was headed.

It took about forty minutes to drive back to my house, and who knew what condition she would be in by the time I got there if she was even there at all. I didn't bother to break at the four-way stop into my neighborhood, and I barely made it in-between two crossing cars. Their horns blared behind me, but I paid no mind to it.

I pulled up to my home. The house was dark, and there appeared to be no beat-up truck out front. Hope rose in my chest, and I thought perhaps I was wrong. Yet, it troubled me to think she was still missing. As I headed up the front porch, I saw tire tracks on the side of the house. I followed them, and in the back of my home was the beat-up truck.

"Fuck," I exclaimed. Heat coursed through my body as the adrenaline took over, and I threw open the front door. It was unlocked, and I *knew* I had locked it. No lights were on, and the storm further darkened the home. There was no sign of life anywhere. "Mom?" I called out.

No answer.

I yelled even louder. "Mother!"

Silence.

I walked towards the kitchen being careful which floorboards I stepped on since some were louder than others. I tiptoed lightly being careful not to put too much weight on one foot. My ears perked when I heard the sounds of creaking. It bounced off the bare walls leaving me confused as to where the noise came from. Panic rose in my chest, and I called out my mother's name frantically. "Patricia! Where are you?" Just as I was about to grab a kitchen knife, I felt a sharp pang hit my head. My head went numb before I fell to the floor unconscious.

Chapter Nine
The Universal Truth

The smells of metal and rain greeted me. My eyes were still closed, and I could hear a man humming whimsically a few feet away. I winced as the pulsing in the back of my head vibrated with pain. I tried to lift my head up, but I couldn't move. I attempted to move my arms, and they too wouldn't budge. My eyes shot open, and above me, all I could see was a lone light bulb that swung left to right as the wind blew through the damp room. I recognized the bulb as the one that hung in my basement.

I tried to look with my peripherals and saw my arms were pinned down using leather straps to a bed. Glancing past my hand, I saw the old metal cabinet from the storage closet with some of the old surgical supplies placed neatly on top of a towel. I recognized some of the antique surgical tools like a silver syringe, straight and curved needles, a tiny metal hammer, and other nefarious schematics that I could only imagine what they'd be used for. Besides that, I saw the same brown leather-bound notebook from my dreams. It was the one I saw Lavinia hide in the basement.

While half-conscious, I could see my mother on another surgical table, which I recognized was from the storage room. She was tied up, and she was unconscious. My head pounded, and I closed my eyes as I let out an involuntary groan. I tried to move my wrists to get out, but my muscles were weak.

"Oh, good. You're awake," said the humming voice.

I clenched my teeth to get a better grip on my pain. "Why do you have my mother here trapped?"

"All in due time, Ted."

I tried to open my eyes, but the light made me shrink back in pain. "How do you know my name? Who are you?" As I slowly gained better control of my body, I yanked my bound wrists trying to loosen the straps.

The same bearded man I saw in the beat-up truck stood over me. His piercing blue eyes glimmered with what I could only make out to be glee. "You won't be getting out of those any time soon. At least not without my say so."

"You're Howard, aren't you? The one who killed Lavinia."

The man chuckled. It was a deep and low chuckle that made a shiver run down my back. "Howard is no longer with us."

"Crazy bastard. You're just disassociating yourself from your crimes."

The man leaned over the metal bed that I was lying in. He was mere inches from me. "You still don't get it, do you? *I'm* Dr. Ransteen. The original owner of this house you now reside in." He walked over to his makeshift workbench and picked up one of the icepick-like needles. The silver tool shined against the swinging light.

242

"You're nuts to think you are someone that is dead."

He snapped his head around towards me. "You still don't believe even after all you've witnessed?"

"What have I seen?" I wanted to keep him talking. Anything to keep him distracted, so I could try to get myself loose.

The man marveled at the icepick as he used a cloth to wipe it clean. "In this home, you have seen visions, yes? I had them too when the souls began to pile up. The shadows—They pressed themselves onto you. The dreams made you go crazy. I know it all."

I paused. There was no way this man could know about my dreams unless someone had told him. "How do you know about the dreams?"

The gleeful look left his eyes, and he snaked his head towards my direction. His eyes turned a harsh black. "I know because I have this house marked. I know because you have been trying to divulge my secret just like that Lavinia girl. The souls collected in this home, *stay* in this home. They must stay on this property."

"Why? You're dead, so why does it matter?" I still didn't fully believe what this crazed man was saying, but I couldn't deny that he did know a lot about my dreams. Still, I just needed to distract him, so I could try to escape.

He smiled, and the whiteness of his teeth seemed out of place against the rustic look of his face. "Death is not death, Ted. You *can* live on in other ways if you know how. I found a way to continue my work, and those souls that are bound to this house are bound to the Beast of Eternal Life."

I thought back to my visions and seeing Dr. Ransteen sprinkle his blood across the circle. "If that's the truth, then your soul is bound here too since this is where you died." I kept loosening my straps on my right wrist very slowly.

His charming smile came back, and the whimsical tone of his voice returned. "I know that your mother has Alzheimer's, and I know that it is hereditary." He looked over at my mother as he wiped the towel one last time over the icepick.

I froze in place.

"What I do is I try to find secrets to the human mind," he said. "I can find the secret behind Alzheimer's and heal both you and your mother of this curse." he chuckled. "Of course, I had to improvise with some of my older tools since the police drove me out of my place of residence thanks to you." He made this sound like this was a minor inconvenience for him and sighed. "I had to make do with what I had even if it is a bit outdated." He scowled at the bed I was strapped in and held his lips in a tight line as he looked over his instruments. It was as if he was some artist who didn't have his favorite paintbrush.

"You cannot make any such promises. You couldn't even save your own mother." That seemed to have successfully distracted him from going towards my mother with the sharp tool.

His smile vanished, and his sinister expression constricted his face. "My mother could have been saved!" He raced over to me with his face just inches from mine, and he pinned the icepick against my flesh. "She could have been saved," he said in a calmer tone. "Just like your mother can."

"All you do is experiment on people inhumanely."

"I do what is necessary to find cures. You cannot have the light without the dark, Ted. I am what is needed for the light to survive."

I arched my brow.

Dr. Ransteen straightened his posture and put down the icepick on the workbench. "It's true. I am what is necessary. The universe needs balance, and I give it balance. Think about the past. If it weren't for the Nazis experimenting on the Jews and other prisoners in the Holocaust, we wouldn't have the information we do now about drugs and our reactions to them. Nor the knowledge of the durability of the human body. Even the Hiroshima bomb led to a great understanding of radiation and how we could use it to save lives. A lot of evil, yes, but so much good came from it in the long run." He turned back to me with a hand drill. "You see, you cannot have the good without the bad. You need both in order to exist, and that is the universal truth I have learned since death." He stepped over to the back of my head, where I could no longer see him. I began to shake my wrist furiously causing the whole bed to shake.

"Stay still, or I will drill in the wrong place and have to start all over." He didn't sound the least bit agitated. It was more like a small annoyance to Dr. Ransteen to have to drill a whole new hole into my head.

I still shook the bed. "Why not just put me to sleep to make it easier?"

"I need you awake. I find the brain functions much better when awake."

I began to sway erratically as much as I could when Lavinia appeared beside me. She rested her hand on my wrist and goosebumps prickled across my arm where her cold hand touched my skin.

Dr. Ransteen noticed Lavinia and relaxed the hand drill at his side. He leaned back, smiling. "Well if it isn't Lavinia. You look nice being transparent." All Lavinia could muster as a response was a morose smile. The doctor leaned forward with his eyes wide and a smile plastered across his face. "Oh, you can't talk?" he chuckled. "You should have thought better than to stuff your nose in matters that do not concern you. You cannot do much to help this boy here." He patted my head.

I noticed a slight change in pressure from the straps around my wrists where Lavinia's hand was. I eyed her. She looked down at me briefly and shook her head subtly before snapping her attention back to Dr. Ransteen. He didn't seem to notice our quick exchange.

"You know," began the doctor as he sauntered over to Lavinia. "You were always such a pain to me even in death. But I'm more powerful than you, now. A common spirit cannot do what I can."

She inched herself away from me and slowly went towards the makeshift workbench to position herself in front of the journal. The doctor moved towards her, which gave me time to start loosening my straps more. My wrist was now more easily able to move side to side.

"I will continue my life's mission, which is to purify humanity," he said. Right then, Lavinia vanished with a smile. The doctor's eyes scanned across the room, and when he realized she was not returning, he focused his attention back on me. My wrist was now almost completely free, but I froze when he made eye contact.

246

"Back to our work at hand," he said. "I find that the issue with Alzheimer's is the brain deteriorating faster than the body. Specifically, in the area where memories are stored." The doctor reached his arm out towards the journal. "I have a theory that may fix that, but I have to test it out first. You and your mother will be my guinea pigs if you will." He grinned and spoke as though all this was a normal procedure. It made my blood run cold.

Dr. Ransteen's brow furrowed as he patted his hand on the makeshift workbench. He turned his head searching for something. "Where is it?" he mumbled. He scattered aside the tools that were on top of the metal cabinet. He knelt and searched underneath it. "Where is it?" he exclaimed. He stood up and gripped my shirt in his fist. "Did she take it? Did she take it!?!" I instinctively shot my eyes over to the journal that was clearly on top of the workbench. The doctor let me go and went searching for it.

I knitted my forehead together. I could see it clear as day on the cabinet, but for some reason, Dr. Ransteen couldn't. A thought clicked in my head as I thought back to whenever I lost my keys or phone in the house. Lavinia appeared at the edge of the bed and winked at me. My mouth fell open, and my lips curved in amusement as I saw the doctor struggle to find something that was completely blind to him.

I decided to make use of Dr. Ransteen's distraction to further loosen my wrist. I writhed my arm around until I could finally slip my wrist through. Using my free hand, I unbound the left one. I frantically felt around my head for a way to free myself. I felt screws that poked out on both the left and right side of the metal bar that trapped my head in place, and I began to twist them. The metal pinched tightly against my skin as I struggled to loosen them fast enough.

Dr. Ransteen turned his attention back to me, and before he could react, I had loosened my head free and punched him in the jaw, causing him to fall to the ground. My knuckles screamed with pain. I hastily freed my ankles while he recuperated from the blow.

I hopped off the bed, and my vision blurred as blood rushed to my head. I gripped onto the bed. He grabbed a syringe needle from the top of the cabinet and lurched himself towards me. I fought him off with all my strength and tackled him to the ground. Lying on top of him, I sat up and rained down a couple of blows causing blood to seep out of his nose.

I stood up and ran over to grab the journal stuffing it into a pocket that was sewn onto the inside of my jacket. Grabbing a scalpel from the desk, I went over to the doctor's immobilized body. I used my knees to keep his arms pinned to the ground as I pressed the weapon against his neck.

Dr. Ransteen chuckled and lifted his head to push his neck against the blade further. "You think threatening my life will change anything? I can always find another body." I wasn't a man of extreme violence, so I rethought my approach for a second. He took my moment of hesitation to his advantage and used his body's strength to knock me off of him. It caused my weapon to pierce his skin; he grabbed the scalpel to pull it out of his neck. Bright red liquid oozed out and poured down over his shoulder, but this didn't seem to faze him at all. He charged towards me, and I braced for impact.

He smashed my body to the ground and said, "Tell me where the journal is, and I'll let your mother go." I punched him in the face leaving a bright red mark across the side of it. Shoving the man off me, I ran towards my mother to untie her. My hands shook from pure adrenaline and panic, which made it difficult. She stirred awake. Her head turned, and she groaned. "Teddy?" she asked in a meek voice. "W-Where are we?"

Before I could manage to break her completely free, I heard the click of a gun.

I froze in place.

"Give me the journal." Said Dr. Ransteen.

I swallowed hard and slowly turned around with my arms raised. As I turned, I saw my baseball bat against the wall.

"Where is it?" he screamed with a crazed look of fury in his eyes.

I knew the journal was the only way that'd possibly stop him from continuing his work, and I knew it was the only leverage I had. I had to act quickly, so I kicked over my mother's surgical table, so the backside was facing him. This was to shield her at least a little from the bullets. I ducked down in time before he let out a shot. The sound of it vibrated throughout the room, and a sharp ringing took over my eardrum.

He screamed again. "Where is it?"

I pointed towards the storage room door and said, "It's in there." Dr. Ransteen walked past me with the gun pointed down to the ground. It surprised me that he would turn his back to me like that. Then again, his mind must've only been focused on the journal and not me. I took his mistake to my advantage and grabbed my bat to swing it at him. The doctor heard my movements in time to move away, so I didn't hit his head as I wanted. Instead, I nailed the side of his torso, knocking him over.

Dr. Ransteen pointed his gun in my direction, and I chanced to take another swing hoping it'd knock him over in time before he could pull the trigger.

Pop!

I grabbed my side and fell to my knees. The sounds of my mother's screams were all I could hear. The aching that shook my side snaked itself across my upper body, and I looked down briefly to see that a bullet had grazed my skin, leaving a burning sensation in its wake. I bit down hard as I willed myself to get a better grasp on my bat to swing at the doctor. I yelled out in pain as I swung at him. I hit his backside and heard a crack as he hit the ground.

I stumbled onto the ground. As I lied there, I saw that the far back of the basement, dark shadows started to fall around all four corners of the room. They fully encompassed the entirety of the basement, and goosebumps prickled across my arms as the temperature dropped dramatically. My warm breath huffed out of my mouth with each exhale. I noticed the doctor had realized the sudden change in temperature too, and he stared around the basement at the dark mist that choked the air. I knew this was only the beginning, and the dark shadows would soon pin me down like they always did. The doctor's eyes widened with terror, which made me pinch my brow in confusion. *Why would a spirit possessing a body be afraid of other spirits?*

He let out a frantic breath, and I followed his gaze to the wall behind me. Smoke manifested out of thin air against the wall. The smell of smoke made me jump into action. I grunted and clenched my teeth together as I forced myself up, holding my side. That was when the flames appeared against that far wall of the basement, and I was mesmerized by the shock of it all.

The flames were controlled by an invisible force that glided across the brick wall. It zipped up and across. The line of flames dipped and curved. My mouth fell agape when I began to make out words:

Paulton Edwards.

Sasha Greensfield.

Marcus Smithson.

Janet Barton.

Jacob Cruz.

These were the names of every victim that Dr. Ransteen ever experimented on in the mansion. Amongst the already dark mist, a pure black abyss took form in one of the corners of the basement. It grew and blanketed over the smoke. I could have sworn the flames got bigger and became increasingly out of control as the dark mass circled the room.

I knew what was coming next, so I scrambled towards my mother. I pushed myself to finish untying her. Dr. Ransteen's face was white as a sheet, and he paid no mind to us as his gaze stayed glued onto the sight before him. The smoke that filled the room made it almost an impossibility to see us anyway.

Once my mother was freed, she crawled over to me. "Are you okay?" she whispered. I put her arm around my shoulder to help her up, and we shuffled towards the stairs. I groaned in pain, and my vision blurred from the screaming ache at my side. I clung to the injury hoping it'd relinquish some of the throbbing.

I heard Dr. Ransteen's frightened gasp, and I snapped my head over towards his direction to see that the black mass began to break off into pieces. The pieces shot up in the air before swirling down towards the ground forming cloaked silhouettes.

The doctor pointed his gun and shot at them rapidly until all I could hear were the clicks of an empty chamber. The silhouettes darted towards him at lightning speed. The heat of the fire burned at my skin, and I limped up the steps with my mother as fast as I could. As we made our way out of the house, I could hear Dr. Ransteen's screams of pure terror.

As I limped off the front porch, a few police cars followed by an ambulance came racing down the street towards my home. I fell to my knees once I reached the grass. "Teddy!" My mother exclaimed. Her voice shook, and she knelt by my side as tears fell down her cheeks. Her hands trembled as she applied pressure to my wound. I yelled out in pain, which made my mother burst into more tears.

The cops got out and immediately pointed their guns at me. "Put your hands up!" One of them commanded. I winced, and my arms shook as I slowly lifted them, but my right arm couldn't go up nearly as high as the other.

"He's injured. Can't you see?" My mother yelled. "Help us!"

At the corner of my eye, I could see the smoke rising out of the basement window. The police noticed it too, and one of them called into his radio that was attached to his shoulder, "We will need the fire department out here as well." The officer spoke to me next. "What happened here?"

"There's an intruder in my home," I whispered. "I've been shot."

The police lowered their weapons slightly, and the main officer nodded his head to the other policemen to silently communicate that I was not the perpetrator. They released their weapons back into their holsters, and the EMTs came racing to my aid. They had a stretcher for me and placed me on it before carrying into the ambulance. Another EMT tended to my mother.

As the stretcher was pushed into the back of the vehicle, the bright fluorescent lighting inside made my eyes ache, and I shut them momentarily. "It's just a flesh wound," I said with my eyes closed. "The bullet grazed me." I could hear the sirens of the fire truck approaching in the distance.

"You're lucky it didn't go through you or hit a major artery. You will need stitches," said the EMT.

"Are you the homeowner?" asked a voice.

I squinted my eyes open and nodded at the main officer who was standing outside the ambulance. The EMTs pushed my shirt up and began cleaning the wound. "I own the home," I said wincing from the burn of the rubbing alcohol. "There's a man inside the home. Tell the fire department when they get here."

"What happened?"

I swallowed hard as the EMT began to stitch me up. It gave me a lot of pain, but once it was all cleaned up, the injury didn't look like much. There was no way I could tell this cop about the spirits and the fact that it was Dr. Ransteen's soul who used black magic to come back from the grave. Instead, I settled on saying, "He took my mother. She went missing in the woods, and when I went to find her, I found him at my house with her tied up. He took me by surprise by hitting me on my head. I passed out."

"You mean you could have a concussion?" asked the EMT.

I managed a nod but didn't pay much attention to their worry. It'd seemed like such a small issue now. "He had me tied up to this operating table when I woke up."

"How did you get free?" asked the cop.

"He lost his journal, which had all the experiments he was going to do on me. He had a property that was found yesterday with bodies. While he was distracted, I broke free." My hand shook as I reached into the inside pocket of my jacket and took out the book.

The cop tilted his head to one side as he reached for the journal.

"I fought him to get my mother and I out of there."

"You think he's the one that's been kidnapping all those mentally ill patients?"

"Yes, I do. I think that's what attracted him to my mother."

The cop nodded as he studied the journal. "The EMTs are going to transport you to the hospital. The fire department will get him out, and we'll question him if he's alive."

Right then, the fire department's red lights glimmered across the other homes in the neighborhood as it parked itself right outside my house. The officer approached the firefighters to tell them there was a man still inside. They set to work hosing down the house where the basement window was. The EMT slammed the ambulance doors shut, and as we drove off, I could see a couple of firefighters haul out Dr. Ransteen. He appeared to be weak but alive. His chest heaved as he coughed, and he collapsed to the ground.

Chapter Ten
Freed Souls

I was snug in my blanket, and I winced as I slowly sat back on the couch at my parents' home. The feeling of my mother's poorly knitted blanket scratched at the back of my neck. My injury was still tender, but it wasn't anything that Advil couldn't fix. "Mind if we watch the news?" my mother asked.

"That's fine. How are you feeling today?" I asked.

"I'm alright." My mother still had bruises on her wrists from being tied to the operating table.

I could hear the anchorwoman on the television say, "Today Howard Jefferson will be put away for life for the deaths of over fifteen mentally ill patients that had gone missing. Their remains were found on his property. Experts suspect there could be more victims that have yet to be found. Ashes of the deceased were also confiscated along with the sadistic tools he used on his victims."

The news channel played a video clip of Howard being placed into the back of a police car. He didn't have that dark look in his eye anymore like when Dr. Ransteen had control. He had left Howard's body soon after he got captured. He could jump into any body at any moment, so that meant I had work to finish still.

"Howard Jefferson was responsible for the death of his girlfriend, Lavinia Holland, over eight years ago. Investigators believe he had become obsessed with a man named Dr. Ransteen and his experiments during the time that Lavinia had been researching about this doctor's unethical practices. They were living in the same home that was once the doctor's mental institution. Investigators believe Howard began to copycat his experiments."

A darkness twisted in the pit of my stomach. Poor Howard didn't do any of these things, and he still had to pay the price for becoming possessed. That guilt would stay with me forever. The woman on the television went on to say that the investigators found the bones of the missing mental patients from Dr. Ransteen's practice around my property, and they were confiscated. At least one part of the ritual that I had to do to reverse his powers was done. This way, he wouldn't have enough strength to come back so soon. Still, I needed to get back to that house before it was too late.

"Does anyone want any tea?" Christina came into the living room holding up a tray of mugs with a steaming teapot.

My Mom sat up and smiled. "Oh, thank you, dear. Your help has been appreciated. My husband can't care for both me and Teddy."

Christina grinned as she gently placed down the tray on the coffee table. "It's no problem. When Ted finally decided to ask for my help, I jumped at the chance." she laughed lightly. "He can be stubborn."

My mother giggled. "Oh, don't I know it."

My cheeks burned hot, and I chewed on the inside of my cheek. "Yeah, yeah."

My mother gave me a playful smirk. After she took a sip of her tea, she asked, "When will your father be back from the store?"

I looked at my wristwatch. "He left about an hour ago. It takes time to get up and down the mountain, so he should be home in another hour or so. Later, today, I have to stop by my house to pick up a few things."

"Are you allowed back there yet?" my mother asked with concern. "Isn't it still a crime scene?"

"Is it even safe to go in there after the fire?" asked Christina.

I sat up to reach for my tea. The soreness in my side was numbed by the pills, which made moving around easier. "I won't go down into the basement. I just need to handle a few things. Besides, they already collected all the bodies. I'm sure it's fine now."

"I'll go with you then," said Christina. She had been a big help to my family and me this past week. She was one of the first people to visit me in the hospital, besides my father and sister. She stayed by my side the entire time while I was there, and during my brief stay at the hospital, I had come to rely on her. She was so much more than a girl I was dating. She'd become someone I could depend on, which was a new concept for me. Why she wanted to help a man she barely started dating, I had no clue. I tried asking her once, and all she did was smile and kiss me.

Christina and I decided to leave before sundown once my father came home from the store. I put a sledgehammer into the trunk of Christina's car, and she drove me down to Saratoga Springs.

"I can't believe you've been through all this," she said after a few moments of silence.

I watched the passing oak trees as we sped down the mountain. "Neither can I sometimes."

"You went to save your mother, right? And then got caught up in all of that."

I pursed my lips together. I didn't know if I'd ever tell her the truth because even, I had a hard time digesting it all. "Yeah. Something like that."

"I'm glad you're safe now." She looked over at me and reached out her hand to hold mine. That simple touch soothed me, and I tenderly tightened my hand around hers.

Once we reached the mansion, I noticed the left side of it was charred from the basement window, and the blacked streaks hiked their way up the side of the house like spikes. The yellow tape was gone from the front door, which led me to believe the home was no longer involved in the investigation. I had Christina open the trunk, so I could take out my father's sledgehammer. I winced as it dangled at my side.

"Do you need my help?" asked Christina.

I shook my head.

Once inside, I knew where to go. I first went to the kitchen to grab a knife, and then I went straight downstairs to the basement.

"I thought you said you weren't going to come down here," said Christina.

"I know, and I'm sorry I lied. I just didn't want my mother to worry." I saw the ruined brick from the fire. It was still standing, but it was now discolored and weakened. "Stand back," I said to Christina. I lifted the hammer and groaned as I hit the brick. I dropped it to my side and took a few breaths.

"I can help," she said. Worry seeped into her voice.

Again, I shook my head and clenched my teeth as I lifted the hammer to hit the wall again. This time, the brick broke more easily. All I needed were a few broken ones. I dropped the hammer to the ground and began ripping out the brick. A cloud of dust puffed out, and I coughed. "Hand me a bucket," I said. "There should be one somewhere in here."

Christina looked around the basement and found an old tin bucket to hand me.

I used the knife to stab at the mortar to loosen the bricks up and take them out easier. As I did so, a rush of brownish-gray dust poured out, which I used the bucket to collect.

"What is this?" asked Christina. "Is it from the fire?"

I used my hand to scoop out the rest of the ashes. I felt a heavy weight lift from not just me but from the house itself. The sun seemed to shine brighter through the small window. "It's a long story, but I'll explain it one day. It's to free the house of a heavy burden," I said.

Even though she didn't understand, she still gave me a small smile. "Want my help?"

I gave in and handed her the bucket. "Hold this as I pour the ashes into it."

I knew what I'd do with the ashes of the victims. I'd take them to a beautiful place to be free. Where they could go wherever they wanted and roam the Earth if they so pleased, and I knew that releasing them in the ocean would be the only way to do that.

I noticed that behind some of the bricks were those symbols that were used by Dr. Ransteen to encase the souls. I made it a point to smash those later just in case. "I know this may look silly or superstitious," I said. "But after everything I've been through, it's impractical not to be."

Later that day, we picked up some flowers and visited the Saratoga Springs cemetery. We walked up to the markers where Lavinia and Monica were laid to rest. They had recovered Monica's remains and buried them next to her sister. After we placed the flowers over their graves, I stood there next to Christina, and I held her hand. Then, the thought of what Dr. Ransteen said took over my thoughts:

You can't have the light without the dark.

Everything in life caused a ripple effect. Could it be that everything that happened to me was to ensure that I got what I always wanted? The girl of my dreams, being able to take care of my mother and finding out who I was as a person and what I wanted out of life. Was what happened to me, Monica, and Howard that necessary evil? I looked at Christina and began to smile. I was where I wanted to be, but I knew that in my eyes, the world would never be the same.

The End